JENA PARKER RETURNS

Betty Swem

 iUniverse®

Jena Parker Returns

iUniverse books may be ordered through booksellers or by contacting:

iUniverse
1663 Liberty Drive
Bloomington, IN 47403
www.iuniverse.com
844-349-9409

Because of the dynamic nature of the Internet, any web addresses or
links contained in this book may have changed since publication and
may no longer be valid. The views expressed in this work are solely those
of the author and do not necessarily reflect the views of the publisher,
and the publisher hereby disclaims any responsibility for them.

Any people depicted in stock imagery provided by Thinkstock are models,
and such images are being used for illustrative purposes only.

Certain stock imagery © Thinkstock.

ISBN: 978-1-4759-9319-6 (sc)
ISBN: 978-1-4759-9321-9 (hc)
ISBN: 978-1-4759-9320-2 (e)

Library of Congress Control Number: 2013909853

Print information available on the last page.

iUniverse rev. date: 11/11/2020

CHAPTER ONE

"No!" Jake screams. Two bullets hit him, one in the chest and the other in the head. "Stop, Jena! It wasn't me!" She hears Jakes voice echo in her head as she tosses and turns.

"Wake up, Jena." Jake shakes her. "Wake up. You're dreaming." Jake pushes Jena. She opens her eyes.

"Jake?" Jena stares at Jake in disbelief that he is still alive. She's breathing hard. "Oh, Jake." Jena looks around the room. The gun she used to kill Mr. McNeil is on the table next to her. She looks back at Jake, and then she gets out of the bed slowly. "You're alive, but ..."

Jake removes the covers. "Yes, you killed Mr. McNeil ... and possibly a few other people."

Jena shakes her head. "My mom?" she asks.

"She's dead, Jena," Jake replies.

Tears run down Jena's face. "No! God no!" Jena looks at the bed, blankets, and sheets. "Did we?" she asks.

"Yes, we made love last night and, Jena, it was perfect."

Jena sits on the bed. "I killed you last night, Jake." She looks back at Jake.

"You were dreaming, Jena," Jake says. Jake touches her on the shoulder. He tries to hug her.

"No! Stop! Get away from me," Jena screams.

"What's wrong, Jena?" Jake asks.

"What's wrong? I'm a damn killer, Jake. I killed my—" Jena stops. "I killed my mother ... Why would I do that?"

Jake rubs his hands through his hair. "I don't know, Jena, and I don't care. I love you."

"Oh, you love a killer? A person who could kill her own ... mother."

Jena begins to remember her father's horrible death. She gets angry and remembers why she killed Mr. McNeil. *He deserved every bullet he got*, she thinks.

Jake walks over to Jena's side of the bed. He sits down next to her. "Jena, I don't have all the answers," Jake says. "I don't know what happened to make you do the things you did. What I do know is that I love you and I'll do anything for you." Jake kisses Jena on the cheek and then tries to kiss her on the lips.

"Don't!" Jena gets up from the bed. "I have to go," she says quietly.

"Go where?" Jake asks.

"I don't know, Jake, just away from you. From this place." Jena picks up the gun.

Jake stands up. "Jena, please put the gun down."

She points the gun at Jake. "You don't know who I am, Jake. Who I've become." Jena has both index fingers on the gun's trigger. Jake steps toward her. "Stop! Don't move, Jake," she says.

"Jena, you don't want to do this," Jake pleads.

"Really? I don't? You don't know what I want or what I care about." Jena walks closer to Jake. She puts the gun to his head.

"Jena, I love you," Jake says.

"Love. Me. You love me. I don't think you do. I think you've been obsessed with me since we were kids. I think you've wanted to have sex with me, but you don't love me. How could you love someone who has killed her own mother and is capable of killing you? No, you don't love me ... and that's why you have die."

"Jena, *no!*"

"Yes, Jake, with everything that's happened, you have to die. I can't have you constantly reminding me of the things that I'm not proud of."

"Jena, please. Don't, Jena, please—" Jena fires two shots into Jake's head. He falls backward to the bed.

Jena suddenly wakes from her dream. Jake is lying next to her, still asleep. She pulls the covers back and realizes that they are both naked. She looks around the room, fearing that this moment is also a dream. The blowing wind from the hotel room window convinces her that this moment is real. The gun that killed Mr. McNeil is still on the table next to her bed. She slowly gets up and dresses, staring at Jake the entire time. She grabs the gun from the table and places it in her bag and then slips on her shoes and coat. The wind blows her hair from side to side. She reaches back into the bag for the gun and points it at Jake. With the wind still whipping at her hair, she stands firm and continues to point the gun at Jake. Exhausted from the night before, Jake doesn't stir. Jena puts the gun down.

Jena remembers spotting Mr. McNeil at the dance club. She remembers how she flirted with him in the cab and in the hotel room—and how she killed him just before Jake rushed into the room. The look on his face. The look of love and fear.

Jena puts the gun back into her bag. She backs away, slowly opens the hotel room door, walks out, and gently closes the door. A couple is kissing in the hotel hallway as Jena passes. The girl stops and stares at Jena as she walks past. Jena gives her an evil look. She stops.

"Is there something wrong?" Jena asks. The couple just stares at Jena, and then the girl shakes her head.

"Get out of here," the guy says to Jena.

Jena pulls out her gun. "You talking to me?" Jena points the gun in the guy's face. "I don't think you're talking to me."

"No, I wasn't talking to you," the man says. "I was talking to myself."

Jena looks at the girl. "Are you scared?" Jena asks. The girl looks at the man, afraid to speak. "I asked are you scared?" Jena raises her voice. The girl nods her head. "What's your name?"

"Candy," she reply.

"Candy," Jena says. "Your name is Candy?"

"Yes."

"Well, Candy, get the hell out of here." Jena points the gun at Candy and pushes her. Candy runs down the hall. Jena points the gun at the man. "What's your name?"

"My name is Paul."

"Paul … Well, Paul, today is your unlucky day." Jena fires a shot at Paul's left leg. Paul falls to the floor. People begin peeking out of their hotel rooms. Jake opens the door. Jena sees him and runs.

"Jena! Jena come back!" Jake yells and tries to run behind her, but Jena is gone. Jake goes back to help Paul.

Candy is standing over Paul. "Don't help him," she says. "He's an asshole." Candy kicks Paul.

"Well, talk about kicking a person when they're down," Janice, one of the guests, says.

Jake rushes back to the hotel room. *I have to find Jena,* he thinks. He frantically gets dressed, quickly grabs his things, and leaves the room. *Jena, my love, I know you're confused and I know you're not yourself, but I will find you.* Jake stops. *I will find you.*

Jake rushes out to the New York streets and screams Jena's name. "Jena!" He cries out. "Jena! Where are you?" People pass Jake by and stare, but he doesn't care. He is desperate and willing to do or say anything to be with Jena again.

*   *   *

Jake searches for Jena for days, but there is no sign of her anywhere. He passes a police station and stops, but he realizes he can't report Jena as a missing person because of the murders she has committed.

He doesn't know what to do. Just then he looks up and notices a flashing sign advertising a psychic palm reader. Jake contemplates his options as the flashing lights blink back and forth. He finally walks in the door.

A lady with a wrinkled face and a scarf wrapped around her head is sitting at a table. She looks at Jake, glaring at him with her dark eyes. "My name is Jaslin. How can I help you?" Jake just stands there and doesn't say a word. As if she could sense Jake's desperation, Jaslin stands up and gestures to Jake with one of her arms. "Please, have a seat." Jake sits down in the chair.

The two of them sit and stare at one another for at least a minute. "I know why you're here," Jaslin says. Jake looks away to avoid Jaslin's eyes. "Please look at me," she says. "Look at me and know the truth," she continues. "Know the truth about the one you love." Jake's eyes widen. "That's what you seek?" she asks quietly. "You seek the one you love ... and the one you fear." Jake doesn't speak. "Your lips don't move, but your eyes," Jaslin glares at Jake, "yes, your eyes tell me all the truth I need to know. You want to know where she is, don't you?" Jake shakes his head. "You want to know if she is," Jaslin pauses, "bad?" Jake swallows. "I must tell the truth," Jaslin says. "You may not be satisfied, but the truth is all I know and is all I will tell anyone. The truth in itself can be a lie. A lie and the truth can be one in the same. She is good, and she is bad. She is a woman scorned and a woman who has no path. The pain in her is deep ... too deep for you to reach. She is falling—falling slowly. Just like a bird flying through the sky, she is free."

"Will I find her?" Jake asks.

"Yes," Jaslin answers. "You will find what you want to find, but it may not be real."

Jake stands up. "Oh, come on. You haven't told me anything," he shouts. "Just a bunch of nonsense." He slams his fist on the table. "Where is she?"

Jaslin stands. "I've told you a lot, but you are not open to listening. She is here."

Jake looks around the room. "Here? Where?"

"Wherever you are, Jake, that's where she is."

"How did you know my ..." Jake pauses.

Jaslin continues. "Wherever you are, Jake, she is with you. You will always be able to find her. Find your Jena."

Jake is shocked. He reaches in his pocket.

"Don't," Jaslin says. "I don't want your money. You will pay a price, but it will not be here."

Jake stands with his head down for a moment. "I don't know what price I have to pay. I love her," he says. "Love has no price."

"Everything has a price," Jaslin says.

Jake rushes out of the building. He walks down the deserted street. *I will find her*, he thinks to himself. *I will find you, Jena.*

CHAPTER TWO

J ena sits on the city bus with her bag in her lap. She stares out the bus window and flashes back to a memory from when she was five years old.

"So, Daddy, what kind of animal is that?" Jena asks her father.

"Oh, Jena, this isn't an animal. This is just a ladybug." Mr. Parker picks up the bug and hands it to Jena. "Here—see, it won't harm you," he says.

Jena slowly reaches for the ladybug. "Are you sure, Daddy?" Jena asks. Mr. Parker smiles at her and nods his head. Jena holds the ladybug gently in her hands. She grins at her father. "It's just a little old tiny bug looking for a friend. I'm holding it, Daddy," Jena says. "I'm holding it!" The young Jena smiles at her father. "I love it, Daddy. It doesn't want to harm anyone. It's just a little old bug." Suddenly she's back on the bus.

"Do you mind if I sit here?" Jena looks up and discovers an old lady with a cane staring at her. Jena shakes her head then turns back to stare out the bus window.

"My name is Joan," the old lady says. "What's yours?"

Jena turns to her. "Jena," she says.

"Jena," Joan says. "I like the name Jena. It sounds so sweet." Jena turns away. "I bet your mother was just beside herself trying to come up with a name for you," Joan continues. "I remember when my daughter was first born. I didn't quite know what to name her, but as soon as looked into those big baby-blue eyes I knew. I knew she had to be called Lucille. You know, like Lucille Ball?" Jena continued to stare out the window. Joan got quiet. "I lost Lucille about six years ago." Jena turns back to look at Joan, whose eyes begin to well up with tears. "Yeah, she left me. Here. She was such a nice young lady, although she wasn't really young at all. She was sixty-five."

The bus stops, and Jena stands up to get off. "So this is your stop?" Joan asks. Jena stares at her. "You don't say much, do you?" Joan asks.

"No," Jena replies, and then she walks down the aisle of the bus and steps off. Joan stares out the bus window as Jena walks away. Just as the bus is getting ready to leave, Jena turns around and looks back at Joan. She walks up to the bus window so Joan can read her lips. Jena whispers, "Lucille is better off." Joan moves back from the window with a surprised look on her face while the bus pulls away.

*   *   *

"Papers! Anyone need a paper? How about you, ma'am—would you like a paper today?" Jena walks past without saying a word. Scott, the paper guy, gets upset. "Oh, what does a guy have to do these days to get someone to buy a paper?" he yells.

Jena stops, turns around, and walks back toward Scott. "Shut up!" she yells. Scott looks shocked. "Do you think that anyone wants to buy your pathetic paper?" Jena asks. "Why would anyone want to read this paper? It's depressing and loaded with columns of bad news and poor advertising. Someone's always trying to sell you something—someone like you."

"Look, lady—" Scott tries to speak.

"I said shut up!" Jena says.

Scott stares at the coldness in Jena's eyes. He quickly packs up his newspapers. "I'll just find me another corner," Scott says.

"Yeah, you do that," Jena says. Scott hurries up and leaves. Jena reaches in her bag for a piece of paper with an address on it. *This is it*, she thinks. In front of her is a cathedral church. Jena stands in front of the building and stares for a moment. She begins walking up the long steps of the church. Statues of angels and godly figures surround the church entrance. When Jena walks inside, she sees it is full of beautiful paintings of Christ, angels, and other holy figures. There is a red carpet leading up to the altar. Two altar boys stand at the front entrance.

"May we help you?" they both say simultaneously.

Jena shifts her gaze back and forth between the two boys and realizes they are twins. "Yes," she says, "I'd like to see the priest. I'd like to attend confession."

One of the altar boys turns. "Follow me, and I will take you to him." He walks slowly in front of Jena; Jena patiently follows. He takes Jena to a booth located near the front of the church. "Here," the altar boy says. "He is in here." The boy slightly bows his head and then slowly walks back to the front of the church.

Jena walks into the booth. There is a priest sitting inside, but Jena can barely see him. She opens the window to speak to him. She doesn't say anything for a moment. The priest doesn't say anything either. Jena blinks her eyes.

"Forgive me, Father, for I have sinned."

A deep voice echoes through the confession booth window, "Yes, my child."

"I have sinned, and I'm here to confess," Jena says quietly.

"My name is Father John, and I will hear your confession," he says. "Go on, my child."

"Father, I committed a horrible act of revenge on the man who killed my father." Jena pauses. "I don't have a family anymore, Father. My father is dead. All of them are dead. Some by the hands of another, and ..." Jena pauses again.

"Yes—go on, child," Father John says.

"Father, will the Lord forgive me?"

"The Lord forgives everyone who confesses and ask for forgiveness."

Jena leans forward. She remembers the gun fire echoing in her head when she shot Mr. McNeil, and the feeling of contentment rushes back to her. She peeks through the confession booth window. "Father, what if a person isn't truly sorry?"

Father John pauses before answering, "You mean you aren't sorry you shot me?" Jena stares closely and realizes that the priest is Mr. McNeil. Mr. McNeil leans closer to Jena's face. His nose presses against the confession booth window. Jena looks at him with fear. "Of course you're not sorry. You meant to kill me, and you'll kill again and again because you're a killer, Jena. You were a killer long before I killed your father."

Jena is eye to eye with Mr. McNeil. "I killed you once, and I'll kill you again."

"You can't kill a ghost, Jena." McNeil begins shaking the confession booth. "You can't kill me anymore." He is laughing— harder and harder. Jena suddenly wakes up on the bus. Old lady Joan is sitting next to her.

"So see, dear, that's my life summary in ten minutes," Joan says. Jena stares at her and looks around the bus with a startled expression on her face. She is breathing hard. The bus stops, and Jena rushes to get off. Still breathing hard, she hurries to exit the bus. The bus driver doesn't say a word as he opens the door. Jena's bag falls to the ground. She reaches to pick up her bag and glances back at the bus. Old lady Joan gives her an evil grin, and then everyone on the bus stands up and stares at her. The driver steps off the bus. Jena begins to run down the street.

She runs until she reaches a corner store. There is a Chinese woman working behind the counter. Jena goes inside. A bell rings. A man wearing a long leather jacket enters the store behind Jena. Jena walks over to the drink cooler. The man moves toward the counter and points a gun at the woman.

"You give me everything you got!" the robber says. The woman freezes in fear. Jena leans back against the cooler. The man turns to Jena and says, "You better not move." The robber turns back to the Chinese woman and points the gun at her face. "Move faster, lady. You're in America. This is America, and you better give me what I want," the robber says. The scared Chinese woman scrambles to get the money out of the cash register. She is so nervous that she drops most of the money on the floor. "Pick it up!" the robber yells.

A gun fires. The robber is shot in the shoulder. He quickly turns toward Jena as she fires the next shot through his head. Blood spills over the store counter and on the Chinese woman's face. The woman screams. Jena points the gun at her. "Shut up! I don't want to kill you," Jena says. "At least not today." The Chinese woman continues to scream as she falls to the floor in fear. Jena puts her gun back in her bag, grabs a cola from the cooler, and walks out of the store.

CHAPTER THREE

J ena, where are you? Jake ponders as he desperately searches New York's streets, stores, and alleys. He is physically and mentally exhausted, so he walks back to the hotel room, plunges onto the bed, and falls asleep.

Police officers begin to surround the corner store where Jena shot the robber dead. Jena manages to wave down a cab driven by a Middle Eastern man wearing a white turban on his head.

"Where to?" the cab driver asks. Jena hands the driver a piece of paper. "Okay," the cabby says as he presses heavily on the gas pedal. He eventually pulls up to the hotel where Jena and Jake had stayed. "That'll be fifteen dollars and ninety-four cents," he says. Jena hands him a twenty, gets out of the cab, and closes the door without saying a word.

There are several people walking past the hotel. Jena quietly looks around to make sure there are no cops in the area. A man is entering the elevator. He sees Jena coming and holds the door, but Jena walks past the elevator straight to the stairs. The man gives her a strange look, shakes his head, and then lets the elevator door close.

The hotel is quiet. While Jena ascends the stairs, she remembers the night she and Jake made love, the horrible dream she had about killing him, and the moment she left him. She wonders to herself,

Why am I going back to that room? Am I hoping that Jake will be there waiting for me to return? If he isn't, is he out pounding the streets searching for me? Can he possibly understand why I killed? Exhausted from searching for Jena, Jake is crashed out on the hotel room's bed. Jena uses her room key to open the door. She sees Jake lying motionless on the bed. He doesn't hear the door opening. She slowly closes the door and walks to the edge of the bed, puts her bag on the floor, and gently lies down on the bed next to him. Facing him, she watches him sleep. She studies his face, his lips, and the movement of his eyes under his eyelids. *I wonder what he is dreaming about,* she thinks. Her thoughts begin to wander back to when they were ten-year-olds playing at the lake; that was when she first knew in her heart that Jake loved her. In her mind, she is transported back to when the two of them were sitting near the lake, tossing rocks and talking.

"Tim was a jerk today," Jena says.

"Yeah, he's always a jerk," Jake says. "I never wanted to be his friend, but Mom was friends with his mom so ..." Jake pauses. "Well, you know how that goes." Jake stares over at Jena. Jena looks away. She sighs and then looks back at him. "It's not your fault, Jake." Jena reaches over to touch Jake's hand. "You didn't know that he was going to tell the whole school your secret."

Jake throws a rock in the lake. "Yeah, now the whole world knows." He throws another rock.

"It's not that bad," Jena says.

Jake stops throwing rocks. "No, I guess not," he says. "I mean, it's not a real big deal that I accidently wet the bed," he quietly says.

Jena shakes her head and tries not to laugh. She moves closer to Jake. "Jake, everybody wets the bed at least once."

Jake looks over at Jena and says, "Yeah, but the whole school doesn't know about it. I knew I should never have let him spend the night ..." He pauses again. "Jena, have you wet the bed before?"

Jena's mind says no, but her lips lie. "Of course, Jake," she says. "Once I had this really weird dream that I was going, but in my dream I was on the toilet and when I woke up I was in my bed."

Jake smirks. "You thought you was on a toilet?"

"Yeah, the dream seemed so real."

Jake begins to feel better. "Yeah, yeah," he mutters and then turns to Jena. The sunlight beams in Jena's eyes, and Jake can't take his eyes off her. Jena stares back at him, and the two of them lock eyes for over a minute. Jake finally turns his head, and Jena puts her head down. "So ..." Jake stands up and reaches for Jena's hand, "we better get back before your mom calls my mom," he says.

Jena stands up and brushes the dirt off her shorts. "Yeah, I guess so," she says.

"Jena, you know you're my best friend?"

"Of course I know that, Jake."

Jake smiles at Jena, and Jena smiles back. They both begin walking toward home.

Jena shoves Jake. "I bet you can't outrun me," she yells and begins to sprint.

"Oh, no fair! You're cheating!" Jake screams as he tries to catch up. They both run through the wooded field, leaping over flowers and zigzagging through trees.

*   *   *

Jake opens his eyes to discover Jena staring at him, smiling. He is shocked and mesmerized by her presence. "Am I dreaming?" he asks.

"No," Jena replies. She begins to lean toward him.

"Please don't move, Jena," Jake asks. "I just want to look into your eyes. Those beautiful eyes." He gently reaches over to touch her face. He brushes her hair back. "You're beautiful, Jena."

Jena blinks her eyes and has a sad look on her face. She leans forward. "You still think I'm beautiful after everything I've done?" She looks down at Jake.

Jake leans forward. "Yes, I do."

Jena stands up and reaches for her bag. "Jake, we have to leave New York. There are police officers all over the place, and I killed a man earlier."

"Jena!" Jake stands up. "What happened?"

"He was robbing a store, and clearly he was going to kill me and the clerk—so I did him in first." Jena turns around. "And I can't say I didn't enjoy it, because I did."

"How did you know I would still be here?" Jake asks.

"Jake, I knew you wouldn't leave New York without me, and I couldn't just leave you here to wonder. So I came back for you. I've put you in a terrible position." Jake turns around to face the hotel door. "Jake, we have to leave now! I'm surprised the police don't have this place surrounded." Jake walks closer to Jena.

"Maybe that's because this is New York and there's probably five million other murders going on," he says.

"Maybe," Jena replies.

"Where are we going to go, Jena?"

Jena reaches in her bag and pulls out the letter her mother had given her right before graduation. "Home," Jena says. "It's been only a few days. I'm sure my family hasn't buried my mother yet." Jena speaks sharply, "So you're going to take me home, Jake." Jake turns to look at Jena, but then he puts his head down. Jena pauses. She walks slowly toward him. "Are you afraid of me, Jake?" She smiles at him.

"No," he answers as he moves closer to her. He touches her face. She tries to look away. "Don't look away from me," he says in a soft voice. He kisses Jena gently on the lips. "Despite everything, Jena, I love you."

Jena breaks his gaze and walks away from him. "Jake, we have to go," she says in a demanding voice. "I don't want to miss my mother's funeral." Jena walks out of the hotel room and heads toward the car.

Jake turns and walks to the car with his hands in his pockets. He stops to stare at Jena as the wind blows through her hair and brushes her long coat open. He thinks back to the days when they were on the school bus together and he couldn't stop staring at her and daydreaming about her.

Jena opens the car door. "Are you coming, Jake?" she asks.

Jake snaps out of the daydream. He smiles at her as he walks to the car, gets in, and starts it up. "Jena, before I drive you back home, please promise that you won't run away again." Jake looks over at her. Jena looks away. "Promise me."

Jena is silent. Jake's voice fades away, and she is back in the hotel room pointing the gun at Mr. McNeil as he lies on the bed, filled with terror and fear. She hears his voice. "Jena … Jena Parker," he says.

"No. My name is Jena Gray." She can hear her name *Jena Gray* repeat over and over again in her mind. Then all of the thoughts of the tragic memories of the past sink in like a deep stab wound as she finally accepts the person she has become.

CHAPTER FOUR

She isn't Jena Parker anymore; she is Jena Gray. *Nothing Jake or anyone else could do or say can change that now,* she thinks. "The police are looking for me?" Jena turns to Jake and asks.

"Yes," he hesitatingly answers. "Yes they are, Jena. My mother has already been questioned over ten times about my whereabouts …" he says as he turns to Jena, "and yours. They're even trying to link me to the murders you've committed."

Jena frowns and turns away. "You had nothing to do with it," she says in a hard, rushed voice.

"As long as I'm missing, they'll assume I'm with you and they'll assume I played a part in the murders."

"Jake, you don't—"

Jake quickly pulls over to the side of the road and stops the car. He stops so quickly that they both bounce around in the car. "What were you gonna say, Jena? Were you gonna say, 'Jake, you don't have to be here' or 'Jake, you can leave'? If you were gonna say that, then you might as well save your words because I'm not going anywhere." He squeezes the steering wheel and pushes down hard on the gas pedal, propelling the car back on the highway.

Jena sighs and rolls down the car window. The wind blows her hair sideways as Jake stares off down the road. The two of them remain silent for hours, Jena staring off at the side of the road as Jake drives. Jake steals glances at her while trying hard not to lose his focus. *What is she thinking about?* he wonders to himself. *Does she even think about me at all? Does she remember our friendship, how much I love her? How much I've always loved her?* Jake peeks over at Jena. Jena is still staring out the window, almost as if Jake no longer existed and she was just traveling in some soundproof capsule. *The woman I love is a killer—not a born killer, yet a killer just the same. She's a young, beautiful girl who once had a bright future ahead of her. Now she's torn and transformed.* Just as Jake has this last thought, Jena turns and stares him directly in the eyes without saying a word. Jake quickly looks away. Jena turns back and resumes staring out the window.

"Are you hungry?" she asks.

Jake pauses and then breathes hard. "A little," he answers.

"Well, let's stop," she says.

"Okay," he replies. They pass a road sign. "Well, the nearest food and gas is in ten miles." He looks over and discovers her gazing at him with cold eyes.

"I guess we're stopping in ten miles," Jena says. She continues to stare at Jake as he drives. "Don't be afraid of me, Jake," she says as she scoots closer to him. She touches his leg and runs her hand up to his crotch and squeezes it. "I'll never hurt you."

Jake shakes his head. "Jena, you have a strong grip."

She smiles at him. "So does that mean you want me to stop?"

"Umm, yes ... no, I mean I ..." Jake is caught off guard by Jena's boldness.

Jena lets go of Jake's crotch and then whispers in his ear, "We'll finish this later." She turns and scoots back to her side of the car. Her hair blowing in the wind again, she goes quickly back into her own time capsule. Again there is nothing but silence in the car between them—at least in spoken words.

Jake's thoughts about Jena are out of control. He can't think of anything but holding her gently in his arms and making love to her like he had before. His mind returns to when he was in bed with Jena. He fantasizes about her laying there naked. Her body so beautifully formed. His hands all over her soft skin. He leans down, kisses her, and begins caressing her breast. She turns her head to the side as he kisses her neck, breasts, stomach, and between her thighs. As his tongue massages her inner lips, Jena moans with excitement and grabs his head, pulling it closer to her. Jake kisses her thighs again, her stomach, her neck, and then he passionately kisses her on the lips as he slowly penetrates her. Jena breathes out softly and then lets out a harder breath. She grabs him tightly as he penetrates slowly and softly.

Jake tries to focus on driving, but his mind keeps drifting back to that night. He grips the steering wheel tightly.

"Jake!" Jena yells. "Watch out!" Jake's focus returns to the highway in time to see the deer in front of them. He swerves almost off the road to avoid hitting the deer. He pulls off to the side of the road. Jena is staring at him with a shocked look on her face. She gives him a mean look. "What the hell is wrong with you?" she asks him.

Jake is breathing hard—less from the almost-fatal accident than from the thoughts of him and Jena. Jake sits silently for several seconds before even looking at Jena. "I'm sorry." He looks over at her and then looks to the other side of the road, where the deer was standing. "I'm sorry I wasn't paying attention."

"Really," Jena snaps at him.

"I had something very important on my mind, Jena," he answers back.

"Yeah—what?" she asks. He drives back onto the road. "What were you thinking about, Jake?" Jena refuses to let it go.

Jake doesn't answer right away. He spins back onto the road and starts driving again. Jena looks back out her window. "You," he finally answers. "I was thinking about you and me last night." Jena looks over at him, looks down, and then looks back out the window. "I was thinking about how lovely you looked—tender, sweet—and how much I really ..." Jake swallows. "How much I love you, Jena. I love you so much."

Jena doesn't say a word. She leaves Jake hanging on his thoughts of her without her expressing any thoughts of him. Jena suddenly leans forward. Jake is looking her. "Jake. Jake!" she yells. "Stop the car!"

"Why?" he asks.

"Because there's a guy walking out onto the highway, and I don't want you to hit him." Jake looks back to the highway. A young guy with a backpack on his shoulders, a jacket in his arms, and an iPod in his hand is waving them down. Jake speeds up. "What the hell are you doing, Jake?" Jena yells.

"I'm speeding up. I'm not going to stop."

"Why not?"

Jake slows down and stops just inches from hitting the walker. "So you want to pick up a hitcher?" Jake asks her.

"Yes," she answers. Jena opens her car door, gets out, and walks up to the hitchhiker. The two stand in the middle of the road and stare at each other. Jena grabs his bag. "You need a ride?" she asks.

The man gives her a flirty look with a slight come-on smile. "Yeah. I would say me walking out in the middle of the highway would be a great indicator of that."

Jena frowns and tosses his bag back to him. "Really? I would say that you almost got your ass killed. If it wasn't for me telling Jake"—she points at Jake—"to stop, you would be spread out across this highway and we would be halfway down this road. Now I'll ask you again." She leans her head slightly to the side. "Do you need a ride?"

The hitchhiker quickly answers, "Yes!"

Jena waves for him to get in the car. The hitchhiker pulls the backseat down to hop in. Jena grabs him. "No. I'll get in the backseat. You get in the front."

He looks at her strangely. "Okay, will do," he says. The hitchhiker hops in the front. Jena gets in the back.

Jake looks back at her and then at the hitchhiker. "You got a name, guy?" Jake asks.

"Yeah—Matt."

Jena leans up. "Matt what?"

"Matt Ross." Jena leans back. Matt asks, "Where are you guys headed?"

"Home," Jena answers. "We're headed home."

Matt shakes his head. "And ... umm ... where's home?"

"Where are you headed, Matt?" Jake asks.

Matt pauses. "Well, I'm not really headed anywhere. I'm kind of a loner—a drifter." Matt puts his bag on the car floor. "So wherever you guys go or however far you're willing to let me ride is where I'm going." Matt looks back at Jena and then looks at Jake.

Jake puts the car in gear and drives off quickly. "We've got to make a food, gas, and whatever-else stop," Jake says. "So, you cool with that?"

Matt nods his head. "Yeah, man, I'm cool with whatever you guys do. I mean, I'm the one hitching a ride." Matt leans back comfortably in his seat. "Hey, man, when you hitch you got no complaints."

Jake peeks at Jena in the rearview mirror; she stares back at him and winks.

CHAPTER FIVE

"Five miles to the next gas and food stop," Matt says as he gets comfortable in his seat.

Jake drives a few more minutes and then the five-mile sign appears. "How did you know that, Matt?" Jake asked.

"Oh, I've traveled this road a few times," Matt says causally. Jena remains silent. Jake glances at her in the rearview mirror.

"Well, here's our stop," Jake announces. "I'll get the gas first and then we'll eat." Jake pulls into the gas station, gets out, and begins pumping gas.

Matt turns around to start a conversation with Jena. "So, that's your boyfriend?" Jena just gives him a blank stare. Matt is persistent. "You are a very beautiful girl. I'm sure that's your boyfriend."

Jena leans up and stares Matt right in the eyes. "So what if he is?" she answers. "What are you going to do about it?" The look in her eyes makes Matt a little uneasy. Jena leans back in her seat just as Jake gets back into the car. Matt turns around. He makes quick conversation with Jake.

"Hey, umm, I'm a little low on cash, but when we get to the restaurant I'll hit up an ATM."

"Yeah," Jake replies, clearly unconvinced. Jake drives to the diner.

"Oh, look. We're at Kyler's Diner—the home of the best hot and fresh breads and all-you-can-eat soup," Matt says in a sarcastic voice. "Wow, only in the middle of nowhere would a bunch of hicks think that all-you-can-eat soup could be a delightful meal." Matt continues to make jokes. "You know, I once ate at this place that said they had the best burgers in town. Turns out they were serving up ground-up rat meat. Man, I ate one of those rat burgers and puked for an entire week." Jake and Jena both remain silent. "Man, just thinking of that makes me want to puke."

"Can we not talk about rat burgers right now?" Jake asks as he gets out the car and lets Jena out from the back.

Jena walks over to Matt's windows and leans in and whispers to him, "Maybe you would have been better off being spattered all over the highway."

Jake grabs her. "Let's eat, Jena."

She opens the car door for Matt. "Yeah, Matt, let's eat some nice rat soup."

Jena and Jake walk into the diner. Matt grabs his bag and follows them. Jena, Jake, and Matt find a table. Five huge truckers walk in behind them, laughing and joking.

"So what are you carrying today, Bob?" one of the truckers asks.

"Oh, just some hot items," Bob says. They all sit down.

"Hot items? What hot items?"

"Hot like your momma, boy ..."

"Oh, we doing 'your momma' jokes?" The biggest guy in the group suddenly stands. "Oh, don't any of you talk about my momma. Don't say anything about my momma." The biggest trucker has a serious look on his face. The entire table is quiet. Jena, Jake, and Matt overhear the truckers' conversation.

"Good lord, Big Papa, calm down," Bob says. "No one said anything about your momma." Big Papa sits back down while eyeing all of them. "Yet ..." Bob laughs, and the other three guys chuckle real hard. Big Papa begins getting up again. "Oh, sit down and get some all-you-can-eat hot soup in this hot-ass desert." Big Papa sits down, and they all laugh, joke, and chuckle some more.

The restaurant has ten tables, all filled with waiting customers. There's only one waitress, and the owner, Kyler, is the cook and the cashier. There's a TV right on the cashier's counter. Its signal flickers in and out, and Kyler has to pop it a few times to get the picture to come back into view.

"Damn it, Kyler," Big Papa yells out. "Every time we come in this place we have to wait. You say you're going to get more help, and here we are again—and here you are with just one damn waitress."

"Calm down, Big Papa. I'm just trying to run a local business," Kyler yells back. "I leave the truckin' to you guys, so you leave the cooking to me."

"You call soup cookin'?" Big Papa yells back. "Hell, I can make a can of soup. Besides, it's hot as shit in this desert. Who the hell wants soup, anyway?" Big Papa says loudly.

"Obviously you, Big Papa, because you're back again," Kyler yells. "So just wait until Rosa gets to your table."

Big Papa gives Kyler a dirty look. "I better get some hot and fresh bread too," he yells out. The truckers start laughing. Rosa finally gets to the truckers' table.

Jena eyes the entire diner, watching everyone talk and wait patiently for Rosa to take their orders. Matt looks at her. "You looking for someone?" he asks.

Jake quickly butts in. "So, Matt, how long have you been just wandering around the world?"

Matt scratches his neck. "For a while, man. I mean, I don't really have a home," he says. "I'm a loner, and I like it that way." Matt focuses back on Jena. "Jena, you are the quietest female I've ever met." He laughs. "I mean, most the women I've been around—and that would be a lot—couldn't shut up. But you, you are so calm and quiet," he says.

Jena gives Matt a mild smile. "You ever heard of the quiet before the storm?" she asks while giving Matt a devilish look. Matt backs off.

Rosa finally reaches their table. Jena and Jake order while Matt looks nervously around the diner. He watches while Kyler cashes out his customers. His eyes lock in on the exchange of cash.

Rosa asks Matt, "What'll you have?" Matt is still distracted by the cash out of the customers. He quickly reaches in his bag and pulls out a gun just as Kyler cashes out another customer. The customers are all frantic, whispering and crowding around each other. Kyler tries to reach for the shotgun he keeps under the counter.

"Don't reach for that gun," Matt yells. "I know where you keep it, and I'll blow you away."

Big Papa and all the other truckers stand up, ready to fight. "You don't want none of this, son," Big Papa says with his fist clenched. Matt points his gun back and forth from between Kyler and the truckers.

Matt's a little nervous, but he tries to act tough. "No, you don't want none of this," Matt says. "Now sit down and shut up." He points the gun around the room. Jake has an angry, intense look on his face, but Jena is calm.

A man yells, "Put down the gun!" Matt points the gun at him, back at Kyler, and then around the room.

"Give me the money, man," Matt yells.

"I ain't giving you shit," Kyler yells back, still reaching for his shotgun. Matt feels trapped. He glances down a little, and in that one second Jena is standing behind him with a gun pointed at his head.

"Put it down, Matt," she says in a calm voice. Matt is still pointing his gun at Kyler.

Kyler grabs his shotgun and points it at Matt. "I'm going to blow you away, son."

"Shoot 'em—shoot 'em!" Bob the trucker yells. The tension in the room grows: Jena pointing her gun at Matt, Matt pointing his gun at Kyler, the truckers all ready to fight, and Kyler ready to shoot off his shotgun.

The TV clears, and there's a news bulletin. As the newsman begins to speak, Kyler peeks up at the TV. The entire restaurant is suddenly listening in. Jena's picture is flashing on the TV. "Wanted for multiple murders in—" the picture flickers off and then on again "—and New York, Jena Parker." Everyone in the room stares at Jena. Kyler cocks his shotgun. Jake stands up. The truckers move in closer.

Bob yells out, "That's her! That's Jena Parker."

"Oh my God, we're all going to die!" a woman yells out while clinging to her daughter.

"Don't kill me!" Matt says as he panics.

"Girl, you better put down that gun," Kyler says.

Jake grabs Matt's gun from his hand and points it at Kyler. "Put it down, man," Jake says in a commanding voice.

Another news flash comes on the TV, and Matt's picture flashes across the screen. "Also wanted in Larmont and Fairmand Counties for burglary and murder is Matthew Ross." Everyone in the diner looks over at Matt. Kyler is ready to shoot. Jake stands next to Jena.

"Oh shit, we got two mass murderers in this restaurant!" Bob yells out.

"I just hit the button. The cops are on the way," Kyler says.

"Jake, let's go," Jena says while scoping the room. Jena and Jake back out of the diner together with their guns pointed.

Matt turns toward them with his arms in the air. "Please don't leave me here!" Matt pleads.

"Leave 'em or let 'em stay—either way, all three of you are going down," Kyler says.

"Put down the weapon," a woman pleads. "For the love of God, just let them go." Kyler ignores her.

Jake and Jena back out the door. The truckers are ready to jump Matt. Matt continues to plead with Jena. "Jena, please don't leave me here. They're going to kill me."

Jena glances over at Jake. A woman jumps in front of Kyler. "Back up, Matt," Jena says. "Let's go."

Matt grabs his bag and rushes out with Jena and Jake. Jake rushes to start the car while Jena covers them. The truckers follow them slowly. Kyler rushes out from behind them. Matt jumps in the passenger seat, and Jena gets in the backseat. Jake drives off quickly.

Kyler and some of the truckers jump in his truck, two in the front and two in the back. Jake is driving over a hundred miles an hour. Kyler is behind him, and so are the cops.

"Drive man, drive!" Matt yells. Jake steps on it and manages to get a speed advantage over them. Matt puts his head down in relief. "Oh, man, that was close," he says.

"Pull over, Jake," Jena says.

"What?" Jake answers.

"Pull over!" Jena yells.

Matt turns around. "What the hell?" he says to her.

"Jake, pull this car over now!" Jena yells.

"Man, don't pull over." Matt tries to grab the wheel. "Don't pull over. She's crazy." They spin out along the side road. Jake manages to stop.

"Get out!" Jena tells Matt.

"What? But you just saved me!" Matt looks confused.

"Get out!" Jena points the gun at him.

"You're not going to shoot me," Matt tests her. "I don't care what that TV said. You're not a killer."

Jena shoots a bullet through the front passenger window, right past Matt's face. "Really?" she says.

Matt runs out of the car. Jake spins off. Kyler and the cops manage to catch up, but they stop to capture Matt. Kyler holds a shotgun on Matt while the truckers hold him down and the sheriff handcuffs him.

"Matthew Ross, you have the right to remain silent. Anything you say …" the sheriff reads Matt his rights as he handcuffs him. Jake drives off as fast as he can. Jena lies down in the backseat, puts the gun on the car floor, and stares out the back window.

CHAPTER SIX

Jake tries to calm down. "Shit! Shit!" he grips the steering wheel tightly. "What the hell was that?" he says out loud. He peers in the mirror at Jena, worried about her. She is calm and staring out the back window. "Jena, are you all right?" Jake says in a panicky voice.

"I'm fine," she says while continuing to stare out the window. Jena's thoughts drift off, away from Jake's panic. Jake is like a blur in the mirror. It's almost as if they're sharing the same space in two alternative worlds.

As a child, I used to dream of being someone famous. Jena sees herself as a child playing with her dolls and smiling with her dad. *Now I am,* she thinks to herself. *All that I was seems like a distant memory. A hoax. A clown laughing at me, taunting me. I saw my dark side several times, but I looked away and pretended that it wasn't me ... How could I become this person?* She asks herself.

Jake is still talking in the background. His words are like bubbles popping in the air. Jena doesn't hear his voice anymore. She doesn't even believe she is sitting in a backseat of a car. When she looks back at Jake, she sees herself in a transient state with the road being just a black image of a gateway and her body floating toward it. There is a force pulling her into this black hole—a force she can't stop. It pulls her back in slow motion, past her shooting of Mr. McNeil, past her sitting with the doctor on the train, past her opening the door for the hotel clerk, and past her father as he stood there in the fog in her dream.

"Daddy ..." Jena reaches out for him as the force takes her. "Daddy ...," she calls. She can feel her body drifting further into the darkness of the force. Her eyes begin to get heavy, her body limp. She is exhausted, paralyzed, and drifts into a deep sleep.

Jena is ten years old, sitting at the top of their house stairs watching her parents slow dance to their favorite song. "If I can't have you, I don't want nobody baby. If I can't have you," Jena's father whispers in Kitty's ear as they dance. He kisses her softly on the lips. Kitty smiles and rests her head back on his shoulder. He kisses her on her forehead, and the two of them dance romantically as Jena watches. Jena smiles at the gentleness her parents share together and dreams of one day having a love like theirs—so passionate, so tender.

Jena gets up and begins to walk to her mother's room, but Jena is now a teenager. She stops and stares at her mother's empty bed and tries to walk into her mother's room, but the force won't allow her to. She is instantly pushed backward. She can feel her body swaying back and forth while she giggles with excitement.

Jena, age five, swings back and forth as her dad pushes her higher and higher. She giggles loudly. Her hair sways in the cool breeze, legs lifted high in the air. Her mom claps her hands and smiles at the two of them. The swing stops and Jena runs off into her mom's arms, reaches to kiss her on the cheek, opens her eyes, and she's in seventh grade and kissing Jake's cheek.

Jake had picked up her books after Ken knocked them out of her hands. He gently handed the books back to Jena, and she leaned over to give him a kiss on the cheek. "You're my hero," she whispers to him. Jake smiles at her. After school that day, they walk down to the lake where they always meet to talk. The cool, warm breeze blows through Jena's hair while Jake sits next to her, gazing at her long eyelashes, her lips, her slender shoulders, and her legs. She turns slightly toward him and smiles as the sun reflects off her smooth lips, wet from her lip gloss.

"Thank you for picking up my books," she says while smiling.

Jake is shy and only smiles and tries to distract himself from her by throwing rocks in the lake. He glances over at her. Her body starts to levitate. He is amazed, caught off guard, and tries to grab her legs to stop her from leaving. "Jena! Jena!" he yells. "What's happening?" The sun suddenly turns dark, and Jake struggles to hold on to Jena's legs. Jena looks down at him frantically holding on to her. She tries to reach for him, but the force is pulling her away. "Jena!" Jake cries. "Jena, please don't go." He grips tightly to her, but his hands begin to slip. "Please!" He can no longer hold on and is forced to let her go. She drifts away into the darkness. Jake stands there with his arms raised up high, crying, and then he falls to his knees. Jena is gone.

She floats somewhere in the darkness and just drifts. There is no one and nothing around her: no sound, no people, no mother or father, and no fear. A tiny light, as small as a pinhead, shines through the darkness. She fixates on the light and lies in transit watching it. She has is no sense of time. Eventually, her body begins to drop. She reaches for the only thing she has—the tiny light—but the faster she falls, the less the light is in sight, until it's gone and only darkness surrounds her. The darkness and Jake's voice blurs together a little. When she can hear him clearly, she opens her eyes.

"Jena," Jake calls. He has pulled over to the side of the road, out of sight, and he gently touches Jena's arm. "Jena, are you all right?"

Jena is silent, but she feels relieved and happy that it's Jake's face she awoke to. She reaches for him, pulls him closer, and begins kissing him softly and squeezing him tightly. "I've been waiting for this moment all day," she whispers softly in his ear.

Jake kisses her gently on the lips, and then they both gaze deeply into each other's eyes. He reaches for her face, touches it, and rubs his hands down her cheek, along her neck, to her breast while gently caressing and kissing her. Jena stops for a second and navigates Jake on to his back in the backseat. She sits on top of him, removes her blouse, and throws it in the front seat. He reaches for her breasts and gently squeezes them and leans up to bury his lips in between them while removing her bra. He pulls her to him, his hands conforming to her like soft butter, rubbing every inch of her body, every sensual part of her. She breathes softly as he kisses her neck and smoothly removes her pants and panties and his own. She grips him tightly, and he assists her, squeezing her deeper into him. Jena moans softly, harder, and then harder. Her nails dig deeply into his skin, lightly piercing it just enough to induce a little pain and unforgettable pleasure. Jake gently turns Jena around on to her back. He stops to stare at her. Her eyes blaze up at him like the moon shining on a bright night. Her hair is pushed back, showing off her lovely shoulders. Her naked body is exposed to his obsessed eyes. Every movement is an enchanted feeling for him, like horses running in slow motion, pushing them together. He leans into her and they both hear the angels' music. Nothing but music—soft, angelic music—in rhythms that pulse as slowly as the heart of Sleeping Beauty. The motion of their bodies is like ripples of ocean waves flowing over and over again. Though all is silent, to them it is like roaring thunder a hundred times over, nonstop hard raindrops, and then back to sun all in one moment that seems to last for hours and hours.

"I love you, Jena," Jake moans and murmurs through his passion. "I love you so much."

"Jake," Jena says softly. She reaches for his hand. "Squeeze me … squeeze me … hold me, please. Oh, I … I …"

"Jena, are you all right?" Jake asks. "Jena? Jena?"

Jena slowly wakes up. "Jake?" She looks around the car. She breathes out. "Wow. It was so real."

"What was real?" he asks.

"I was dreaming, and then I woke up and we started …" She looks out the car window.

"We started what, Jena?"

"We were making love." She reaches for Jake's face. He is surprised. "I thought it was real," she says. "I mean, I had just woken up, and then we started … but …" Jena stops talking.

Jake kisses her. "It can be real, Jena," he says. "It can be real right now."

Jena stares at him. She leans in close to his face. She stares at him as if it was the first time she had ever seen him. "You're right, Jake. It can be real." She kisses him and then slowly removes her shirt. Her brushed-back hair accentuates her beautiful shoulders. Jake's eyes shine as bright as the moon. She whispers in his ear, "Yes, it will be as real as I dreamed it—even better. I'll make sure of it."

CHAPTER SEVEN

Jake resumes their drive home. The car is once again silent, as Jena stares off out the window.

"This has been a long ride, huh?" Jena says while waving her hands out the car window, the wind pushing it back while she defies it.

"Yes, but we are almost home," Jake says quietly. "Jena, we're going to have to be careful. The police are looking for you ... and me. We can't afford to be seen. We are very lucky to have gotten this far without getting caught," he says while looking around the road suspiciously. They pass a road sign: fifty miles to Maplesville.

Jake utters, "Jena, last night was ... so beautiful. You're beautiful. I'm not leaving you, so don't ask me too." Jena is silent. "We have to find somewhere to hide until we can sort all this out," Jake says.

"Jake, I'm going to my mother's funeral. I think about her. I think about what I did. I know murder is an awful thing to do to your own mother, but my mom died the moment my father left her—the moment that gun fired and killed him. I would have run a hundred miles to avoid seeing her face. I knew she would never be the same again, no matter how much I wanted and needed her to be. Watching her suffer was like watching her fall from a hundred-story building in slow motion." Jena reaches in her bag. Jake watches her. She pulls out the letter her mother gave her after graduation—a letter she never opened. Jena holds the letter lightly in her hand, looks up at the car ceiling, and then puts it back in her bag.

Jake comforts her. "When you're ready, you'll open it."

Jena looks over at Jake as they pass the next highway sign: thirty miles to Maplesville. Jake reaches for Jena's hand, but she pulls away. "I'm not afraid, Jake. I'm not afraid anymore. If anything," she looks out the window, "they should all be afraid of me."

Jake turns off onto a side road. "We have to find another car. The police are looking for us, and by now they have to know what we're driving. Jena, I'm sorry, but I'm going to steal a car tonight."

Jena shakes her head. "Wow, you're worried about stealing a car when I've just killed a few people only a few days ago." She sighs.

Jake pulls slowly into a wooded area. There is a house sitting by itself. The lights on the porch are dim and flicker on and off. A pickup truck sits under an outside garage, and an old car is parked on the grass near the house. Jena and Jake sit still and stare out at the lonely, broken-down house.

Jake slowly opens the car door and steps one foot out. He glances back at Jena. "This is it," he says as he steps out of the car and then gently closes the car door. Jena follows him. They both stand staring out at the house. A slight wind is blowing, and Jena's hair sways in the breeze. Her coat is brushed back by the motion of the wind. Jake looks over at her, swallows softly, and reaches for Jena's hand.

She turns to look at him, squeezes his hand, and kisses him gently on the lips. "What a boy will do for love," she whispers to him.

He softly touches her face, the wind blowing both of them closer. "Not a boy, Jena—a man. I'm a man now. I was a boy a long time ago, but now I'm a man in love. So deeply in love. A love like those told about in fairy tales, movies, and books. But this is no fairy tale or movie. This is me and you, my love." He leans in to kiss Jena, but he stops to just watch her with her eyes closed, her beautiful hair swaying in the wind, and her soft lips waiting for his embrace.

She opens her eyes. "No kiss," she says.

He hugs her tightly. "I just wanted to look at you. Look at your beautiful skin, your face—everything about you is my armor." He places his forehead on hers. "We'll take this journey together." He grabs her hand and walks toward the truck. Jena stands on the lookout as Jake searches for the keys. While Jake continues to search for the keys, Jena wanders off closer to the house. She walks to a window and peeks in.

There is a man standing in the doorway of a room. He is angry and yelling at someone. Jena can barely see the other person. The man grips his fist and walks swiftly toward someone. A woman with her clothes half torn off runs from the end of the room, trying to get away from the man. She is crying and begging for him to stop. He hits her, and the blow from his fist knocks her to the floor.

"Please stop!" she screams. "Please don't do this, Carl. Please stop," she says again.

"You shut up, Maggie." He reaches over and grabs her up by the neck. "You shut up now!" He pushes her against the wall and begins hitting her over and over again, and then he tries to kiss her.

She begs, "Please. STOP IT!"

"You asked for it, Maggie," he says in a deep, mean voice. He rips her dress; one side is hanging almost completely off. Her nose is bleeding, and her face is battered and bruised from his hard fist. He reaches to hit her again. A gun cocks. He turns around with hand ready to strike. Jena is holding a gun on him.

"Don't do it," Jena says in low voice.

"Who the hell are you?" Carl yells. "Get the hell out of my house, you little bitch." He lets go of Maggie. She crawls into a corner, as he walks toward Jena. Jena fires a shot and barely misses.

Jake runs toward the house screaming Jena's name. "Jena! Jena!"

Jena holds the gun on Carl. She looks down at Maggie, who is curled up in the corner crying. Her face is almost beaten in, her clothes torn off, and there are bruise marks all over her body.

Carl walks, big and bad, toward Jena. "You think you can come in someone's house and pull a gun on them? Huh?"

Jena walks toward him, pointing the gun directly at his head. "Yes. I do," she replies. She peeks over at Maggie, who is too afraid to look at her.

Jake reaches the room. "Jena, put the gun down."

"No, Jake. If anyone deserves to die, it's definitely this creep." Jake looks over and sees Maggie crying in the corner.

The room is still and then, just like a circle, the room winds around and around. Maggie in the corner, Jake at the door, Jena with the gun pointed at Carl, and Carl standing defiant. The room spins around and around. Maggie in the corner, Jake at the door, Jena with the gun pointed at Carl, and Carl's face changing to Mr. McNeil's. Jena's eyes grow black as coal. The room darkens. Maggie in the corner, Jake at the door, Jena with the gun, Carl on his knees.

"Stand up, Maggie," Jena speaks gently to Maggie as she looks over at her. "Stand up, and don't be afraid." Maggie stares at Jena. Carl looks back at Maggie to intimidate her. "Don't be afraid, Maggie." Jake moves toward Maggie. "No, Jake, don't," Jena says. "Let her do it on her own."

"Maggie, don't you listen to her," Carl says. Maggie stops crying. She looks over at Jake and Jena.

Jena keeps the gun on Carl. "Come on, Maggie, stand up. It's okay. It's okay." Maggie looks around the room at the broken lamp, down at her torn clothes, and then back at Carl. She slowly manages to stand on her feet, her body shaking and fragile from the beating. She fixes her clothes the best she can. Jake looks away. She walks to the mirror and begins to cry of shame. "It's okay, Maggie," Jena says.

"Maggie, look at you," Carl taunts her. Jena lets him stand while still holding the gun on him. "Yeah, look at you," he continues. "You're ugly. You're fat. You're hopeless." Maggie breathes in hard and stares at herself in the mirror in horror and in shame. Carl looks back over at Jena.

Jena walks a little closer to him, still holding the gun tightly. She begins to tell a story. "There once a man named Mr. McNeil, who lived next door. He was an awful man, a terrible soul who stole the heart of a little girl." Jena walks closer and closer to Carl. Carl stands still while listening closely to Jena's story. "Mr. McNeil was a man of the unknown, a nameless figure, faceless, and destined to face justice. He had no future, because he was a man on a plane—on a plane to nowhere, to destination unknown. How do I know?" Jena is face-to-face with Carl. "I know because I was on the plane with him, and I made sure he never, ever landed ..."

Jake steps close to Jena. Maggie is right beside Carl. She grabs the gun from Jena and shoots Carl twice. He stares her in the eyes as he falls to the floor. Maggie stands holding the gun over his still body. Jake is in shock and doesn't move. Jena stands alongside Maggie—both of them standing over Carl's bleeding body, both of them with emotionless stares on their faces.

A cool breeze flows through the room. Jena and Maggie both sway as they glare down at Carl. Jena kneels down toward Carl and whisper to him, "Now you go. You go and tell them that I'm coming." She looks up at Maggie, the gun still gripped tightly in her hand. Jena slowly stands up and gently takes the gun from Maggie's hand.

Maggie blinks twice. She is focused and is in her right mind. "Will you help me bury him?" she asks, looking at Jena and then Jake. Jena looks over at Jake. He steps slowly toward them. Jena, Jake, and Maggie lift Carl's heavy body and carry it to the backyard and lay him down. Jake grabs a shovel and digs a grave for Carl as Jena and Maggie watch.

CHAPTER EIGHT

J ake is exhausted from all of the shoveling. He climbs to the top
of the grave, lays the shovel down, and gives Jena a look as if to
say it's time to put Carl's body in the grave. Carl's dead body
lies still on the cold, black ground. Maggie is watching the night
sky, avoiding looking at Carl lying there with blood streaming down
from his shirt to his pants. Jake reaches for Maggie's hand as Jena
stands near her and touches her shoulder. Maggie turns to stare at
Carl, walks slowly toward him, and kneels down. Jake walks away
in disappointment with himself for being a part of Carl's death.

Jena stands over Maggie. "Maggie," Jena calls.

Maggie stands up. "I'll do it." She looks at Jena. "I'll do it by
myself. He's my problem." Maggie reaches for Carl's arms. She tries
to drag him, but his body is too heavy. Jena turns to look at Jake; he
walks farther away. Jena leans down, grabs Carl's legs, and both she
and Maggie struggle to carry Carl to the grave. They throw him in.
Jena grabs the shovel and begins to cover Carl's body with the dirt
Jake had dug. She lays the shovel down when she is done.

Maggie stands next to her. "Thank you," she says to Jena. Maggie
begins to cry. "I'm not crying because I'm sorry," she says. "I'm crying
because I'm so happy. Happy that my beatings will stop. That I won't
have to look at another blooded face in the mirror. That I won't have

to hide from my family and friends because I'm too ashamed to tell them the truth." Maggie continues to break down in tears.

Jena doesn't cry or show any emotions, she just points out into the night. "Can you see that, Maggie?"

Maggie looks out into the night. She is confused. "She what?" she answers in a sobbing voice.

"Freedom," Jena says as she turns to walk away. Maggie turns to watch Jena leave. The wind blows, her body movement flows in sync with the wind, and Jake waits for her as he always has, his hands reaching for her, waiting, and longing to hold her, no matter the consequences. No matter the risk or what the end holds. He wasn't thrilled about what he had done, but he wasn't going to leave Jena. Maggie saw in Jena's body movement Jena's sheer confidence that the man she was walking toward was a man that loved her, adored her, and would do anything to keep her—even dig a grave for a woman's lowlife husband whom he didn't even know.

"Wait!" Maggie yelled. Jake and Jena turn around. Maggie walks toward them. "The keys to the truck are hidden under the door mat," she walks toward the house. Jake and Jena follow. "I hide them there just in case one day I'd ever get the courage to leave this hellhole of a place." Maggie gets the keys. "I want you two to take the truck." Maggie looks off to the long, winding road that leads to her house. She hands Jake the keys. "Take the truck and drive. Drive and drive to wherever you two want to go." Maggie smiles as she looks at Jena and Jake. "You two drive on. Drive."

She's inspired by the love Jena and Jake have for one another. A tear drops from one eye. She gets a sudden burst of energy and runs toward her front door. "I'm getting out of here," Maggie says loudly. "I'm going to my sister's, and I'm getting out of here. I'm burning this damn place down to the ground. Everything …" she stops to look around her yard, "everything … Now, you two, come on in, wash up, and be on your way. Don't you worry about me." She wipes the tear from her eye. "No, don't worry about me. I'm getting out of here." Maggie runs into the house, calls her sister, slams the phone down, and runs around the house packing whatever she can take with her.

Jena and Jake wash up in the kitchen. Jake turns to Jena. "You think she'll be all right?" he asks.

Jena watches as Maggie packs her things. She is no longer crying and her face has a glow of light to it. Just like a child being born, Maggie is living life for the first time in a long time. Jena turns to Jake. "She'll be fine. Let's go."

They both walk out of the house without saying good-bye to Maggie, and they jump into the truck. Jake drives away down the road. Jena puts her arm out the window. The cool breeze runs up the sleeve of her coat, up her arm, and a burst of wind flows through to her hair. She closes her eyes. Mr. McNeil's face flashes through her mind. She opens her eyes quickly.

A car speeds past them on the road. The driver honks the horn twice to alert Jake to get out of the way. It's a woman wearing a black hat, an angry look on her face, driving like a drunk who's had way too many beers. The woman spins the car's tires and drives out of control. The dust and wind kick up as she zooms past Jake and Jena.

Jake stops the truck. "Whoa …," he says. Both he and Jena get out of the truck, stand in the middle of the dusty road, and watch as the woman's car roars up to the house. She leaves the car running and gets out carrying two cans of gasoline. Maggie runs to the car, throws her stuff in, and grabs a gasoline can. They both start sprinkling gasoline all over the place. They both act like two children running loose in a kids' park, laughing and talking loudly. The woman lights a fire all around the house area.

Jake begins to run toward the house; Jena holds him back. "Let it go, Jake," she says. "Let it go." They watch as Maggie and her sister burn down the house, burn the car, and burn everything else in sight. Black smoke fills the air, and Jena knows the firemen will soon come … and then the cops.

She turns to Jake. "Jake, let's get go. There's nothing else we can do here. This is Maggie's moment." Jena glances over at Jake and speaks firmly to him. "This is her moment, and she's earned the right to celebrate it the way she chooses." Jena gets back in the truck. Jake follows. He puts the truck in drive and spins off down the road.

Jena glances back at the burning house in the rearview mirror. Maggie and her sister are jumping up and down and hanging onto each other as everything burns. And although a man is dead, a woman is somehow alive again—and for Jena, justice is done. Jena continues to watch until she can no longer see the burning house in the mirror. She rests her head back, breathes softly, and then closes her eyes.

Jake drives cautiously to avoid being noticed and stopped by the cops. The highway is dark and empty; ten or fifteen minutes pass between them meeting any other car. Jake turns on the radio just as Jena doses off. The radio announcer makes an all points bulletin: "The Maplesville police have apprehended Matthew Ross, who is wanted for burglary and murder in several other counties. They are holding Matthew Ross without bail." Jena opens her eyes widely. "The Maplesville police department is also looking for Jena Parker, wanted for multiple murders, and Jake Paterson, who is considered an accomplice to those murders. We will keep you updated as we receive news on these two murderous individuals." Jake turns the radio off. Jena closes her eyes tightly. The inevitable outcome seems to strike both of them at the same time, and neither of them utter a single word.

Jena dozes off again. Just when she gets comfortable sleeping, a car races past them, honks the horn three times, and a woman sticks her head out the window. It's Maggie. She is smiling and waving out the passenger window of the car. Jena's eyes began to get heavy as Maggie's sister's car fades out of sight.

Jena's eyes blink slowly as Maggie's hand wave becomes a reoccurring event in slow motion. Even when Jena closes her eyes, she can see Maggie's hand waving, her smile, and her sister's car speeding past in slow motion. Everything in slow motion. Jake turns to look at them and then back at her in slow motion.

Jena's eyes blink in and out, watching the world around her resist gravity and pull her away from reality until she is no longer in the car. She is back on the plane, where she sits next to a man who has a strong resemblance to Mr. McNeil. He sits next to Jena, who is trying to recognize her surroundings. The man laughs out loud.

Jena looks at him. "You're dead." She smiles.

"Am I?" he says as he chuckles.

"Yes, you are," she answers.

"Well, I'm here. You're here," he says.

Jena stands up and turns toward him. "Yes, we are both here, but only one of us is leaving." She leans down to get close to his face. "And it's not you."

Mr. McNeil is quiet for a moment, and then he laughs again. "Maybe that's a good thing," he says. "Maybe I like it here. Maybe it's you who's the unfortunate one." He laughs again. Jena stares at him. "Look at you. You killed me, and you still don't have any peace. You still wander in and out of this fictitious plane. Why do you come back?" Jena struggles to answers. She looks around the plane. The man gets confident. "Yeah, why do you come back?" He picks up a newspaper that was sitting in the back of the seat in front of him. He crosses his legs and begins reading the paper. "Let's see what's happening today. Oh," he says, "Matthew Ross was caught by the Maplesville police department. Ha, ha." He laughs. "And look, murderer Jena Parker is still on the loose. Oh, if the police department could just get on this plane. Ha, ha. Jena Parker?" He chuckles hard, looks up from the paper laughing, and stares at Jena. "Don't they mean Jena Gray? Ha, ha." He laughs uncontrollably.

Jena snatches the paper from his hand and rips it up. "No," she says. "They mean Jena Parker." She leans close to him. "I'm leaving." She walks to the front of the plane. "You want to know why I come back here?" She looks around the plane, and all the passengers disappear. She turns around to look at Mr. McNeil with a mean expression on her face. "I come back here because this is my plane, my rules, and you're just a simple man trapped here," she says in a commanding voice. Mr. McNeil stands up. He tries to move, but he can't. "See," Jena says. "You're not like me. You're nothing. You're my nothing, and that's what you'll always be to me."

Jena wakes up. Jake is out of the truck, standing next to the lake where they used to meet as kids. Jena sits up, looks around in amazement, opens the truck door slowly, and steps out. She knows that she is home.

CHAPTER NINE

J ake is throwing rocks into the lake. He has a depressed look on his face. Jena walks toward him. He doesn't look at her; he just continues to throw rocks. Jena suddenly remembers all the moments she and Jake shared together at the lake when they were children. She remembers waiting for Jake at the lake one day after school, and she is transported back to that day.

Jake is running late. Jena looks around while she waits for Jake. When Ken taps her on the shoulder, she is startled.

Jena stares at Ken. "What are you doing here?" she shouts.

Ken smiles while circling her. "Umm, I guess you're waiting for Jake?" Jena walks away. Ken follows her. "So you can't speak to me?" he says.

"Yes, I'm waiting for Jake. But you didn't answer my question. What are you doing here?"

"Well, I just wanted to say hello. What's wrong with that?"

Jena smirks. "Well, we don't really speak to each other, and neither do you and Jake, so I'm just wondering."

Ken stops and begins to back away from Jena. "What, you think no one knows about you and your lover boy's favorite spot?" Ken says in an angry voice.

"He's not my lover boy," Jena says. "He's my best friend."

"Oh … friend." Ken laughs. "Anyway, your friend has after-school detention, so I thought I'd be nice enough to come all the way out here to tell you. Well, so much for niceness." Ken walks away.

Jena just stares at the lake. She kneels down, picks up a few rocks, and begins throwing them in the lake. She is back, and Jake is still throwing rocks in the lake. He kneels down.

Jena stands over him. "What's wrong?" she asks. Jake turns his head and looks off into the distance. Jena kneels down next to him. She gently touches Jake on the shoulder.

He looks down at her hand, back up into her eyes, and then kisses her hand. "My mom called." He sighs. "She left me a message. My dad is in St. Mary's Hospital. He passed out at work, and right now the doctors don't know what's wrong with him." Jake stands up. "My mom is pleading for me to come home." Jake almost breaks down. A tear drops from one of his is eyes. He turns to Jena. "Jena, my mom said your mother's funeral is tomorrow." Jena turns around quickly. She tilts her head down slightly and closes her eyes. Jake walks close behind her. "Jena, I have to go see my father." Jake grabs her. Tears begin to flow from his eyes. He puts his head on her shoulder.

"I understand, Jake," Jena says softly. She turns around to face him. "I'm so sorry." She looks down at the ground. "I'm so sorry that you have to be here with me when your family needs you. You have to go now." She pulls away from Jake.

"No," he says. "We will go together."

Jena turns around with a surprised look on her face. "Jake," she says. "The cops. We can't."

Jake walks quickly behind her. He grabs her arm. "Yes, we can." He holds her tightly. "I won't leave you behind. Never, Jena." He squeezes her. "Never." Jake looks deeply into her eyes. He kisses her softly on the lips. They lock eyes for more than a minute. No words. No movement. No sound. Just the locking of their eyes. Jena reaches for his face with both hands and, just like the wind, she rushes to kiss him. She kisses him like never before. Long, deep kisses. Jake is lost in her. "I love you," Jake says to her. Jena stares him down. She kisses him again, over and over again. "You're my family too, and I will take care of you until the world stops for me—and even then I'll spend the reminder of the time searching for you until I find you again so I can take care of you and love you." He holds her closely. "My world will never stop, for you are my everything—my every moment and my only reason."

Jena is taken by Jake's words. "What will we do?" she asks. "Where will hide?"

"We'll go to my parents' house and hide in the basement. My mother is at the hospital, so she won't be around." Jake looks off again. He grabs Jena's hand to lead her to the truck.

Jena suddenly stops. Jake turns around. She lets go of Jake's hand. "Jake, I will go to my mother's funeral."

"Jena, you—" Jake begins to speak.

"No. Don't say I shouldn't go, because I will go." She walks past Jake and turns back around. "I will go to her funeral, and no one—not you, not the cops—no one will stop me." She gets into the truck.

Jake leans on the truck's hood. He puts both hands on the truck and stares through the front window at Jena. "Okay," he says while nodding his head yes. "Okay." He walks over to Jena's door, opens it, and kisses her on the cheek. "Okay." He kisses her hand, closes the truck's door, and walks with his head down to the driver's side. They both take one last look at the lake. The stillness of the moment sets in, and they both can feel that their journey will begin a new chapter the moment they leave the lake. Jake drives away.

Darkness has set in, and Jake manages to drive through his neighborhood without being noticed. The streets are empty. Only the wind shares the space with him and Jena. His house is dark, and his mother's car is gone. Jake passes his house and stops.

"There's a car garage down the street. We'll park the truck

there and walk back." He looks over at Jena and smiles. "Maybe this would be a good time for you to wear that famous red hat of yours."

Jena doesn't find the humor in Jake's joke. "Yeah," she says as she looks away.

Jake pulls up to the parking garage window. There's a tall, slim man sitting in the booth reading a newspaper. Jake slowly pulls forward. The man doesn't look at him, he just sticks his hand out the window and shoves the parking ticket in Jake's face. Jake quickly snatches the ticket and drives off. Jake parks the truck on the highest level in the parking garage. He shuts off the engine and sits still for a moment. He turns to speak to Jena, but she grabs her bag and opens the truck door before he can say anything.

Jake gets out, walks up to her, and reaches his hand out to her. "Everything will all right," he assures her. "You'll see."

Jena just stares at his hand for a moment, her heart slightly racing. The inevitable awaits as she looks up to gaze off into the night. She takes Jake's hand, and they both begin to walk back to his house, cutting through backyards and alleyways just as Jake had done when he was a kid.

Jena and Jake stop in the dark near his neighbor's house. Jake checks out the area. "Looks clear." Jake reaches for the extra key, hidden under a plant near the back door. He opens the door. The house is dark and quiet; no one appears to be inside.

Jena reaches for his shoulder. "Find some lights before we trip over each other," she says.

"I'm looking." Jake manages to turn on the living room lamp. He stares around the room. Jena stands close to him. She walks up to look at the pictures on the mantle: Jake's father and mother, his brother and him, and him and Jena as children.

Jena looks back at Jake. "We were once kids," she says softly. "Innocent kids, young and full of life's energy. Just dreaming of being teenagers, graduating high school, going to college." Jena walks away from the mantle. She shakes her head. "But now look at us. I'm a killer, and you're wasting your life chasing after me."

Jake walks over to her. "I'm not chasing after you, Jena. I'm standing by you." He reaches for her, but she shies away. "It doesn't really matter what you say or do, I'm not leaving you." He turns Jena around. "I know you're afraid."

Jena jerks her arm away. "I'm not afraid, Jake," she says abruptly. "I just don't want you to let your life go to shit for me. Look around. This is your home, your family … and what are you doing? You're playing Bonnie and Clyde with me." Jake looks down. Jena walks upstairs to Jake's room. He follows. She opens his door, walks in, and circles the room. Jake stands in his doorway. Jena sits down on his bed. She remembers the night her father was shot and killed by Mr. McNeil. She closes her eyes tightly. A small tear falls from one of them. Jake sits next her.

"I remember everything," Jena says. She lies back on his bed; Jake lies back alongside her. "I remember, Jake. I was so torn, broken, and ripped apart. It was the most unbelievable moment in my life." Jena's tears begin to fall. "That night … that night was the end of my life the way I knew it." She quickly sits up.

Jake follows and grabs her shoulder. "Jena …," he calls.

"No. Please." She sobs. "I miss him so very much. I try to forget, but my father … my mother …" Jena's tears are flowing like a waterfall out of control. "What happened to us, Jake?" She stands up. "What happened to my family? Why were we so cursed?"

Jake wipes a tear from Jena's face. He soothes her by caressing her face. He hasn't seen her vulnerable in such a long time. Somehow, the old Jena had come back; Jena Parker had returned. Jake knows that this is a moment that has to be savored. It marked the moment that Jena had returned home, had returned to being the girl around the corner. The best friend. The crush. The love of his life. He caresses her cheeks, hair, and shoulder. He can see and feel the pain and confusion in her eyes. Her tears are like a bullet lodged in his heart. He wants nothing more than for her to know that he would do anything to put her pain in a box and throw it away in the deep ocean, a hidden treasure meant to never be found again. "I love you, Jena," he says. "Please tell me now that you love me too."

Jena looks at him. She sees the compassion in his eyes, his sincere emotions, and the death of his own life in order to make her happy. She looks away.

"Jena, please—I need to hear you say it." Jena turns her eyes down. Jake moves in closer to kiss her. She doesn't say anything, but she doesn't turn away from his kiss. His lips enfold hers like soft pillow feathers or cotton candy. Jake's room door opens wider.

"What are you doing?" Jake and Jena both look up in sheer surprise to see Ted, Jake's brother. He had been asleep and was awakened by their voices. Jake stands up. Ted's face is red. They both just stand and stare at each other like two men ready to brawl in the Wild West. Ted quickly runs up to his brother and gives him a hug. His eyes watch Jena as she stands and stares.

"I'm so happy to see you, brother," Ted says as he hugs Jake harder. "Man, I just thought something really bad happened to you." Ted looks up at Jena.

Jake hugs Ted back. "I'm good, man," he says. "I'm good."

Ted stands back a little, still taken by the moment. "Dad, man." Ted rubs his hand on his head.

Jake turns around to look at Jena. "I know, man. Mom called."

Ted breaks down. "Man, he just passed out." Ted tries to hold back his tears.

Jake walks over to him, squeezes his brother's shoulder, and hugs him again. "It's okay, man," Jake consoles him. "It's okay."

Ted looks over at Jena. "I can't believe you brought her here, Jake."

"Back off, Ted." Jake stands in front of Jena.

"Look, it's not that I don't like you, Jena." Ted leans past Jake to look at her. "I do. I mean, I don't know whether to believe the shit I heard or not, but it's Mom." Ted walks around the room. "Mom broke down over Kitty's death, and now Dad is in the hospital." Ted continues to explain, "I mean, man, things around here are just wicked. I just think Mom is going to lose it if she finds out Jena is here. This whole thing is falling apart." Ted sits down on Jake bed. "Hell, I'm falling apart, and I'm still in high school."

Jake tries to console Ted. They both continue to talk about their dad, their mom, Jena, and where Jake has been the last couple of days.

Jena wanders out of the room. She walks around the upstairs, remembering when she was little and her mom would bring her over to play with Jake. She remembers her, Jake, and Ted running through the house as their moms chatted downstairs in the kitchen while baking cakes, pies, and cookies. The aroma from the chocolate chip cookies baking in the oven would fill the entire house, and the three of them couldn't wait for the cookies to be done. Gooey chocolate morsel sticking to their fingers and faces, the three of them would laugh uncontrollably at cartoons or at the silliness of their parents' crazy clothes and conversations.

Jena wanders into the Paterson's bedroom. There is a black dress, hat, and shoes laid out. Pictures of Jena's mom and Mrs. Paterson are pasted all over the bedroom mirror and dresser—pictures of when they were little girls, of them as teenagers, and of the Patersons and Parkers as couples at the local bowling alley. Jena walks up to the dress. She touches the fabric. She looks back at the pictures of her mom and then back at the dress and shoes.

CHAPTER TEN

J ena walks back to Jake's room. Ted and Jake are still talking. She stands in the doorway.

Ted stands up, walks over to her, and gives her a big hug. "I've missed you, girl." He squeezes Jena really hard. Jena smiles a little and hesitates, but she eventually gives in and squeezes him tightly back. "I don't know what really happened, Jena, but I know you, so I'm gonna just be the friend I've always been to you." Ted gently pinches her cheek. Ted turns to Jake. "Hey, you guys, you don't have to worry too much tonight. Mom won't be back until early morning." Ted looks at Jena. "She's ... umm ... coming back to get ready for the funeral tomorrow morning." Jena stares out Jake's window as the darkness of her murderous actions dawns on her.

Jake won't let her slip back into a deep depression again. He walks over to her. "We're going to the basement now."

Ted watches as they both head down toward the basement. "Hey," Ted calls. "Umm ... I'll make dinner."

Jake gives him a weird look. "You—make dinner?" He laughs.

"Umm ... well, I don't know, man. Hey, I'm a decent cook now," Ted says in a joking voice.

"Sure," Jake says as he smirks at Jena and then walks down the steps. "I guess we really don't have a choice." Ted laughs as he shrugs his shoulders and closes the basement door.

The basement is a little chilly, dimly lit, and full of the Paterson family's old furniture, toys, clothes, and other household items. Jake flops on the couch and laughs; he almost falls over the side to the floor.

Jena laughs out loud. "You klutz! Ha, ha." They both laugh loudly. She flops down next to him. "So this is home?" she says smiling.

"I guess." Jake chuckles. He starts bouncing up and down on the couch, trying to keep Jena in a cheery mood. "Remember, Jena?" Jake keeps bouncing. "Remember when we were kids and how we just bounced and played on our parents' furniture?" Jena's body is shaking from Jake's bouncing. She tries not to laugh, but she can't help herself. "Oh, come on, Jena—bounce with me."

Jena thinks back to when she and Jake were children. His words echo from the past. Little Jake's voice flashes through her mind. "Come on, Jena—bounce with me." Jena starts bouncing up and down on the couch. The two of them together, acting like little children, bouncing up and down on the couch, laughing, giggling, and being playful with one another.

Suddenly the basement door swings open. Jake and Jena quickly stop. It's Ted. "Hey, what are you guys doing?" Ted asks.

Jake and Jena are relieved that it's Ted and not Mrs. Paterson. They look at each other and burst out into loud laughter. "You trying to scare us, guy," Jake asks.

Ted starts laughing. "I realized you guys didn't want to add me in the fun, so I thought I'd add my own fun." The three start laughing together just like they had when they were kids, splattered with chocolate chip cookie dough all over them, bouncing up and down on their parents' furniture.

Jake's eyes beam with excitement as he watches Jena laugh out loud. He stops everything to watch her. He studies each and every detail of her smile, the way her hair flows, the widening of her eyes. The bus rides, the talks at their school lockers, and the afternoons at the lake all flash before him. He understands that life isn't just pieces of moments; it's every moment—and his moment is lost in Jena's eyes and her smile. His smile fades, not because of sadness, but because he wants to freeze this beautiful moment just like a red rose frozen in the winter woods. Still red, still beautiful, and still alive, even if the cold had stopped its moment. It still wants to be noticed. To live. To breathe. Jake is convinced that Jena wants to live again. He can hear it in her laughter, feel it in his heart. He is ready to battle anyone and anything that gets in the way of her happiness.

Trying to rush Ted off, Jake says, "Aren't you supposed to be cooking us something, dude?"

"Oh, now you're longing for my cooking?" Ted jokes. "Just a minute ago, you weren't sure if I could cook." Jake and Jena stare each other with smiles on their faces. "Okay, I get it—you just want to be alone with Jena." Ted heads up the stairs and peeks down at them as the door closes. He raises his eyebrows just before the door shuts.

Jena gives Jake a shy look as he moves in close to kiss her. The basement door swings back open just before Jake lands the kiss. Ted does a funny little dance and closes the door again. Jake tries to move in for the kiss again.

Jena stands up. "I think I'm going to take a shower while it's safe." She laughs to herself as she walks up the basement steps.

"Yeah … umm … me too." He walks behind her. "You go use the bathroom in my room, and I'll hit the hallway one."

"You like to follow me, don't you, Jake?" Jena laughs.

"I'm not following you. I just happened to need a shower, just like you."

"Yeah, yeah. You just make sure you stay in your shower," Jena says playfully.

"I'll try." Jake leans in his room's doorway.

Jena sniffs his armpit. "You stink."

Jake sniffs his armpits. "Yeah, I guess it's not sexy, huh?"

Jena laughs. "Not really."

Jake watches as she enters his bathroom and closes the door. He thinks to himself, *Jena's back. My Jena is finally back.* Jena turns on the shower. Steam fills the bathroom. She carefully steps into the shower. The hot water races down her skin. She stands under the showerhead with her hand braced against the shower wall. The water drills down her on her hair, body, and feet. She looks up. "Shampoo and a razor," she utters. "Just what I need." She stares at the shampoo and razor before grabbing them. *I guess I should probably ask Jake what he is doing with a razor in his shower,* she thinks as she laughs to herself.

The hot shower makes Jena think about Jake. The heat of the water reminds her of the heat they shared when they made love. The soap suds slowly glide down her body, just like Jake's hands when he gently caressed every inch of her. Jena touches her own body just as Jake had—first the neck, chest, breast, stomach, thighs, and then her vagina. She heats up just thinking of Jake. She closes her eyes and imagines him on top of her. His movement ... his motion ... like a hard ocean wave crashing up against a rock, over and over again. She tightly closes her eyes and imagines him thrusting into her, tossing her over, playing with her, and giving her everything. All of him, over and over again. Like a caged tiger, her face is filled with desire as both hands press up against the shower wall.

Jake pulls back the shower curtains. He is naked, and his body is dripping wet. Breathing hard, he stares at Jena's naked, wet body. The hot steam surrounds them. He steps into the shower and presses his body up against hers. He begins kissing her softly and then harder. Jena parents' song jiggles in her mind. Jake looks at her as he gently plays with her nipples, squeezes her breasts, and leans down to kiss both of them. He licks her neck with the tip of his tongue, kisses down her chest, her stomach, and then gently kisses between her thighs. His hands smoothly slide up her thighs, waist, and back to her breasts. He grabs her to him like a man in charge who knows what he wants. He kisses her deeply. They are locked in a deep, passionate kiss as he hands discover every intimate inch of her.

There's a knock at the bathroom. "Hey?" a voice calls. "Jena? Time for dinner." It's Jake. He leans his face up against the bathroom door. "Are you all right?"

Jena comes back to reality. She turns off the water. "Yes. I'll be out in a minute." Jena grabs a towel.

"Okay," he answers softly. "I've put some of my clothes out for you."

"Okay, Jake. Thanks."

Jake can see the steam roll out from underneath the door. He places his hand on the door.

Jena can still feel him standing outside the door. She places her hand on the door. "I'll be downstairs soon." Jake smiles as he walks away.

Jena slips into a towel. Jake has laid out some of his clothes on the bed: black sweat pants and his favorite football team T-shirt. She slips on a pair of his socks and fantasizes for a moment that she's Jake's wife, in their room, in their house. Everything seems so perfect, but she knows it isn't. Jake's father is in the hospital, her mother is dead, and she is a fugitive on the run from the cops. She knows no matter how much she wants things to be perfect, it never will be.

Jena walks toward Jake's room window, opens it, and sticks her head out to feel the cool breeze. *If only snow would fall right now,* she thinks. *Beautiful white snow crystals and shooting stars all at once. What a fantasy,* she thinks. *What a gift that would be to brighten the world I live in now.* Jena closes the room window. Her tension is back. All that was so happy, so peaceful disappeared out the window the moment she opened it. An upside-down world is what she sees and feels. Even the magical moment that she and Jake so recently shared felt like it happened a lifetime ago when it happened only an hour ago.

She looks around Jake's room, walks out to the hall, and then looks once more into his room—as if it would be the last time she sees it. She slowly walks down the hall past Jake's parents' room. She stops to glare at Mrs. Paterson's dress for her mother's funeral. *What an ugly dress,* she thinks. *Just hanging there, waiting to be worn by a warm body. Why should a warm body wear that dress?* she thinks. *Why? That dress should be worn by someone cold. Someone not worthy of wearing it. Someone whose heart is as black and cold as that dress.* Jena walks into the Patersons' bedroom, removes the dress from the hanger, and grabs the shoes. She quickly heads to the basement to hide the outfit.

Jake and Ted are waiting for her at the kitchen table. Jake stands up. "What took you so long?" he asks.

"I was just thinking about some things. Life." Jena glances at the food on the table. She remains standing. "There is so much in life that is unexplained. The dark tunnels of life. The dungeons and lost chambers. In the blink of an eye, anything can change your life—for better or worse. Either way, you have to be ready. Ready for it all. Ready for a showdown." Jena looks at Jake and Ted. "You two have a father in the hospital, a mother that needs you, and a world that is still capable of offering you both something." She sits down. "And I ... well, I have a funeral to attend tomorrow." Jake has a worried look on his face. Jena reassures him. "The world is still spinning, Jake, and tomorrow I must face my own doings—and I must face them alone."

None of them have an appetite, although they all pretend they are still hungry. The sun had set, the rain had come, and the wind had blown everything around in the room. The truth could not be hidden—not by laughter, not by memories, not even by love.

CHAPTER ELEVEN

J ena sits at the dinner table with thoughts of her life moving backward like a horrible hurricane ripping through a small town. Jena at the dinner table, in the shower, on the couch laughing with Jake, at the lake, at Maggie's, in the car with Jake, at the hotel with the gun pointed at Mr. McNeil ... running to Jake's ... her mother's bathroom ... frozen across the street, watching her mother on her knees cry with blood on her hands ... the murder of her father. *Walk backward,* she thinks, *and then maybe it'll all be a horrible nightmare. Maybe I'm not a murderer. Maybe my father and mother are still alive and Jake and I are back at school, laughing and playing as we did when we were children. No, forward. There is no walking backward for me.*

Jena distances herself from Jake and Ted for the rest of the night. When the morning comes, she knows exactly what she has to do and the demon she has to face.

Jena stands looking in the mirror the morning of her mother's funeral. She is wearing Mrs. Paterson's black dress, shoes, and black hat with a veil that covers her face. The day of her mother's funeral has now arrived, and it's time for her to face the truth—that backward is really forward and the time has come for her to walk through the pitch-black door.

She grabs the truck keys off the dresser, slips out of the house, and heads down the street to the parking garage. The garage is almost empty. Only the truck and two other cars, which look abandoned, are parked there.

From red to black. The red dress she had worn was so provocative. *Red, the color of blood. The color I dreamed of when I thought of Mr. McNeil's vicious ways. Now a black dress—so black, so cold, and so fitting for a person like me,* she thinks to herself while walking toward the truck. She gets into the truck and glances in the side mirror. *Is my heart really as black as this dress, as this hat, as these shoes? Could I be so cold? So heartless? Or is my heart just hidden, buried underneath the world, and I somehow have to find my way back home?*

Jena turns on the truck engine. The radio instantly plays coverage of a police officer taking questions from a local reporter. "Officer Reyes, did Matt Ross confess to the robbery and murder he allegedly committed?" the news reporter asks.

"This information can't be revealed at this time, because the investigation is still pending," he replies.

"Officer, is Matt Ross being charged by the Maplesville's police?"

"We are working with the other counties as we continue to investigate," he answers quickly.

"Officer Reyes, there has been a rumor circulating that Matt Ross is an accomplice of Jena Parker, also known by the alias Jena Gray. What can you tell us about that?" Jena turns the radio up.

"Though we are not ready to confirm or deny that relationship, I can say that we have received information from this arrest that has aided in our search of Jena Parker. We believe that Jena Parker may currently be either close to or in Maplesville. We will be ready for Ms. Parker if she tries to return to Maplesville. She will be arrested or captured the moment she hits this town."

Jena turns off the radio and spins out of the parking garage. She drives past the ticket booth without paying. The ticket attendant yells as Jena passes, calls it in, and then tries to run after her. Jena speeds off. The attendant stands in the middle of the busy highway, winded and exhausted from chasing the truck. The attendant is hit by a car and is knocked unconscious.

Jena continues to drive to the funeral. She doesn't know exactly how she will attend the funeral without being noticed. She knows her grandmother will be there along with uncles, aunts, cousins, and other family members. The police will probably be circling the funeral site waiting to arrest her and undercover detectives will be watching out for her. She also knows that soon Jake will discover she is gone, and he'll come running after her like a tiger chasing a lamb.

*   *   *

Jake awakens, calls out for Jena, but no answer is sent in return. He can feel the emptiness in the room. There is not a sound or a whisper of her voice. The evidence is clear that she is gone. He hears footsteps upstairs and his mother's voice as she tries to wake up Ted.

"Ted. Ted." Mrs. Paterson shakes Ted to wake him.

"What, Mom?"

"Where's my dress?"

"What?" Ted opens his eyes wide.

"Where is my dress for Kitty's funeral?" Ted sits up. He looks at his doorway. Mrs. Paterson turns around. Jake is standing there with his eyes locked on his mother. "Jake," Mrs. Paterson utters softly in shock. She crosses the floor slowly, trying not to stumble as she walks toward her son. Mrs. Paterson looks up at him as if she has seen a ghost. Her tears drop, one by one, onto her pinstriped blouse and then like hard rain drops her tears flow as she rushes into Jake's arms. "Jake, your father …" She is at a loss for words.

"Mom, it's okay." Jake holds her tight.

"Jake, you have to see him." Mrs. Paterson squeezes him tighter. "He's not good. He's not good at all, Jake."

"It's all right, Mom. We'll go." Jake rubs his mom's back as he stares at Ted. "We'll go together."

Mrs. Paterson calms down for a moment, breathes a deep breath, and then let's go of Jake. She bites her bottom lip, runs her fingers through her hair, and swallows. "Where is she?" She looks at Jake.

"Mom, please."

"Where is she, Jake!" she screams.

"I don't know."

"Yes, you do. She took my dress." Mrs. Paterson circles the room. "My shoes! My hat!" Jake is quiet. "Jake, she's a killer!" She yells louder, "*She's a killer!* How could you bring her in my house?" Mrs. Paterson sits down at the end of Ted's bed. She looks up.

"She's going to Kitty's funeral," Jake says.

She rushes off the bed and tries to pass Jake. "She's going to Kitty's funeral! Oh, my God! What is she doing?"

Jake grabs his mom's arm. "Mom, please calm down."

She pulls away from him. "Calm down? Calm down!" She struggles to pass Jake.

"Mom, stop it! You don't have the facts," Jake pleads with her.

"Yes, I do!" she yells. "She killed three people—and her own mother." Mrs. Paterson begins to shake. "I thought she killed you, too, Jake. Now you're an accessory to murder! Running from the cops and linked with this Matt Ross!" She pushes Jake. "Get out of my way. I have to call the cops."

"No!" Jake yells back. "No, mom, you can't do that."

"Why not?" She stands back from him.

Jake slowly answers, "Because I love her." He walks toward his mom. "I love her, Mom."

Mrs. Paterson looks back at Ted, who has a terrified look on his face. She sits down on the bed. "How could you love a killer?" she asks.

"I love her, Mom, and that's that. I love you too. I love Dad. I even love Ted." Ted lifts his eyebrows surprise at what Jake just said.

Jake sits down next to his mom. "I don't want to hurt or disappoint you, Mom. I've been with her, and the journey we've shared together has been unbelievable."

Mrs. Paterson stares at Jake with a shocked and disappointing look. "You killed too?" She shakes her head and begins to cry.

"Mom, please don't cry."

"Jake, the cops are looking for her—and they're looking for you too. I don't want you to go to jail. You're father's in the hospital. Ted's here alone all the time. You're on the run. I … I just can't take it anymore." Jake holds his mom to try to console her. "I just can't."

Jake gets on his knees in front of his mother. "Mom, let's go see Dad." He holds her hand in his. Mrs. Paterson looks deep into his eyes. Jake's eyes beam bright like the sun. The last time she had seen him, he was a boy going off to college. But in front of her is a man. A man on the run with a woman who is a killer. A man who is still her son, no matter what the circumstance. And she is a mother who wants to protect her young. She glances into Ted's and Jake's faces and decides she has to conceal her anger for Jena from Jake in order to destroy the hold Jena has on him.

"All right," she agrees. She stands up. "Get ready, guys." She slowly starts walking out of the room, eyeing Jake and thinking, *I'll make Jena pay.* Thoughts of Kitty race through her mind. *I'll make her pay for everything she's done.* She stops at Ted's doorway. "I won't go to Kitty's funeral today—not because I don't have a dress or anything to wear, but because I'm too damaged. What little piece of me is left," she turns to face them, "I must give to you two and your father."

She walks out of the room and goes straight to the kitchen to call the police.

Officer Reyes answers the phone. "Maplesville Police Department. Office Reyes speaking."

Mrs. Paterson tries to disguise her voice. "Hello, I won't say who I am, but I have information to report."

"Yes, ma'am. Go ahead." Officer Reyes listens closely.

"I believe that Jena Parker may attempt to attend her mother's funeral." Mrs. Paterson quickly hangs up the phone, leaving the officer listening to only a dial tone.

She places her hands together in prayer. "This one's for you, Kitty. Rest in peace, my dear friend. Rest in peace."

Jake walks into the kitchen. "Mom, you all right?" He hugs her. "I'll be ready soon, Mom." She is quiet. He kisses her on the cheeks before walking away.

*   *   *

Is life really so complicated? Jena wonders. *How can a girl go from being so innocent, sweet, and curious to being a stone-cold killer? What a vicious act of faith, that I could be the one to create such darkness.*

Jena stands in the mist in the woods across the street from the funeral grounds. She watches as people dressed in pitch-black clothing and sunglasses begin to get out of cars and the family limo. No one notices her. She is a dark figure aligned with the woods, just waiting for the right moment to step out of the dark and into the light where everyone can see her, but no one will know who she is and where she came from. She lifts the veil from her face just as the hearse passes by. The shock of seeing the hearse gives her an unsettling feeling—an emotion that is as quiet as the woods she stands in, but causes a deep, thundering thump in her heart. It's like someone had just walked up to her and ripped all of her clothes off to shame her. She is powerless to move while stones, leaves, and tree branches begin to fall on her. Her palms lift to the sky, expecting what she feels she deserves—the true reality of the pain rooted so deep in the vessels of her heart. "Mom," she utters as tears begin to fall from her eyes. The pain of knowing that it is her mother lying in that hearse awakens a spirit in her, just like a swimmer coming up for air from the waters, or like a mother viewing her baby for the first time, or a child looking at her father's smiling face while her hair blows in the wind as he pushes her back and forth on the swings. Jena walks out to blend in with her family. She passes a family car just as her grandmother, Kitty's mother, steps out. Jena looks at her, an old woman with tears running down her face, wearing a big black hat and carrying a big black purse. Granddad Donaldson and Uncle Norman walk alongside her.

"It's all right, Mom," Uncle Norman comforts her as he holds her arm tightly. All of the family is gathered at the funeral site. Cousins, great aunts and uncles, even Jena's dad's sister, Aunt Denise. Jena walks alongside all of her family. With no one saying a word or asking who is who, she manages to finds her way through the funeral crowd to a front row seat right next to her grandmother.

CHAPTER TWELVE

I was five when I last saw my grandmother, Jena silently reminisces. *Her and Granddad came down to help celebrate Mother and Father's ten-year anniversary. My grandmother was always very nice to me. She always sent me beautiful pageant-like dresses and shoes, along with really bright hair bows. I loved getting gifts from my grandmother. My grandfather lost one of his arms in the war. He was a kind person, but I was always frightened to see him walking around with that one arm. I would just hide behind my mother when he'd try to talk to me, and I couldn't keep my eyes off that missing arm. Even now, looking at him, I remember the fear I felt in thinking, "What monster stole my grandfather's arm?" How awful that must have been for him to be a one-armed man. My mother was very close to my grandfather, but she never really got along with my grandmother. She would tell me, "My mother is so judgmental. I can't stand the way she talks about other people. I'm not like her, Jena. She always gave me this look. I never will be like her," my mother used to say to me all the time. She said she would raise me differently than her mother raised her. Looking at my grandmother with uncontrollable tears running from her face, anyone would have thought she and my mother were closer, but I guess the past doesn't matter—even if we lived it with the one we loved in patches or pieces. We still love the*

*ones who are dear to us as a whole, especially when all that's left is a
casket staring back at you.*

Jena's aunt Denise sits next her. She is also wearing a veil over
her face. She doesn't look at Jena, just straight ahead with a black
handkerchief in her hand to wipe the tears away from her eyes. Jena
can hear her aunt sniffling every few seconds. With her grandmother
falling apart on the right side of her, her aunt Denise's unbearable
emotional state to the left of her, and the other family members
crying and moaning all around her, she is truly trapped to endure
it all. She can feel the buildup of emotions raise like the heat from a
volcano about to erupt. She wants to stand up, yell at the top of her
lungs, and run … run to her mother.

The time has come. She can't hold back her tears any longer.
They begin to drop like hail—hard, long, and everlasting. She takes
a deep breath and puts her head down to let her tears fall to the
ground. She lets them fall … fall … "My mom," she utters through
the tears. "My mother." Jena is trembling, lost in sorrow. All of her
family, the friends of her mother, and even the entire area itself just
fades away from her. It is just her, her mother, and the ugly truth;
that's all she can allow herself to see.

Beautiful birds begin to fly over her mother's casket. One of
them lands, flaps its wings, and stares directly at Jena. Its eyes are
as blue as the sky, and its feathers are as white as the snow. The bird
sits quietly on the casket and stares at Jena, and then it flies up in
the air and lands on her lap. Jena's tears fall on the bird's wings. As
it opens its wings, what seemed to be a small bird ends up being a
bird with big, beautiful white wings that glow like pearls and are
capable of soaring like an angel. The bird flies off of Jena's lap toward
the sun. Its shadow grows large over the funeral as it flaps it wings,
flying farther and farther away into the sky.

Jena is overwhelmed by the presence of the bird. It somehow
calms and excites her at the same time. She reaches her right hand
up to remove the veil from her face, but right before she does Jena's

aunt slowly taps Jena's leg. She looks at Jena with tears streaming down her face. She looks into Jena's eyes, but she doesn't say a word; they both just stare at one another. Jena's and her aunt's tears drop at the same time. Their tears fall simultaneously as they look deep into each other's eyes. Jena stops, puts her hand down, and looks back at her mom. Her aunt Denise looks back toward the casket without saying a word to Jena. Jena glances over at her grandmother, who is leaning over, barely able to keep from fainting. Her grandfather and Uncle Norman try to keep her from falling completely apart.

The minister walks to the podium to begin the service. The family who are seated stand up. Her aunt Denise slowly stands up. Her grandmother is too distraught to stand on her own. Jena's grandfather and her uncle try to help, but she is so traumatized that her legs are weak and heavy. Other family members try to console her by talking to her, patting her shoulder, and wiping her tears. The minister watches and doesn't speak until the family has Grandmother Donaldson to her feet. Everyone is standing, including Jena. Her aunt Denise glances at her. The minister is ready to start.

Just as he begins, a police car pulls up to the funeral site. Two men get out: one wearing a police officer uniform and the other in a dark-blue suit, a long black coat, and dark shades. They talk as they stand by the police car. Uncle Norman looks over at them. He signals to the minister to start without him. The minister begins to speak to the family.

Norman approaches the police car with an angry, depressed look on his face. "Why are you guys here?"

Officer Reyes and Detective Martin walk over to Norman. "We got a call."

Norman gives them a much angrier look. "About?" he asks sharply.

Officer Reyes steps in closer to him. "Someone called the police department with a tip saying that Jena Parker may be attempting to attend this funeral." Officer Reyes scopes out the crowd.

Norman looks back at his family and then back at the officers. "Look, this is a funeral." He holds his head down in despair. "A funeral. A goddamn funeral." He holds his hands up in the air. "My mother doesn't need to see cops at her daughter's funeral."

Officer Reyes gets mad. He puts his hand on his gun. "This is official business."

"No," Norman says loudly. "This is a funeral. So please leave." Norman points at the officer.

Detective Martin gives Officer Reyes a quick look. Officer Reyes moves in closer to Norman. "You're not going to tell us how to conduct this investigation."

"Investigation of what?" Norman yells.

"The murder of Katherine Parker by her daughter, Jena Parker."

Norman steps up to Officer Reyes. "There's no proof that Jena killed her mother." He points at the officer.

"Put your hand down, mister."

Norman frowns. "Don't tell me what to do." He clinches his fist.

Detective Martin steps in between the two men. "We are here to follow a lead," Detective Martin pleads. "That's our job." He gives Norman a meaningful look. "Your niece is wanted for multiple murders. And it is a fact that she is a suspect in the murder of own mother."

Officer Reyes pipes in, "That's right. So what proof do you have that your niece didn't kill her own mother?"

Norman pushes Officer Reyes. "Just as much proof as you guys have that she did!" he yells.

Officer Reyes and Norman begin swinging at one another. They both scramble around fighting in the dirt. Detective Martin does his best to break up the fight. Some of Jena's other uncles run over to help break up the fight. Jena's great-uncles Paul and Ray grab Norman and pull him off of Officer Reyes.

"You're under arrest, pal, for assaulting an officer of the law!" Officer Reyes yells.

"You interrupted my sister's funeral." Paul and Ray are holding Norman. The minister has stopped speaking, and the family is standing, staring at the fallout. "What are you going to do," Norman yells, pointing at his family, "check all of my family looking for her?"

Officer Reyes stares over at the family. Almost all of the women have black veils over their faces. He looks over at Detective Martin.

Norman, breathing hard, starts crying. "For the Lord's sake, this is my sister's funeral." He breaks down crying, falling to his knees. "Have some respect for my family. For her. Please ... please," he pleads as he cries. "Have some respect for my family."

Officer Reyes brushes himself off. He tries to calm himself, but he's still angry. He looks over at Detective Martin and then gets in the car.

Detective Martin looks over at the crowd. He sees Jena, but he doesn't know it's her. He feels bad and wants to apologize to Grandmother Donaldson. He walks over to her. Jena is still sitting next to her. "Ma'am," he speaks to Grandmother Donaldson. "Ma'am," he speaks to Jena. "Ma'am," he speaks to Denise. "I just want to apologize for coming here today."

Jena stands up. Denise stands up next to her. Jena's grandmother is crying and doesn't answer or responds to Detective Martin's apology. Jena walks past Detective Martin. "Excuse me," Jena politely asks. Detective Martin steps back to let her pass. She walks to her mother's grave, stops, and stares at the casket. Detective Martin turns around and stares at her. He begins walking toward her, but Grandmother Donaldson grabs his hand. She stands up.

"Thank you, but please leave now," she sobs. "I'd like to bury my daughter in peace."

Detective Martin nods his head. He steps back. Jena remains at her mother's graveside, just staring at the casket. Her aunt Denise walks over to be with her. She pretends to talk to Jena. Detective Martin walks to the car, and he and Officer Reyes leaves the funeral.

The wind picks up just as the funeral ends. Jena is still standing next to her mother's casket, and Aunt Denise is standing alongside her. To the side of where Jena's mother will rest is Mr. Parker's grave. Denise is so overwhelmed by Kitty's funeral and her brother's grave that she leaves without saying good-bye to the family or Jena. The family members all begin to leave the funeral, but Jena is still standing, staring at her mother's grave. Jena's grandmother stays behind and stands next to her, waiting for Kitty's body to be placed in the ground.

"You want to say something to me?" Jena asks her grandmother.

"We all know it's you," she answers. "I knew it was you the moment you sat down next to me."

"Then why didn't you speak to me?" Jena asks.

"Well, I was never very close to your mother, so I'm sure she told stories about me. I decided that I'd let you be."

"And the cops?" Jena looks at her.

"They say you killed her. Did you kill your mother, Jena?" her grandmother asks.

Jena is silent. She removes the veil from her face. "I set her free. One may call it murder, but my mother died …" Jena gets choked up. "She died the moment my father was murdered. But you wouldn't know that, would you, because she never spoke a word after that night. You two never spoke to each other anyway, so you will never truly understand how silent and distant she became after my father died. I have to live with my demons," her tears begin to fall, "and, well, you have to live with yours."

Jena kneels down to touch her mother's casket one last time. "Good-bye, Mom," she utters softly through her tears. She walks away, leaving her grandmother standing alone.

CHAPTER THIRTEEN

I n the air. Up in the sky. The plane flies and flies. Sit down in your
seat quietly, because where the plane takes you can be unpredictable
so you have to ready for anything. In flight, the plane begins to
fall. Everyone's afraid. Everyone grabs hold of something or someone.
We tighten our seat belts, floatation devices in hand, as the roof of the
plane rips off and people, one by one, are lifted out of their seats into
the sky, into the cold air. Lifted up like air balloons drifting away to an
unknown destination. Everyone but me. I'm still in flight, waiting for
my plane to land—waiting for Jake to save me. What if I loosen the seat
belt? I let the floatation device float away, and I just run up and down
the plane like a child playing in a playground as it continues to go down.
I go down with it when it crashes and burns to the ground. I'm still in
flight. Jena Gray. Jena Parker. Jena Gray. Jena Parker.

"Wake up, Jena," Jena's mother's voice whispers to her. Jena
quickly wakes up and finds herself in the truck. She's in the middle
of the woods just two miles from the funeral site. She looks at herself
in the mirror, grabs her bag, and changes her clothes. Her mother's
letter falls out of the bag. She picks it up from the ground and grips
it tightly in her hand. "Mom," she says as she puts the letter back
in her bag.

Jena walks around the woods barefoot. She admires the trees, weeds, and small animals roaming around. "Nature at its best," she says. Jena hears a buzzing noise coming from the truck. She walks back to the truck, leans in to reach under the seat, and grabs the cell phone. She answers it.

It's Jake's voice on the other end. "Jena." She is silent. "Jena," he calls her name again.

"Jake," she finally answers.

"I'm at St. Mary's hospital with mom and Ted." Jena remains quiet. "Mom is a mess ... and Dad ... he's not responding." Jake is quiet. They both refrain from speaking. "Where are you?" Jake finally asks.

She looks around. "I'm in the woods."

"Oh. Well, when are you coming back?"

She hesitates to answer. "I don't know. I don't think I'm coming back, Jake. It's not that easy. We've both been running from the cops, so it's probably better we remain apart." She walks with the phone. "There only looking for me, anyway."

"Jena, they're looking for both of us. Heck, I'm wearing a hoodie, sunglasses, and a hat trying to disguise myself. Look, I know you're at your mother's funeral—"

She stops him. "Jake, I don't want to talk about it. I'm going my own way, so let me go."

"No," he replies.

She hangs up the phone on him. She stands tall, looking around at the forest again. Thoughts of Jake run through her head. Thinking of his smile—so bright, so alive—makes her shed a tear and a few moments of sadness. But she knew that she had to let him go, because he would never let her go. Ever.

Jake calls for Jena, but the ringing of the phone is all he hears. His mother is standing behind him. She touches him on the shoulder. "Let her go, Jake." He turns around and gives her a surprised look. "Just let her go. She comes with too many issues, and right now your father needs you. Your family needs you."

"Mom, do you love Dad?" She is surprised at his question. "Do you love my father?"

"Yes."

"Then don't tell me not to love Jena, because that's like me telling you not to love Dad—and I know that's completely impossible. I can't do the impossible. You can't do it, and neither can I." He pauses and turns around. "You're right that I do need to be here with my family. I'm here, and I'm sorry I wasn't here sooner. I'll be here for you, Mom. But don't ever ask me to stop loving Jena, because that is like asking me to die." Jake walks away from his mother to cool off. He tries calling Jena back, but she doesn't answer the phone.

The phone has been discarded on the ground in the middle of the forest. The forest is dark, with only the light from the moon to illuminate it. Jena is alone, hungry, sad, and confused. She knows she has to remain in hiding but also that she has to find somewhere to go. She cranks up the engine, rolls up the passenger window, and drives out of the woods onto a one-way highway toward town. She drives the highways and back roads in hopes that it will lessen of a risk of her being noticed by anyone, especially the cops—particularly Officer Reyes, who is out to get her at all cost.

She drives and drives until she ends up at the hotel where she once stayed. It is the place where the rude, fat clerk saw his fatal end. Now she is about to step back into what seems like a time bubble. She sits in the truck in the parking lot. The "open" light flash on and off. Not much has changed since she was last here; the place is still run down, and there are cats everywhere. Surely it was a refuge for the wanted, the ones who are hiding or running from something. A dark, hidden spot filled with secrets; each room shared by strangers who lie to themselves at night and pretend to be normal, self-righteous people in the morning.

Jena steps out of the truck. She reaches for her bag, tosses it on her shoulders, and walks slowly toward the hotel entrance. She hesitates before she opens the door. The glass door is cracked. A tiny bell hangs off the handle. Everything seems quiet, still—not like the last time, when the clerk had the television blaring for the entire hotel to hear. She opens the door and walks to the counter. There is a book lying on the counter titled *Cold Reda Gray: Life Is Filled with Mysteries and Then There's Death*. Jena found the title of the book very interesting. The TV is in same spot. The counter and everything else inside looks exactly the same except there is no clerk. Jena visualizes the fat clerk sitting there eating while staring at the loud television, mustard clinging to his shirt. She stands and stares around the hotel's trashy lobby.

A tall men, wearing a wrinkled red silk shirt and a gold chain, walks from the back. He is smiling as he approaches Jena. "Hello, there." The clerk seems overexcited to see a customer. "How can I help you?"

Jena is taken aback. "Umm, I would like a room."

"That's wonderful." The clerk starts searching for his paperwork. "That's great. We love, *love* people at "The Palm Lee Inn hotel." Jena shakes her head. "Yep. We have the best hotel in town." The clerk looks around and so does Jena, both trying to believe his bullshit. "We offer cable TV, comfortable beds, and … breakfast." Jena looks at the small concession stand. "Just coffee and donuts, nothing special." The clerk laughs. Jena has a serious look on her face, but she finds the clerk quite funny. "So, young lady, what floor do you want?"

"Second floor."

He looks at the keys. "Well. Second floor. Let's see. Second floor." There are only three keys left, so Jena can't understand the clerk's prolonged tally count of his available rooms. "Umm." He looks at all three keys. "Well, it looks like all of the rooms left just happen to be on the second floor."

"Great." Jena tries to be patient and polite. The clerk scrambles around to search for more paperwork. Jena's patience is running thin. "Could I just have the key?"

"Sure, sure." He gives Jena a pleasant smile and hands her a key. "But wait—I have to get you to sign some papers, you nice young girl." He grabs the paperwork, and his book falls to the floor. "Oh, sucks." He reaches down to pick it up. Jena stares at the poster hangings on the wall behind where he had been standing. There's a scratched picture of her with big "WANTED" posted on it. The clerk catches her staring at the picture. "Yeah, that's Jena. Jena Parker." The clerk looks at the picture and then back at Jena. "Hey, you look like her. You guys could be twins. Yeah, twins."

"Twins?" Jena says.

"Yeah," the clerk says as he stares at Jena. "Ah, but no way you're her. I mean, what are the chances of her returning to same place where she committed murder?" The clerks laughs. "I'm not that lucky. I mean who am I? I'm nobody. Just a silk shirt–wearing hotel clerk who wants to be a writer."

"A writer?" Jena seems curious.

"Yeah, see." He shows Jena the book. "This is my book. *Cold Reda Gray: Life Is filled with Mysteries and Then There's Death.* Isn't that a catchy title?" Jena nods her head. He starts rifling through his paperwork. "Man, I just love this book. I mean it's my own work, but I just love it." The clerk looks back at Jena's picture posted on the wall. "You know, I'd love to write a book about her."

Jena looks up at herself on the wall. "Why?"

"I mean, she is so mysterious. She kills the clerk at this hotel, kills a doctor on the train, and—oh, she was obsessed with that McNeil guy who killed her father." The clerk stares starry-eyed at Jena's picture. "But most intriguing of all, I just heard that she killed her mother too." He hands Jena the paperwork. "Can you imagine that?"

"Are we finished?" Jena asks in a subdued voice.

The clerk keeps talking. "I'd write a good book about her. I'd name it *Cold Jena Parker.* Although that would have to wait, because I'm currently working on my sequel to this book." He holds his book proudly in his hand. "You know what I'm going to call it?" Jena lifts one eyebrow. "*Cold Reda Gray: Reda Jones Returns.* She returns to get revenge on all the ones she didn't kill." The clerk smiles at Jena. "By the way, my name is Franklin." He reaches out his hand to Jena. Jena reaches her hand out to shakes his. "Franklin, good luck with your book." He shakes Jena's hand. Jena signs the paperwork, hands it back to him, and opens the door to leave.

"Oh, and thank you for choosing our lovely hotel!" He yells as she starts to walk off. Jena closes the door.

"Geez, I finally found someone crazier than me," she says to herself as she walks to her room. Jena finally reaches the hotel room. She slides the key in to open the door. The room is an exact replica of the room where she once stayed. The room where she caved-in to her impulse to see the sight of blood. Where the coldness in her heart began. Where the light dimmed to dark and then to pitch black. Jena throws her bag on the bed and waits. Was the clerk going to come to her room? Was his niceness just a way to soften her up so she could bare her innocence? *He doesn't really know me,* she thinks as she undressed. She stands in the bathroom doorway naked, staring at the tub and visualizing the fat clerk splattered with blood, dead on the floor and herself naked in the tub. She stands and thinks, *Life is a mystery, filled with the unknown. It's a mystery that can take you far away from your reality. It is almost like there's an insane part of you that is only revealed when you actually look at yourself in the mirror for more than one minute; there it is, that creature that lives inside you—even when you laugh and try to hide it. I stand as proof of that mystery and the unknown. I'm proof that the dark does live among the light. I'm dark, and I'm light. The only thing is … I don't which one I will be tomorrow.*

CHAPTER FOURTEEN

J ena watches as her other self submerges herself in the tub full
of bloody water. Looking through an hourglass of suppressed
memories, it was time to come face-to-face with her true self. It
was here, in that tub. It was here that she murdered that clerk and left
him lying on the floor, bare naked and bleeding from every corner of
his flesh. She glances at the clerk on the floor and then back at herself
in the tub. Jena watches herself stare off at the bathroom wall. She's
staring at herself staring out into the nowhere, the nothing, the black
space corner of the bathroom. Then it happens, in the flicker of the
eye. Jena's body begins to slide deeper down into the tub. Her body—
still, lifeless, and as cold as the clerk on the floor. Her hair submerges
in the bloody water, then her face, and then her entire body is goes
under. Jena watches as her other self sinks completely under the water.
She doesn't do anything to stop her. She wants her to die. She knows
if she had died right there, then that is where this horrible story would
have ended. But it wasn't where the story ended.

Jena emerges from the water, laughing and giggling to herself.
She starts playing with the water, washing her body and her hair.
She looks at the clerk on the floor and laughs at him, even throwing
bloody water on him. Jena watches herself show no mercy, no fear,
and no regrets. She gets out of the tub and walks over and stops to

look at her present self. "Now it's your turn," she says as she walks past. "It's okay. A little bit of blood won't hurt you. Go on—touch him, feel him. He's not alive, and neither are you. You're dead inside, and there's no coming back from it." They both stand naked watching the blood flow from the clerk. They stand face-to-face. "Get dressed," Jena tells herself. "We have a guest coming."

The two Jenas put on identical dresses: the unforgettable red dress. So spectacular on her—well fitted, and perfectly made for a master of murder. It empowers her to be who she wants to be outside the world of the simple Jena. It is the dress of death, worn along with the red hat of doom.

Someone is coming; both Jenas are ready for him. There's a knock at the hotel room door. They look at one another, smiling back and forth at each other. They have very much anticipated this moment, and the Jenas can hardly wait to invite their guest inside. Both of them take one last look in the mirror, readjust their red hats, and blow kisses at themselves in the mirror.

Jena walks confidently to the door. She opens it, and there is a man standing in the doorway with red flowers in his hands. He's wearing a dark-blue suit, red tie, white shirt, and black shoes. The roses cover his face as he attempts to surprise Jena. She smiles and leans to the side to peek at him. He pushes the roses toward her to play at hiding his identity for just a while longer. Jena reaches for a rose. She removes one and turns to hand it to her other self, but there is no one there. She turns around, and it's Matt Ross standing in the hotel room doorway. He is grinning, waiting to be invited in. His face is smoothly shaven, his curly blonde hair nicely cut, with his big baby-blue eyes daring her to say no. She gives a seductive look, smells the beautiful red roses, smiles, and waves to signal him to come in.

"They're beautiful," she says while smelling the roses.

He looks at her. "You're beautiful."

Jena blushes. She walks closer to him, looks him up and down, and then softly touches his red tie with the edge of her fingertips. "I like this color."

He looks at her dress, admiring her tall, slender figure and slightly exposed cleavage. "I like the dress." He brushes his hand smoothly over her waist. "I also like what's in it." Matt puts one hand in a pocket and slowly walks around the hotel room. Jena watches him. He stands in front of the mirror admiring himself, adjusts his tie, and then blows a kiss at himself. He turns to Jena. "Are you disappointed, surprised, or happy to see me?"

Jena looks down. "Well, I'm not surprised. I kind of knew you were coming." She lays the roses on the bed. "I'm definitely not disappointed. I wanted you to come." She walks over to him. "So I would say I'm happy to see you." She runs her hand down Matt's face.

Matt circles her slowly. "Happy?" he questions her motive. "Are you sure?"

She begins to circle him. "Yes. I'm completely and utterly sure." She kisses him on the cheek.

"Show me," Matt says. "Show me just how happy you are to see me."

She stares at him as his big blue eyes try to trap her and his mischief begins to settle into her. "You don't trust me?" she asks.

"It's not that I don't trust you, Jena. I just know a lot about you."

"You do?"

"Yes," he says. "I know that you and I are a lot alike. We both like the color red, and we both have mysterious behaviors." He gets up close to her face. The blue in his eyes deepens. "But mostly the similarity comes from the fact that we both love to murder people." He grabs Jena's arm. She snatches it away from him.

"You're wrong about me, Matt. I don't like to murder people. I'm just a simple girl trying to find her way through life." Matt looks confused. She reaches her hand out toward Matt. "Come with me." Jena takes hold of Matt's hand and tries to show him who she is inside—her true inner self—not a murderer, not a wicked person, just a simple girl wanting to live a simple life.

Matt appears to be interested and mystified by her. They lie side by side on the bed. Matt gazes into her eyes. Jena tells him a story. "When I was a child, I dreamed of flying a plane."

Matt looks over at her and smiles. "You?"

Jena laughs. "Yes, me. I wanted to be a pilot." He laughs. "Why do you find that so funny?"

"You're a beautiful girl and, well, you can be anyone you want to be. I just find you wanting to be a pilot kind of … funny."

Jena smiles. "Well, I did. Flying a plane to me is like getting to be a bird flying in the sky. Just imagine yourself being a pilot of a plane with all those people in it. All aboard awaiting their arrival at their destination, and you're the one responsible for getting them there. Flying high up the sky." Jena daydreams. "Just cruising along the skyline in the clouds, above the world, above the world below where …" she hesitates.

Matt looks at her. "Where?" Matt gives her a curious look.

Jena sits up. "In the sky above the world of people full of hatred. A world where a man could kill another man for no apparent reason at all." Matt sits up as Jena continues. "A world where a girl sees her mother on her knees, hands bloodied, crying her heart out because her husband has just been murdered by scum." Matt gently touches Jena's shoulder. Jena's voice deepens. "A world where a man stands in the middle of a highway to stop a car so he can catch a ride as he plots to commit robbery." Jena gets to her feet and looks over at him. Jena looks around the room. "A world like this, Matt. The world you and I live in." Jena leans down to stare him straight in the face. "Your world. I wanted to be a pilot so I could fly above your world." She turns around. "And now my world. I never wanted to be in this dark, cold cave. And now that I am, I don't know how to escape." Matt walks slowly to Jena. He hugs and holds her tightly. "Do you understand, Matt?" she whispers to him. "Do you understand what

I'm saying to you? I wish you could have seen my life as a child, laughing with my parents, at the lake with Jake … my childhood. I wasn't always like this. I wasn't born to be this way. I was meant for something better. My father was meant to be alive. Everything that happens to you is a domino effect with the consequences only ending up being a circle. A maze." A tear drops from Jena's eye onto Matt's suit coat. "Here I am, back at the hotel where it all began—where my life shattered into blood droplets of never-ending rain."

Matt kisses her on the cheek. "I'm here for you, and I'll never leave your side. You and I are meant to be together. Jake doesn't understand who you are, but I do."

Matt's magical hold instantly fades from Jena. "Jake," she whispers. "You're not Jake," she says.

"No, I'm not, but I can love you just as much if you'll let me. You won't have to worry about protecting me or if I'm judging you. We're the same, Jena."

Jena walks to the mirror. "I don't want to be this way, Matt." Matt frowns. "Why not? What's wrong with the way we are?"

"Everything is wrong with the way we are!" she yells. "Everything! I was supposed to live a simple life, not be on a murderous quest."

Matt feels rejected. He carries on in an angry tone, "This is who we are, and you're going to play the role of queen of the murderers as I play king." They both circle each other, and the rooms follows them—spinning around and around. Matt's anger grows. "I do know you, Jena. I know you killed that clerk. Look at him lying there with blood spilling from him as though he's been beaten to death. Beaten to death by a murderer. I know you killed that helpless doctor on the train. Stole his medical bag, and took it to off your own mother." Jena's face grows as red as her dress. "I know that your obsession led you to go to New York to chase down Mr. McNeil, just so you could murder him for revenge. Yeah," Matt bites his bottom lip, "I also know that you'll kill again, and again, and again, because that's who you are. That's the kind of freak you've turned yourself into."

Jena tries to take control of herself. She turns around to stare at herself in mirror. Her dress doesn't seem as bright and sexy as it was before. Her hat is crooked, so she removes it. Self-pity springs instantly over Jena's mood. Jena reaches her hand out to Matt. He is skeptical at first. Jena seems sincere. "Please take it." Matt submits to her despite his distrust. Jena guides Matt from the hotel room to another place. "Sit, please."

Matt looks around in disbelief. "Why are we on a plane?" He gives Jena a strange look as she walks slowly toward him. "How did we get here?"

"Matt, all of those things you said about me may be true," she adjusts her red hat perfectly on her head, "but there is one thing you don't know—something that you're just not quite aware of at this moment. You don't know that this is just a dream. I'm dreaming about you. This whole thing isn't real." She laughs as she walks closers to him. "Even so, it is still a fact that you're such a creep—such a low, desperate person—to have the gall to come into my dream to try to seduce me to your level of amateur, manipulative ways. I wanted to be the old Jena," she walks closer and closer to him, "the Jena that I once was. It seems just yesterday, but that's the thing—yesterday is gone. I don't know if I'll come back, but what I do know is that I'm going to find you ... and I'm going to kill you." She backs Matt up until he fumbles and takes a seat. He sits down next to a man reading a newspaper. He's face is covered. Jena leans up close to Matt's face. "And you're right—you're not Jake. You'll never be him, so consider yourself forewarned."

The man puts the newspaper down. "Sit tight, young man, because once you're on the plane, you're never getting off." He puts the newspaper back up.

"Now go. Go and tell them, Matt," Jena says. "Tell them I'm coming. I'm coming to get you, Matt Ross—and I'm coming for them too."

CHAPTER FIFTEEN

Jake is frantic, almost beside himself worrying about Jena. Hidden by the hoodie and sunglasses, Jake sits by his father's bedside hoping that he opens his eyes and praying that his love is somewhere safe. The room is quiet. Jake, his mother, and Ted are motionless and silent as they watch Mr. Paterson lie like a corpse in the hospital bed.

Ted stands up. "Mom, I have to step out. I need some air." He looks at Jake.

"I'll come with you, man," Jake says. Jake and Ted leave the room and head down the back stairway. "I don't know how much longer I can keep up with hiding my identity." Jake stops in the stairway. "Sooner or later ..." he sighs, "sooner or later they are going to come looking for me at this hospital."

Ted looks depressed. "Man, Mom can't take any more bad news. Dad's life is on the ropes."

"I'm not sure if I'm much help sitting around here just waiting to be captured, and Jena is out there somewhere."

Ted steps down one flight of stairs. "Face it—your life is shit, man."

Jake steps behind him and takes off his shades. "Yeah, my life is shit—but I've got to find her. Ted, give me your cell."

Ted gives Jake a sour look, reaches in his pocket, and passes Jake the cell. "Meet me outside when you're done, man." Ted walks outside the hospital's back door. Jake holds the cell in his hand. He searches for a number, finds it, and hits dial.

* * *

Five guys are standing outside of a night club eyeing some college chicks when one of them receives a call. "What's up, Ted?" Silence.

"Not Ted. Jake."

"Jake? What the hell, man." Ken walks away from the crowd. Where the hell have you been? Where's Jena? Did she kill all those people? Her mother? That guy on the train?"

"Cool down, man. I need to talk with you. Now isn't the time to play twenty questions. I've been to hell and back. Right now, I need your help." Silence.

"With what?"

"I know we aren't best friends … I'm not sure if we are friends at all … but I'm in hiding, man, and so is Jena."

"Where is she, Jake?"

"She's here in town somewhere. I have to find her before the cops do." Jake pauses. "After I find her, we need a place to hang. My dad's in the hospital."

Ken speaks quickly, "I heard, and I'm sorry. Your dad is a real cool guy. My dad and mom went to see him yesterday." Silence.

"Can you help me?"

"Yeah," Ken doesn't hesitate. "Yes. I'll do what I can. Look there's a masquerade party going on at the campus tomorrow."

"Party?" Jake says. "How's that going to help me? Help Jena?"

"Hey, come see me tonight. We'll find Jena, and then you guys come to the party tomorrow," Ken tries to convince him. "I mean, you'll be all dressed up. Everyone's going to be here—Chance, Carol … everyone—but no one will know who you guys are."

Ken turns to look at his friends. "This is a way for you two to stop running for a moment. Have a normal atmosphere for a moment. I'll find you a place to hang, but I want to see you guys. We'll get some costumes, sit back, and enjoy some real fun." Ken waits for Jake to respond. When he doesn't, he continues to try to convince him. "We'll worry about the cops and everything else later. Jake, if Jena is going crazy, then maybe she needs to be around teenage kids her age. Maybe this will snap her back to reality. Meet outside the college library in an hour."

"That's an hour away. And I don't have a clue as to where she is." Jake is frustrated.

"Meet me here, Jake." Ken ends the phone call and holds the phone tightly in his hand.

Jake walks up to Ted. "Take me to the college library."

Ted hands him the keys. "Take yourself." He walks away.

"Ted?" Ted stops. "I love her. Take care of Mom and Dad. I'll be back."

Ted turns around. "I know. Just put gas in the car." He walks inside.

"Ted?" He turns around. "I'm out of cash."

Ted shakes his head. "Man, the cash is in the dash. Jake? I love her too, man. I hope this all is just a bad dream." Ted walks inside.

Jake rushes to the car. He begins the hour drive to reach the college campus. Thoughts of Jena race through his mind. He remembers the night they first made love, after she had murdered Mr. McNeil in cold blood. The fear he felt watching her point the gun after her murderous act. Realizing how sexy and attractive she was when he finally saw her in the nude. Watching the shapes of her body—nipples hard, tall and slender legs. So dominate, so beautiful, and so deadly. At that moment, he didn't know if she was going to turn and shoot him too or not. All he could do was believe that the love he felt for her would make her recognize him and remember their life leading up to this tragic moment. Somehow this released her into his arms, where he bared himself to shed light on the darkness she felt. He was overwhelmed with passion, held up to that point deep within a part of him but never recognized by the brightly lit yet dark eyes, which flooded the gates like red roses falling from a dead tree. The moment of the death somehow became the moment of life for Jake. It was the first time his love was truly revealed, no longer hidden from her, and expressed in the most profound way possible: hot, unexplained and unbelievable, passion.

On a dark road in the middle of nowhere, Jake finds himself lost in deep thought. He is so aroused by the mere thought of Jena that he stops in the middle of the highway. Time slips away from him. He feels powerless and anxious about finding Jena. *Where could she be?*

Suddenly there's a knock on Jake's car window. A middle-aged man wearing a red wig, donning awful painted makeup, and dressed in a clown suit peeks in the car. "Hey, you all right?" Jake keeps his hand on the steering wheel and shakes his head. The man moves in closer. "You realize that you're parked in the middle of the road," he looks around, "in the middle of nowhere?" The man seems confused at Jake's silence. "Are you hurt? On weed? Umm ... what's wrong with you? You're parked in the middle of the road—like I said—in the middle of nowhere." He takes off his wig.

Jake thinks back to the prom night when Jena dressed as a clown. He breaks his silence. "Do you realize that you're parked in the middle of nowhere dressed up as a clown?"

"Yeah. I realize that. So what! I'm trying to help you. I'm headed to a masquerade party." He starts wiping his face and gets makeup on his hand. "Damn, now my makeup is screwed!" the man yells.

"What if I told you the party was tomorrow night?"

"Really? Come on?"

"Yep," Jake says. "Tomorrow."

"So I'm dressed up as a clown, in the dark, in the middle of highway, in the middle of nowhere, and there's no party?"

"Nope, not tonight."

"Damn." The man walks back to his car swearing, "Damn. Damn. Damn." He gets in his car and zooms up beside Jake. "No party?"

"None," Jake replies.

"Damn. All this work I put into my makeup. Damn. Damn. Damn. Well, I guess I'm headed to the nearest hotel." He walks back to his car and throws his wig off to the passenger side of his car. Jake looks back at the man's car. The man spins off, stops, and backs up. "You sure? These kids called me. They said the party was tonight."

Jake shakes his head. "I know—damn, right?" Jake says smiling.

"Yeah. Damn." The man spins off.

Jake follows behind him and laughs to himself. His thoughts swing back to the prom night when Jena was dressed up as a clown. He remembered that even as a clown she was still beautiful to him. Stunning. Even a clown suit couldn't hide her natural beauty, the beauty the shined from her heart when she burst out in laughter. That night was one of the best nights of their lives, even though they brushed off the traditional celebration of horny heads dancing at the prom. They wanted to make a stand against the ridiculous fighting among friends over cheating and backstabbing and rebel against the typical high school ballroom gowns and the boring bow ties that are found in the trash within one hour of the event starting. *What a night that was*, Jake thinks. First picking Jena up at her house, cracking jokes as they anticipated the facial expressions of their friends when they walked into prom. The jaws dropping, the fingers pointing, the fake outburst of laughter when the room full of pranksters was pranked. Jake remembered how Jena tried to back out of it at the last minute.

*   *   *

Jake is driving and can't stop fidgeting with his hat in the mirror. Jena stares at him with a strange look from her clown made-up face.

"That hat isn't going to change. Stop messing with it."

"It has to be straight, Jena. I can't go in there with a crooked hat—I'd look stupid."

Jena grins. "Jake, you look stupid anyway—with or without the hat ... or the outfit." They both laugh. "Maybe crashing the prom isn't smart." Jena takes off her clown nose and plays with it in her hand. "I mean, our friends being all mad at each other is no real reason for us to just blow off the prom." Jake is quiet. "That was a very horrible night, watching Chance and Carol fight over Ken," Jena's voice saddens. "Chance was so heartbroken, finding out Carol was cheating with Ken."

Jake rolls his eyes. "Well, that's not all that happened that night." Jena looks over at him. Jake's voice changes, "Ken came on to you, confessing his undying love for you." Jake is jealous. "I never trusted him. Even in middle school, he was just a freaking asshole. I probably didn't like him when we were babies either. I bet we were in the same baby room at St. Mary's hospital." Jake frowns. "He was probably crying, and I was probably telling him to shut the hell up."

Jena is amused by Jake's jealous behavior. "Do you think he was wearing a clown's suit? Why didn't you get out of your little baby crib and show him some muscle, muscle head?"

Jake laughs. They both get quiet for a moment.

"Breaking the ice, clown face."

"Weirdo."

"Fake nose."

Jena looks over at Jake. "Ridiculously tall and uncalled for hat."

Jake laughs and thinks of a comeback. "Peanut head."

They both laugh at each other as Jake pulls into the high school gym parking lot. "I take it you just couldn't think of anything else?" She laughs loudly.

The moment had come: the prom. The stars are blazing in the night sky as they both sit quietly in the car watching their peers drag themselves into the prom like robotic zombies all looking for brains they don't have. Yet somehow walking into those doors made them think they made a smarter decision than them. For a moment, Jena and Jake's zombie outlook on two teenagers who had been dating since the ninth grade changed to recognizing a romantic couple full of sincerity and gentleness for one another. They were sharing this moment together, walking into the prom like a prince escorting his princess. Jena couldn't help but think that that could have been her and Jake. Jake was obviously having the same thought. He glances over at Jena, watching her gaze starry-eyed at the couple.

"That's Ann and Rich," Jena says.

Jake nods his head. "Yeah. Wow, they have been dating since we were in ninth, right?"

"Yeah," she says slowly. She looks over at Jake, who takes has hat off. "You don't want to go in, do you?"

Jake looks out his window. "Not really." He touches Jena's hand. "The truth is that I wanted to take you to prom. I wanted to share this night with you, to make you feel like a princess."

Jena gently squeezes his hand. "Jake, proms, props, and people all gathering together were never important to me. This is prom. This is our prom. We didn't choose to celebrate it the traditional way. We chose to give each other a long-lasting gift of laughter in these ridiculous, sweaty, hot outfits." She looks into Jake's eyes. "I feel like princess—even in this clown's suit. There are many different ways of feeling beautiful, feeling free. I'm as free as a bird right now because I have such a caring and wonderful friend like you."

Jake is mesmerized by Jena's words. He gently presses his thumb against her cheek. He starts the car. "Jena," he calls.

"Jake, I know. I truly do know, and that is why I will always, always have a special place for you in my heart."

Jake tries to hold back his emotions. "Well," he puts the car in gear, "you're still a peanut head." They both laugh.

"After all that?" She laughs.

He grins from ear to ear. Never had he believed that Jena would break the cold ice to give him a little hope that one day she could love him just as much as he loved her—deeper than the earth's core, higher than the sky will allow the human eye to see, and farther than man has ever walked toward the end of the never-ending earth then back around to do it all over again. *I'd do this all over again for her. Live this life again just to have her speak those words to me that commends me with the highest gold medal for my boyish crush. Gosh, I love her,* he thinks. *I love her so much.*

He starts to back out of the parking spot with the biggest smile on his face. Jena is his girl/friend/everything else to him, and no prom dress or *Saturday Night Fever* outfit would change that. Love is love. Life is love lived in the face of another who loves you back, and that's what he has this night with Jena—a shot at love. Jake's mind is in a twilight state. He backs out without looking and almost runs down someone.

"Hey!" someone yells from behind the car. It's Ken, all dressed with no one to prance inside the prom with. He has his hands on the back of car as if he was Superman and could stop it from leaving tire tracks on his polished getup. He walks swiftly up to Jake's window and leans in, smiling. "Trying to turn me into a zombie, dude?" He peeks at Jena's and Jake's outfits. "Wow," laughing out loud, "you two look like freaks." He laughs.

"Umm, you want something?" Jake asks.

"Yeah, just wanted to say hello. We are somewhat friends."

Jena doesn't look at Ken. "I don't know about being friends."

"Come on, guys." Ken stands back from the window. "We are most likely going to college together, so we might as well be friendly. I know I'm a jerk."

"Really?" Jake says sarcastically.

"I shouldn't have cheated on Chance. And, Jena … I'm sorry for coming on to you." He pats the window seal and walks away. Jake watches him as he walks into prom like a lonely pimp who just realized the power he felt was only in his head. For once, Ken looked human to him. Just seeing him alone, sorrowful, while still dressed up for a night of entertainment suddenly shined a bright light on him. It made Jake remember when he, Ken, Chance, Carol, and Jena were all hanging out laughing when they were younger—when high school's ruthless competition to be popular or to be a fantastic lover wasn't important, and when friendship came naturally without everyone pushing for the best stooge's award.

*   *   *

Jake tunes back to reality. He continues his drive toward Northwest University to meet Ken. His only mission is to find Jena, hold her in is arms tightly, and keep her safe within the world they've built—their prom night, their sacred love. "Jena," Jake softly utters her name as he drives on down the road.

CHAPTER SIXTEEN

The loneliness from the long ride traps Jake deep in thought. *How can all of this be happening?* he thinks. *It seems like we were all just in high school waiting for the big graduation day, and now I'm hiding from the cops, the love of my life has left me, and I'm stuck looking at a broken taillight belonging to the worst clown I've ever met. What a life.* He laments his decision to take Jena to New York. If only he'd have said no, he could've just taken her into hiding somewhere where no one would have found them, where he could have loved her for eternity without fear of losing her or, even worse, having her captured by the cops and taken away forever to live as prisoner. *I have to find her.* He presses down harder on the gas pedal. *Where could she be?* He passes a road sign: two miles for hotel, gas, and food. *Hotel?* He thinks hard. *Would she go back to where it first started? What are the chances?* The road exit is coming up. Jake quickly turns off the road.

He pulls into a rundown hotel's parking lot. The lights are flashing "Vacant Rooms." *I don't remember the name of the hotel,* he thinks. *Oh well, it's worth a shot.* He gets out, puts his hands in his pockets, and looks around the parking lot for the truck. There's a truck, but it's not Maggie's. It's a red, beat-up truck, parked on the curve like a drunk just decided, "Here, this is where I'll park." He walks toward the hotel.

The clerk is standing at the front desk reading a newspaper. Jake opens the door and hears the sound of a cheap bell attached to the doorknob. He stands at the counter for at least thirty seconds before the clerk acknowledges him. Jake notices a wanted sign with a scratched photo of Jena on it. The photo is upside down, but he can tell it's her.

"You know her?" the clerk suddenly asks.

Jake looks back at the clerk. He shrugs his shoulders. "No."

The clerk walks over to put the photo right side up. "I guess more people would recognize her if the damn picture was posted right." He has a smoker's laugh, yellow teeth, and a bald spot on the top of his head.

Jake tries to make small talk. "So you got vacant rooms, sir?"

"Sir? Just call me Clark."

"Okay. Clark, you got vacant rooms?"

"No," he grins. "All the rooms are taken."

"But your sign says—"

Clark cuts Jake off. "That sign is broken. It always says vacant rooms."

Jake folds his arms. "But your parking lot is empty."

Clark looks out the window. "Yeah, so what? Not everyone has a fantasy car. Some people walk. Hell, on this road, hitchhike," he rambles. "Hell, nowadays that's the way to go. Just live like there's no tomorrow. No car, no house, no bills," he stares Jake in the eyes and lifts his eyebrows, "no wife ... now that's the life for me. That's the good life." He starts snapping his fingers, echoing his words, "That's the good life."

Jake glances back at the wanted poster. He tries to be clever. "That girl, who is she?"

"Oh man, she's, umm, some chick who killed a few people." Clark leans over the counter. "They're just making a big shit out of what she did, but I don't buy it. Hell, my photo should be posted up there, because I've done a lot of shady shit in my lifetime. A lot." Clark scratches his bald spot.

Jake has a sympathetic look on his face. "She looks like an ordinary person—just a simple young girl."

Clark stares at the photo. "Yeah, I guess. But if she's anything like me, looks can be deceiving."

"So she hasn't come through here," Jake fishes for information.

"Nope. If she had, there would be photos of me and her posted on that wall right next to that stupid wanted poster sign." Clark gets heated. "I wouldn't turn her in. Heck, I'd probably join her in getting even with some people."

"Well, I've gotta go find me a hotel." Jake backs away.

Clark follows him out the door. "There's another hotel at the next exit. It's not too far from the university. A lot of kids go there to hang out, you know."

"Thanks." Jake gets into the car.

He drives off, gets back on the road, takes the next exit, and pulls into the hotel parking lot. There are several cars, trucks, and campers parked at the hotel. "The Palm Lee Inn," Jake whispers to himself. Jake walks inside.

A clerk wearing is standing at the counter with a big smile on his face. "Hello. How are you?" He's extremely polite—the total opposite of the last clerk, whose negative outlook on life seemed to ooze out of his pores. Jake sees that Jena's wanted photo is pinned up on the wall. The clerk runs up and shakes Jake's hand. "Wow, it's great to see you."

Jake is surprised. He's never had anyone great him with such enthusiasm, let alone a hotel clerk. "Hi," Jake says as he shakes the clerk's hand quickly and then puts his hands in his pockets.

"So, looking for a room? Oh, by the way, my name is Franklin Bosler."

Jake thinks he's funny, but he tries to stay focused on finding Jena. "Frank," he thinks out loud.

"Yeah, Frank. What a name, right?" Frank walks back to the counter. "Yeah, my mother and father named me Franklin. I think it's a good name. I'm named after a great man." Frank stands with a huge grin on his face. "Hey, I know the parking lot looks full, but I've got rooms left. Yeah, nice rooms." Frank's grin shows all of his teeth. Frank catches Jake glancing at Jena's wanted poster on the wall. "She's a beauty, huh?" Frank sighs. "A killer beauty."

"Yeah, she's quite good looking." Jake tries to look away. His eyes zoom in on Frank's book lying on the counter. "*Cold Reda Gray?* That's an interesting name for a book." Jake picks up the book.

"You like to read?" Frank is excited.

Jake puts the book down. "Yeah, some books interest me."

"Well, you're going to like this book. It's about a girl who has all these tragic things happen to her that it ultimately turns her into a killer."

Jake nods his head. "Sounds interesting."

Frank starts scrambling for paperwork. "So, what floor do you want ... first ... second?" Frank hands Jake the paperwork and a pen.

"I'll take the second floor."

"Well, the second floor is the most popular floor. Earlier I had a young lady request the second floor, too, and a few other college students. Oh, these college students always seem to love the second floor. Must be something special about that floor." Frank eyes Jena's picture. "Oh, I know—that's the floor where Jena Parker murdered the previous clerk that worked here. Those kids are going to that room thinking that there's some sort of supernatural powers there or something." Franks pops his hand on his forehead. "Dumb me. I should've figured that out, since I'm so fascinated by murder mystery. Hey, that's why I wrote this book."

"I'm curious about the girl. The girl, was she good looking?" Jake steps closer to the counter.

"Oh, yeah." Frank puts his book under one arm and walks up to Jake. Jake stares at the book tucked tightly under his armpit. "She was sort of strange, but certainly she was good looking. She looks a lot like this girl who's wanted for multiple murders."

Jake has a wild look in his eyes. "What girl?"

Franks points at the poster of Jena. "That girl. Jena Parker, the notorious murderer, wanted by the cops, wanted by the FBI, wanted by me because I want to interview her for my next book. She's popular." Jake reaches in his pockets. Franks backs up slowly. "Hey, you don't have a weapon do you?" Frank says, obviously scared. "I mean, there's not a lot cash here. Just maybe a few bucks."

Jake has a puzzled look on his face. "What? I don't have a gun. I was just looking for my money for the room."

"Oh, yeah." Franks laugh out loud. "Man, it's these murder mystery books I'm writing. They make me paranoid—although the last clerk did meet his doom at this very place."

Jake pulls out cash he'd nabbed from Ted's car dash. "How much?" Jake puts the cash on the counter.

"Twenty-five dollars for a luxury hotel night stay." Frank picks up the cash and starts counting.

"I don't need luxury," Jake says. "I just need a room."

Franks hands Jake a five dollar bill. "You gave me too much. Now sign that paper. Here's your key. You've just got yourself the best room in town!"

Jake scribbles his initials on the paperwork: JP. He dashes out the door to find Jena, frantically looking at the rooms, trying to figure out which one she is in.

Franks steps outside, his book still tucked under his armpit. Jake looks at him. "She's in room 201." Frank hands Jake his book. "Here, take this too. I'm sure after a good, hot night of fun, you'll probably want a good book to read."

Jake snatches the book and runs like a tiger chasing a deer in the wilderness. He stops and stands still at the door with the book under his arm. His heart is racing like a clock ticking out of control. He taps on the door, whispers Jena's name, knocks louder, and then plays with the doorknob.

Jena awakens slowly from her dream. She still isn't sure if she is still dreaming or if the knock is real. She lies still for moment, trying to balance her reality from her dream. "Matt Ross?" she utters. "How did he find me?" She quickly gets up from the bed to face herself in the mirror. *This is it. This is my dream. Matt Ross is coming to face me down.* She wonders if she should use this moment to take Matt out or use this moment to redeem herself. She opens the door. "Jake?"

He rushes her into his arms, and the book falls to the floor. Jena is shock, relieved, and confused all at once. "Jena, please put your arms around me." He starts to cry. "Please put your beautiful arms around me."

She squeezes him back tightly. "You found me," she says, still shocked. "You found me." Without a moment to spare, Jake kisses her lips. All of the worry, fear, and uncertainty fade as he pours all of his soul into a long passionate kiss. Jena can't break free of his passion; it cages her up like an animal stuck in a cage with another animal that is protecting its territory and nurturing it, as it rules the land it stands on. Jake wants to take control of Jena's passion, to let her know that running isn't going to stop his love from existing, that it is only going to make it grow bigger and stronger and resistant to even her efforts to push it into the shadow. Nothing could break the kiss. It is a moment within a moment that has its own timing, not determined by destiny or circumstances, yet a simple point of love.

"I had to find you." Jake's face is drowned with tears. "It was no choice to me." He kisses Jena's face. "No choice."

Jena begins to cry. "What are we going to do?" she asks.

Jake pulls her close. "Nothing tonight except be together. I don't care what's going to happen tomorrow." He caresses her hair. "Because all I care about is right now, finally finding you and holding you again." He grabs her face. "Looking into those beautiful eyes, I don't care about tomorrow, Jena. I'll deal with tomorrow, tomorrow."

Jena gently kisses him. He slowly removes her jacket; it falls to the floor. The moment was perfect, the timing just right, and the mood bolstered by the oasis of tranquility. Jake removes Jena's clothes. He kneels down to kiss her feet, legs, and thigh. She looked like a goddess to him, and he is her slave to do as she wills. She watches as he takes off his clothes, never taking his eyes off of her. He throws his clothes to the floor. He takes her in his arms and leads her to the bed. He stares deeply into her eyes. "I don't want anyone else or anything else except you." He kisses her gently on the lips. "Even the moment before this moment is done. I'm just taking every moment with you like it is the only moment."

Jena smiles with passion as she guides his head to her face. Jake massages her entire body with his lips. He gently inserts himself, penetrating Jena with the slowest motions possible without breaking a stride in every level of his strokes.

"Oh, Jake," Jena softly calls.

"Yes—call my name again. I love it when you say my name when I'm making love to you."

Jena's fingernails clutch Jake's back. He tosses her up until she sits upright on top of him. She leans in, her hair swaying in front of his face as she moves her body with his, like waves running smoothly down a river on a warm, sunny day. Jake's eyes close, hands squeezing her waist, leaving his fingerprints deep in her skin. Jena leans her head back. Her hair flows backward as they both move in a consistency reaching the highest peak that any men or women could encounter together as their minds, hearts, and souls merge into a unbreakable bond.

Jena sighs. Jake falls silent, as if he's been given a tranquilizer that just took effect as their bodies, once in limbo, were reborn back to the world. They lie in each other's arms, eyes heavy, bodies worn, and minds at peace.

The hotel is quiet, and there's a light, warm breeze outside. It's three o'clock in the morning, and Franklin is gathering his paperwork together for the shift change. He's in a good mood, singing, until he comes across the signature of one of the hotel guests. A familiar name: Reda Jones. Franklin's face turns beet red. He grabs the paper in both hands and almost rips it in half from his excitement. "Reda Jones. My Reda Jones? Jena Parker?" he utters as he stares back at the wanted poster on the wall.

CHAPTER SEVENTEEN

Jena reaches over to put her arms around Jake. He turns to hold her and glances at the radio clock on the table behind her. "It's five o'clock," he says.

Jena breathes in. "Five?" she says and turns to get out of bed. She sits on the side and turns to look at him. "We should get an early start before the sun rises."

"Sure," Jake says. Jena moves slowly to the bathroom, turns on the shower, and steps in. She lets the hot water roll down her hair and body. The door opens slightly. Jena can see the steam rushing out of it. She turns around just as Jake steps in the shower to join her.

Jena grins and then shyly turns around. "Umm, there's a thing called privacy." She laughs a little.

Jake moves closely behind her, reaches for her waist, and then moves in even closer to her. He holds her tightly as the water runs down both of their bodies. Whispering in her ear, he says, "There's also a thing called love." She reaches her arm up behind to Jake's face and neck. She gently caresses his neck as he holds her tight and whispers, "I don't want to go outside this room. I don't want this moment that we've captured in a bottle to be broken."

Jena closes her eyes and wishes too that they didn't have to leave, but reality set ins. She knows that the world is waiting for her. She has to leave the room in order for both worlds to unfold. "I wish we could stay here, Jake, but we can't." She turns around and hugs him tightly and then steps out of the showers, brushes her teeth, and leaves the bathroom.

Jake is left standing under the hot water, feeling a bit isolated from her but determined to never let her leave his sight again. He finishes in the bathroom and leaves to get to dress. Jena is dressed, looking in the mirror, combing her hair. He watches her every move.

"I like your hair red." Jena looks at him, then back in the mirror.

"I guess it's okay," she says. Maybe it's time I changed it back. She watches through the mirror as Jake is getting dressed. His bare, naked chest is toned like a body builder whose only goal is to make a woman understand that he would be Tarzan and she would be Jane. His jeans are perfectly fitted around his toned abs. He slides on his shirt. Jena turns around, leaning on the small dresser. "I didn't know that you were such a gym fanatic."

Jake blushes. "I wouldn't say I'm a fanatic." He walks to her. "I'd say I was trying to do whatever it took to get your attention."

She checks out his body. "Well, I'd say you got it." She looks over at her bag sitting on a chair near the bed, walks over, and takes out the letter her mother wrote to her. Jake walks over to her. Jena plays with the letter, tempted to open it.

"You should open the letter," Jake tries to convince her. He puts his hand on her shoulder.

"I should ... but I won't. Not now." She puts the letter back in her bag. It's six forty-five in the morning; daylight breaks through the window shades. Jena and Jake are ready to leave.

Jake reaches in his pocket for Ted's cell phone. "Where is my phone?" He looks around the room. "I must have left it in the car. Ken's probably pissed."

Jena stops. "Ken?" She picks her bag up. "Why would he be pissed?"

Jake pauses. "I asked him to help me find you." He gives Jena a pitiful look. "I needed help. I was desperate."

Jena blows it off. "Okay. Let's go."

Jake opens the hotel door. The parking lot is almost empty; just Ted's car and two other cars are outside. Jake looks back at Jena before stepping out and asks, "Where's the truck?"

"It's out back. Do you really think I would have parked it up front?"

He smiles at her. "No, of course not." His foot snags on a newspaper lying in front of the room's door. He picks it. Jena and the stories of the murders she committed are the front page news. Jake doesn't want her to see. He looks around at the other hotel room doors, and there aren't any newspapers in front of them.

"Let me see, Jake." Jena grabs the paper from him. "Jena Parker wanted for multiple murders," she murmurs. She closes the paper and sticks it in her bag.

Jake gives her a look. "Why are taking this garbage?"

She pushes past Jake out the door and stops. "It's not garbage. It's the truth. You can't run from the truth, Jake. It'll always find you. No matter where you go or what you do, the truth will always be there waiting for you to face and conquer it. I must face my truth." She puts her head down. "And maybe someday I'll be able to conquer it." She walks to the car.

Jake follows. Tension fills the air. Jake can feel the enchanted moment they shared last night slipping away. He is crushed and wants nothing more except to make the entire situation go away and for last night's unforgettable love making to be every night for the rest of their lives. Jena gets into the car and closes the door. Jake stands out by the driver's side, peeking in, trying to break the tension. "Are you all right?"

"Yes, Jake, I'm fine." Jake gets inside the car, cranks it up. Just as Jake starts to drive away, the front office door opens. It's Franklin. He's holding up a big poster sign with words written in red: "You're

Famous, REDA JONES!" As the car passes, he holds the sign up high. Jena stares at him; her and Franklin lock eyes. He knows and she knows what the sign really means. Franklin doesn't say a word, yet smiles uncontrollably at Jena. The car jets off onto the long highway—Jena's hair swaying in the wind, one hand out the window, gazing off into the early morning sky. "I'm famous," she utters to herself. Jake is quiet. He doesn't ask questions about Franklin or the sign.

Jena is silent. Thoughts of her mother, father, and the funeral drift through her mind as the wind blows against her face. *Sometimes the sun can be too bright; sometimes it is not bright enough. Sometimes the blue skies aren't as blue as I'd wish they would be, but that's life. The sky isn't always going to be painted blue, and the sun isn't always going to shine just right. Either way, I'm still going to be that girl who killed her mother. Who killed an innocent man on a train. Who killed two men who deserved it, a slob and a father killer. Mr. McNeil took my father's life, and somehow—in the midst of it all—he managed to take my life with him. He ruined me, and I let him. And now the man that I love,* Jena looks over at Jake, *he's ruined too. Both ruined, wrecked, and in love. We are that love story in the movies, written in books, and portrayed by average people who see the movies, read the books, and think to themselves, "Hey, that's us." We are those lovers, but my life is much more complicated than a movie or book. I don't think Jake and I are the modern Romeo and Juliet, because I'm not going to let it end that way.*

"What kind of help did you want from Ken?" Jena says as she gives Jake a mean look.

"To help find you. Like I said, I was desperate." The cell phone rings. Jake looks around for it while still trying to keep one eye on the road; Jena ignores it. In a sad voice, Jake says, "It's under the seat, Jena. Please get it for me. It could be my mom or Ted." Jena reaches for the cell and pulls it from under the seat. Ken's name and number are flashing on the cell phone.

"It's Ken," Jena says in a rough voice.

Jake ignores the call. He takes the phone from Jena. There are at least six missed calls and messages from Ken. A seventh missed call appears on the phone. "Jena, please don't withdraw from me. I need you right now. And you need me."

She doesn't want to treat him badly. "Okay, where are we going?" she asks.

"Hold on." Jake presses down to listen to the messages. Message one: "Jake, where the hell are you? I'm out in front of the library. Call me back." Message two: "Jake, come on, man. It's getting late—let me know what's up." Message three: "I'm about to leave. If you're still coming, call me." Message four: "Hey, I'm headed back to the room. I'm starting to get worried. Hopefully Jena didn't off you too." Message five: "Hey, man, I'm back in the room. Sorry about that Jena crack. I was just kidding. I want to help you find her, so call me back." Message six: "Man, it's two in the morning. I got class tomorrow and a hot chick sleeping next to me. Hopefully you're all right. Maybe you've already found her, which would explain why I can't find you. Anyway, man, the party is still on tomorrow. I've got some costumes for you guys. There's gonna be drinks, hot chicks—Chance and Carol will be there—it's going to be kick-ass, so call me back." The seventh messages pops up: "Jake, man, it's the next day, meaning the last I spoke to you was yesterday. I called your mom---whoa, bad idea. Now she's worried. If you don't contact me today, I'm calling the police—because shit, man, I don't know what else to do." Jake clicks the off button. The phone rings. It's Ken. Jake picks up.

"Yeah. Goddamn." Ken sounds excited. "Oh, thank goodness, man. You're alive! What's up."

"I'm with her," Jake says in a sober voice.

"That's good news, because I was going to call the cops. You're mom called me at least six times. I didn't tell her about Jena. I just told her you were coming here to cool off—clear your head." Silence.

"We're on our way," Jake finally responds. "Where do we meet?"

Ken thinks. "Let's meet at this place called Kings. It's the exit right before the college. We'll meet there to plan. Tonight's the night man—party night!" Ken shouts. His friends in the background start cheering.

"Look, I don't know if we're going," Jake shoots the idea down, spying Jena as she stares out the window. "A party maybe too risky."

"We're going," Jena answers without looking at Jake. "We're going to go to that party, Jake. Maybe we need a little fun."

"Is that Jena?" Ken yells. "Is that her? Oh, man, I know what people have been saying about her, but I'm not judging. I just can't believe I'm about to see her," Jake is quiet, "and you too," Ken redeems himself.

"Hey," Jake says in a firm voice. "No one except you, Ken. We don't need the entire school knowing where we are and where we are going to be."

Ken laughs. "I got it." Ken hangs up the cell.

Jena stares out the window. She's not in the mood for small talk, yet with every passing moment in the car her curiosity grows, wondering what lies ahead for her at Kings. A party? And what dark fields of unfinished business lie ahead?

CHAPTER EIGHTEEN

"This is it." Jake pulls into King's Café's parking lot. He looks around the parking lot, across the street, and in the café for any signs of cops. "Doesn't appear to be any police officers here." He looks over at Jena. "Ready?"

She puts on her hoodie jacket and dark sunglasses. "Yep." Jake puts on his hoodie and dark sunglasses as well. Jena opens her car door first, grabs her bag, and then they both walk in together.

The café has a few stragglers, truck drivers, and one family with a little two-year-old. Jena walks ahead; Jake follows her. They both look around the café for Ken. He's sitting in the back corner of the café alone. Jena spots him and walks over. Ken watches her in amazement. Ken seems nervous as Jena stands near the table. Jake's standing behind her, holding her arm, looking around the room. Ken gestures to them to sit down. He looks suspiciously around the café.

"Are you looking for someone?" Jena asks. Chance walks up to the table. Jena looks at her.

"Don't blame him. I followed him," she says. She pushes Ken over and sits down. The four of them sit for minutes just staring at one another without saying a word. Jena stares directly at Chance and then at Ken. Chance picks up the menu. "Are we going to sit here and say nothing?" She signals to the waitress. "Let's at least order some food. If not, we'll really look suspicious."

The waitress walks over. "Hi, ya'll. Welcome to Kyler's ... Oh, I mean welcome to *King's* café. We have a great special." The waitress points at the menu Chance is holding. "Eggs, bacon, and ham for only $4.95. Comes with a side of biscuits or bread." She smiles at Jake. "We even have raisin bread, too."

They all look at each other. The cook yells from the back. "Tell them about our soup special!" Jena peeks at the cook. She nudges Jake on the shoulder.

"It's that guy from the other restaurant!" Jake whispers to her.

"We'll all have the special," Jena quickly says to get rid of the waitress. "And coffee."

The waitress takes all the menus, smiles, and walks away. "Four SPs," she yells back to the cook.

"What about soup?" the cooks yells.

The waitress gets testy. "Hell, Kyler, nobody wants any damn soup." Jake stares at Jena.

"Wow, you guys are real serious looking with the shades and hoodies on." Ken grins. "I really feel like I'm involved in some espionage shit."

Jena gives him stare. Even through the shades, Ken can tell she means business. "You are." She pulls down her shades for a second. "Ken, we don't have a lot of time to chat."

Jake takes off his hoodie, but leaves on his shades. "Tell us the plan," he says.

"Wait," Chance interrupts. "Where have you guys been?" She looks over at Jena and then lowers her voice to merely a whisper. "Jena, did you kill those people?"

Jena keeps her cool. "Chance, we don't have time to discuss my life right now. Jake and I came here to get away from the madness. Ken said there is a party tonight. I'd like to go to it."

Chance glances at Ken. "It's good to see you, Jena." Chance tries to balance her feelings.

"Here's the plan—" Ken begins to speak just as the waitress comes back with the coffees.

"What plan?" the waitress inquires. They all look at her. She politely puts the coffees down and walks away.

"I didn't know nosy came with the waitress job," Ken says sarcastically. "Anyway, here's the plan." He moves in closer, lowers his voice. "I've got a friend named C. A. T. Tyler." Chance frowns at him. He looks back at her and then back at Jake. "He's a good guy. Cool."

"He's a drug dealer, Ken," Chance says in rude voice. Jake and Jena look at each other.

Ken sits back, just looking at her. "Chance, I would hardly call him a drug dealer. He only sells weed. Nowadays, weed is medicine. So he sells medicine." Chance rolls her eyes. "Now, C. A. T. has agreed to let you guys hang out at his house." Ken gets excited. "He's got a nice, badass house. Hot chicks there all the time." Chance is embarrassed.

Jake smirks at Chance's reaction. "I take it by your reaction, Chance, that you and Ken are back together."

Ken hugs her close to him. "Yeah, man." He kisses her cheek. Jena stares at them both. "She's my babes. Then and Now." Ken gets cocky.

Jena feels a rage at the mere thought that Chance would even consider taking Ken back after he cheated with Carol. Jena clinches her bag. "Give us directions," she tells Ken. Ken slides the directions across the table. The waitress is just coming with their food. Ken's and Jena's hands touch as Jena reaches for the paper. The waitress tries to be nosy. Jena snatches the paper and puts it in her bag.

The waitress is assisted by another waitress. "Here you guys go. Four SPs." The four of them give her a strange look as if to say "Okay, really?" She looks at them. "That's our code word for the today's special." She has a creepy smile on her face, and she stares at them for a second before putting the plates down.

The other waitress gives her a nasty stare. "I do have other tables, Ann."

Ann looks at her. She gets upset. "Just because I have more tables then you doesn't mean that you can insult me in front of my customers." The other waitress shoves the plates at her and walks off. Keeping a smile on her face, Ann gently puts the plates down.

Kyler, the cook, rings the pickup bell. He yells loudly from the kitchen, "Ann, soup's ready!"

Ann smiles at them. "I am so tired of soup." She walks away.

"We have to get out of here," Jena says as she looks over at Jake, who is just getting ready to eat. Bob, Big Papa, and two other truck drivers walk in the door. Jake looks over at them. He drops his fork, gets up, and reaches for Jena.

Chance butts in; she seems desperate to say something. "Can we talk to each other first? Jake? Ken? Could you guys leave me and Jena alone, just for a minute? I think that it would look less suspicious if you guys sit at a different table." She glances at Jena. "This way, Jena and I can talk."

Jena turns to her. "Talk about what?"

Chance stands up to let Ken out. "Just to catch up," she says.

"We don't have time, Chance."

She gives Ken a look. "Jena, please," Chance pleads.

Jena relents. "Jake, I'm going to give her five minutes."

Ken stands up, looks around the room, and walks off with Jake. The two of them stroll to a table at the front of the café. Jake keeps his eyes on Jena.

Chance sits down, eyes to the floor, picks up a spoon, and then puts it back down. She looks up at Jena. Jena makes a bold move, completely removing her shades. "You look different," Chance says.

"I am different."

Chance shows compassion for her. "I'm sorry about your father … and your mother. I won't ask if you really killed her."

"You just did."

Chance looks out the café window. "I'm really not with him—not really." Jena looks at her, lets her confess. "Mr. McNeil is dead, right?" Chance continues to prod.

Jena answers boldly. "Yes. He is dead."

"I do understand, Jena. I understand how anyone could get to a breaking point."

Jena tests her. "So, you could kill someone?"

Chance looks out the window again and then back at Jena. "I could?" She sounds unsure. "I'm sure I could." She thinks back to the night she found out about Carol. "I know I could. I could have killed Ken for cheating on me." She looks directly at Jena. "I could have killed Carol for what she did." Jena tries to believe her. "I could have killed you, Jena, after Ken confessed that he'd had a crush on you all that time." Jena sits and listens to her. "I was crushed. Broken. It was the worst betrayal I'd ever felt."

Jena goes back to what Chance said about her. "So, you could have killed me?"

Chance backs out of her words. "Not really *killed* you, but I felt rage. I felt like I could have easily spun out of control. This is why I think you should turn yourself in."

Jena looks up at the café ceiling, tapping her fingers together. "This is why you wanted to talk to me? So you could tell me a past that I already know and then woo me with your cries and humbleness—just so you can convince me that turning myself in is what's best for me? That somehow my teenage life is over because you've got all the answers?"

Chance gets angry. "Jena, you're just prolonging the inevitable. Sooner or later, you'll get caught," she looks over at Jake and Ken. Jake is staring at them, paying little attention to Ken. "And Jake—he'll get caught, too, and go to jail. You two won't be in the same jail, you know."

Jena plays with her. "What's this really about, Chance? Is this about my murderous actions ... or your jealousy? Either way, you don't matter. What you're saying to me is like water running off a cliff—such a long way for it to go until it hits the bottom, and when it does, all that happens is that it splatters everywhere. Does that seem like a scenario I'm interested in?" Chance looks away. Jena pounds her fist on the table. "You might want to look at me." People in the café turn around to look at them. Jake stands up. Jena gives Chance a mean, angry look. "The person you knew years ago, or even that awful night, is not the person sitting at this table with you." Chance begins to shake, tears begin falling. Jena stands firm. "What? Are you afraid? Do you feel my fire? How hot it burns? Think of when you may have accidently burned your hand on the stove, the pain you felt, and then imagine my life's pain now—that fifty thousand times over. Feeling pain—whether inflicted intentionally or unintentionally—either way, I've claimed it."

Chance sobs, fearing Jena may hurt her. "Jena, you weren't the only one hurt." Her eyes well up and tears fall from them as she frantically runs her fingers through her hair. "I was too. I was ruined. So I ... I do know how fire can burn deep. How we can dig our own holes to bury ourselves in. Hide from shame felt that was not meant for us, but meant for someone else—someone like Mr. McNeil, who may have deserved to have never-ending pain, to fall without ever landing, or just to land and ..." she wipes her face, "and just to have you there to fire two bullets into his chest. He deserved it." She raises her face through the tears.

"I'm the victim of an eternity of burning fire. I pray for rain." Jena has listened, but she shows little compassion for Chance. She doesn't want to remember that night when she was beaten and raped. She gives Chance a cold look, almost as if she has a light shining directly on her. She pulls Chance into her world. "You feel powerless, don't you? Scared? It's a feeling like no other—not knowing what to do, where to turn, or who to trust. Then there are times you just want to pick up something and throw it across the room or even at yourself as you stare at the reflection you see in the mirror. It can be overwhelming." Chance stops crying for a moment, breathing hard as she listens. "Revenge is what you're really sobbing about. That is what this whole conversation is about. You have the urge to break loose from being a caged animal trapped within your own pain, forced to accept it, fighting hard to run from it. You want my secrets. You want to feed off my fire, learn from me, so you can tailgate my journey." Jena is cold. "That's not going to happen. My advice to you is to let your fire burn until it can't burn anymore. Let it light you up until you're so consumed by it that you begin to feel coldness run through your mind, until it numbs your hands, feet, and then all of you. Once you reach that point, you won't need my fire." Jena stands up. Chance's eyes are red, and they follow Jena's every move. She is shaking and obviously fears Jena. Jena turns to walk away.

"Jena," Chance's voice cracks, "I don't want that kind of coldness. There's warmth still out there for you and for me."

Jena turns around. "Really? Where is it?"

Chance looks over at Jake. "Jake is your warmth."

Jena stares at Jake with compassion and then walks to him, leaving Chance drowning in her tears. Kens rushes over to console Chance, who pulls away from him and dashes out of the café.

CHAPTER NINETEEN

J ena walks toward Jake. She can see his face is filled with hope, fear, and love for her. *Why does the light always seem brighter when it's farther away? Just until you get close to it. Then you realize it wasn't a light at all, just the reflection in your eyes of what you had hoped to see—what you wanted to see most—which was something that shines so bright that it melts the cold, hardened ice from your soul.*

Jena and Jake begin to walk out. "Stop!" Kyler is holding a shotgun on them. "What—you think you can come into my café and I wouldn't remember who you two are?" He cocks the gun; customers scream. Ken stands up. "You two aren't going anywhere." Bob, Big Papa, and two other truck drivers stand up, giving Jake tough looks. "This is going to go down a little different from the last time." Bob points at Jake. Ann calls 911. "You two come in my café—eating, talking, and plotting—after you cause me to lose my restaurants in Donner's County."

Ann yells out, "Police got me on hold."

"Sit down!" Kyler yells at both of them. Jake and Jena stand still. Jake tries to walk forward. Kyler points the gun at him. "I said sit down." Ken is speechless; he doesn't know what to do.

Jena walks forward. "I'm not sitting down."

Kyler points the gun back at her. "Girl, you won't be missed." Kyler walks closer. "The cops are looking for you in Maplesville, New York, and now Donner's County—not to mention that I've been waiting to catch up with you and that Matt Ross. He's lucky he's in jail. You're wanted for murder, so who's going to care if I shoot you?" Kyler points the gun around the café. People duck in fear. "Anyone in here care if I shoot Ms. Jena Parker—also known as Jena Gray—killer of four people, including her own mother?" He points the gun around the café again. "Anyone?"

A man in the corner booth stands up and points his gun at Kyler, ready to shoot. "I care," he yells from the back. It's Franklin, the clerk from the hotel. Kyler points his gun on Franklin. Franklin walks closer, pointing his gun directly at Kyler. "I care. I'm not going to let you kill my Reda Jones."

"Reda Jones?" Kyler is confused. "This isn't Reda Jones," Kyler yells. "This girl is Jena Parker."

"Jena, you and Jake leave." The friendly face Jena remembered has been transformed; Franklin looks sullen and mean. He seems out of control.

Jena turns to Franklin. "This is my battle. There's no need for you to get involved." Franklin and Kyler stand face-to-face, guns ready to light up the room.

"No, that is where you're wrong, Jena. You're my Reda Jones— and if you die, she dies. I plan on writing my next book, and Reda Jones ain't dying today."

"You are one crazy, nutty bar fool," Kyler says as he tries to keep his shotgun on Franklin and Jena. Ann is still holding on the phone. Bob stands up. Jena pulls a gun on him. Kyler screams at Franklin, "Do you have any idea of what the hell you're talking about?"

Franklin gets sentimental. His eyes get dreamy, teary. "I know exactly what I'm talking about." Jena is drawn to him as he speaks. "There's only a once in a lifetime chance that you will find a character who can take you out of your simple world of hotel clerk. A character who is so charismatic, beautiful, torn," he looks over at Jena, keeping the gun pointed at Kyler, "full of energy ... dark. And most of all ... deadly." He focuses back on Kyler. "You create a character like that only once in a lifetime. Once. But what are the chances that you will actually get to meet that very same character in real life? Jena Parker is Reda Jones, and I'll kill you before I let you harm her." Jena can see that there is a bit of darkness in Franklin. Behind the cheery face, pleasant attitude, and overexaggerated hotel hospitality, there is a man filled with his own mystery. *His obsession with a fictional character has led him to brand me as a mentor*, Jena thinks.

Jena glances over at Ken, trapped in the back of the café. "Ken, Chance, let's go," Jena yells to him.

"Don't you move, son," Kyler yells back.

Jena swings her gun away from Bob and points it directly at Kyler. "Don't tell me what to do." She points her gun at a window and blows a bullet through it. The window glass shatters over a café table. "Get the hell out of here, Ken!" Ken, Chance, and two other people rush to jump out the window.

Bob jumps to grab Jena's gun. Kyler fires off, hitting Bob in the chest. Franklin fires, hitting Kyler in the shoulder. As he falls backward the shotgun goes off, shells hitting Ann in the stomach. Franklin holds his gun down on Kyler, Jena on the truck drivers. Two waitresses run over to help Ann. Jena walks slowly over to Kyler, who is holding his bleeding arm on the floor. Franklin points his gun at the truck drivers. Jake is standing holding the door open, waiting for Jena in amazement of her instant change. Jena points down at Kyler. "I told you I wasn't going to sit down." She looks around the café and feels a slight uneasiness with the gun in her hand. She puts her gun away. "Everybody, my name is Jena Parker. I've been accused of many crimes, and I can't tell you right now if those crimes were justified or not. What I do know is this isn't the last time you're going to hear my name or see my face. As it haunts you, even when you reflect on painful memories in your life that doesn't involve me, but when you do think of me try to remember someone that hurt you deeply." Franklin listens closely. Everyone gives Jena their attention. "Someone that hurt you so deeply that it made you pause, sit for hours, question everything you ever believed in. *Who you are? Why is this happening to you? Why me?*" she screams. "Why me?" she screams again, spying the entire café. "Think about anyone who made you feel that way, and then think of me. Then try to judge me." She turns to look at Jake, who's surprised to see this side of Jena that he's never seen before. This is the very first time he feels disconnected from her, that he sees her as a different person. He can feel her rage, an unsettling feeling amplified by the scene around him: Kyler shot in the arm, Ann shot in the stomach, Bob shot in chest, Ken jumping out the busted window, and Franklin possessed by his own obsession. Jake's hand braces on the door. Witnessing the truth makes him fear the future.

Jena can see the dissolution in his emotions for her, but she doesn't care. She walks quickly past him out the door and gets in the car. Jake follows and gets in the car. Chance gets in her car and spins out the parking lot. Just as Jake is ready to pull out, Ken pulls up next to them and rolls his window down. He's sweating and excited. "Holy shit." He rolls the window up and zooms off. Jake follows.

Jena rolls the window down so she can breathe in the wind. She tries to calm her emotions. Wind blowing in her face, she turns to look at Jake and wonders, *Did I lose my love? My warmth? The one person who'd give it all up to ride forever with me to hell. Knowing that's where we're headed, he still drives as though heaven lives in these eyes when he looks at me—at least he did until a moment ago, when I know he finally saw the fire that's been burning in me. Is that enough for him to finally leave?* "Now you know," Jena says.

"Know what?" Jake answers quickly.

"Who I am."

"Jena, I saw you after you shot Mr. McNeil, but I—"

She cuts in. "I know you felt he deserved it … but today I revealed myself."

"I know that is not who you are or who you want to be. Don't you want to be with me?"

"Jake, it's either going to be that you're going to live in my hell or I'm going to live in your heaven. I don't know if both can exist."

"Both can't exist. That's why I'm going to give everything I've got to give you heaven, forever happiness, because I know an eternity of my love being draped over you will take away your pain. I refuse to accept anything else. I'm with you all the way. There's no turning back for me now. I love you. That's never going to change. We've just got to figure out a way to get through this, and then we can leave. Maybe get out of the country—hide out in Mexico. I don't know, but I know I want you with me and I want you to want me too." He looks at her. "Do you want me?"

Jena is quiet. "I do want you, but I don't know if your fantasy can be reality." Jake is disappointed, but he still hasn't given up on their future.

Ken pulls up to the gateway of a huge house. He has a code to open the gate, but it doesn't work. He buzzes.

"Yep," a voice answers.

"It's me." Ken sounds frustrated. "The code is not working again."

"Yeah, I know. I just changed it." The gate opens. Ken rolls in; Jake follows. Ken gets out of his car and raises his arms in the air. "Hey, hey—we're here!" Jake goes to talk to him. Ken is still in shock and pumped up over what happened at the café. He and Jake talk in private while Jena sits in the car and ponders whether to leave and never be seen again. She finally gets out.

Ken stares at her. "I'd say you're a badass, but I think you already know that." Ken says as he smiles and winks at her.

Not entertained by his comment, Jena asks, "Can we go now?" She puts her shades back on.

"Sure, but first let me show you guys something." Ken clicks a button on his keys, and his car trunk pops opens. There are four costumes in the back. "Hey," he points, "these are the picks for tonight."

Jena is spying the red dress, shoes, and face mask. She gives Ken a distasteful look. "I guess the red outfit is mine?"

Ken reaches for the dress. "I thought you liked the color red?" Ken hands her the dress, shoes, and mask. Jena folds the dress and sticks the shoes and mask in her bag.

Jake rifles through the trunk, looking over the two male outfits. The Phantom of the Opera was one of his choices. "I'll take this one." Jake grabs the outfit, shoes, and mask.

Ken closes his trunk. "Excellent," he whispers. Ken lays out the rules. "Now, here's the deal. C. A. T. owes me a favor, so I'm cashing in on it by asking him to let you two stay at his house without any questions asked of who you are or what you're doing here. He's a real nice, cool guy—or man, I guess, because he's a little older than us—but he's cool with all the high profilers at the university so no one bothers him, if you know what I mean."

"So he sells weed to staff," Jena says sarcastically.

Ken pauses. "Something like that. Anyways, you guys go on to the room, chill, eat, shower, and change to get ready for the party of your lives!" Ken starts walking. "It's that simple."

Jena looks at Jake. She has on shades, but he knows what she's thinking. No party they have ever attended was ever that simple, and what would make them think that this party would be any different? Ken turns around, waves both his hands forward. "Let's go."

Jena walks first. Jake lags behind, checking his costume for the party. The front door is open, but there's no one there to greet them. Jena stands and stares at the house from the outside. It looks like a white castle, with beautiful angel statues, tall glass windows, and palm trees aligned with the sides of the house. They all step inside, amazed at the beauty of this house. Marble floors, classic paintings, modern inside decor, leather couch and chair. *If selling weed can get you a place like this, then I'm in the wrong business,* Jena thinks. She isn't completely sold on the idea that this guy is just a simple drug dealer. They all turn to admire the living room. C. A. T. has his arms stretched out over the back of the couch. He's just staring at a painting on his wall. No music, no television, no one else in the room—just him staring at a painting of two horses.

CHAPTER TWENTY

"Welcome to my house." He doesn't turn around. "I hope you find everything here to your liking. My servants, Moishe and Mary, will assist you with all of your needs."

"Man, you have servants?" Ken is surprise.

"Of course," he answers back in a low, raspy voice. "What kind of food do you two like?" Jena and Jake look at Ken. "Moishe and Mary can make anything from any country. Would you like silk or satin sheets? Moishe and Mary can provide you with the sheets of your choice. This house has six bedrooms. Please feel free to pick your choice." He pauses. "But I have a feeling that you two may be shacking up together." C. A. T. grins.

"Man, I said no questions." Ken waves to Jena and Jake to make their way to a bedroom.

C. A. T. smirks. "I hardly think that asking about food, sheet, or room preferences can be considered asking questions." He laughs. "At least not the questions you were referring too."

Jena raises her eyebrows at Ken as she and Jake start walking quietly to their room. Jena stops. "Thank you for letting us stay at your house."

C. A. T. is quiet for a second. "You are most very welcome. Feel free to stay as long as you two wish." C. A. T. remains seated, still staring at the painting of the two horses.

Ken walks to the back of the couch, leans down, and whispers to C. A. T., "This is a big favor. Thanks for helping my friends." C. A. T. turns around. There's a large scar over his left eye. "You helped me, so I'm helping you. What would this world be like if we didn't all help each other? Now you and I are back at the beginning of the favors ... I may need you again ... to do me a favor," C. A. T. emphasizes. "When the time comes, I hope that you will not ask any questions either." Ken stands, gives C. A. T. a nod, and walks out of the house. C. A. T. turns around and goes back to staring at the horses.

Jena and Jake walk room to room admiring all the unique decor, statues, paintings, lamps, and furniture. Everything looks expensive. They pass Moishe and Mary on the way to their room, carrying towels and blankets. They both wear servants' uniforms, but they are fancy. Moishe is wearing a black butler's suit. It almost looks like he is dressed to go out. If it wasn't for the fact that he is carrying sheets and towels and is wearing a name tag, he could have been mistaken for the owner of the house. Mary is wearing a beautiful dress that still has the maid style to it, but it looks like she could be going to a ball or a party. Both look straight ahead, but acknowledge Jena and Jake with quick nods. They look like they are just coming from cleaning the rooms, but there aren't any other guests in the house and neither of them appear dirty or tired from cleaning.

Five of the bedrooms are all on the same hall, but so far apart that privacy wouldn't be an issue. Jake leads them down the hall, choosing the middle room facing the side entrance. "I think this room would be best. That way we can get in and out without having to go to the front entrance." Jena nods.

Moishe passes them again in the hallway. He doesn't look at them, just walks straight ahead, turning left down another hall into a room. Jena is curious, and instead of following Jake into the bedroom, she follows Moishe. He is standing in the room dusting off the bookshelf. The room is a large office with a table, leather chair, a small leather couch, and a large bookshelf that seems almost impossible to clean by one person.

Jena stands behind Moishe as he cleans each book delicately. She breaks the silence between them. "Do you like cleaning bookshelves?" Moishe is shocked. He keeps cleaning, never turning around. He is quiet. Jena steps forward. "Books are a great way to get lost in another world." She touches and admires the bookshelf. "Are you a butler or a bodyguard?"

Moishe continues to clean. "Both," he says. "I clean the house, and—if needed—*I clean the house.*" Jena understands.

She walks closer and then stands where she can see the side of his face and body. His suit is perfectly clean, nails manicured, jet-black hair groomed with a stylish haircut. "You look more like a bodyguard," Jena presses.

"I'm whatever C. A. T. wants me to be. Today I'm a house cleaner, tomorrow I may be a cook," he looks at Jena, "and the next day I may have to kill someone. It's a job." Moishe begins cleaning the shelf again.

Jena looks around the room. There's a large window with beautiful satin curtains in front of it. She walks slowly to the window and opens it. The warm breeze brushes against her skin, her hair sways back. Moishe turns to watch her. He steps down from cleaning the bookshelf, walks slowly toward her, and joins her in feeling the warm breeze.

"The night is coming," Jena says. "It is easing its way, but it's coming. The warm breeze here reminds me of being home, in my room. I used to stare out the window feeling the warm breeze against my skin. My neighborhood was always dark, quiet … at least at night. My parents would be downstairs dancing to their favorite song, and I'd be upstairs feeling the breeze, smiling, and listening as they laughed and sang to one other." Moishe stands still, just listening to her. A silence comes over Jena.

"I, too, like the breeze," Moishe speaks. "It calms my spirit. It reminds me of home too. My home far, far away. Sometimes I wish I was back home, listening to the loud music, the kids playing in the street, and my wife yelling at me, 'Moishe! Moishe! Come help in the kitchen.'" Moishe is quiet. "But those days are gone. They are far, far away, just like my home. Now my home and my memories are one. There's no need to go back. My wife and children are dead, and so is my home." Moishe walks away, leaving Jena with her thoughts. He finishes cleaning the bookshelf, and then he walks out of the room.

Jena walks back to the bedroom. Jake is in the adjacent bathroom, singing in the shower, "If I can't have you, I don't want nobody, baby ..." Jena listens to his horrible singing. She smiles, sits on the bed, pulls out the red dress, and stares at it. She thinks back to the last time she wore a red dress. She was in New York and spotted the dress in the window at a little boutique store owned by an old, wise woman. A dress once seen in a dream. A dream that came true, true as the blue in the sky and red as the blood that runs through her veins. It was the chosen dress. The dress to be worn to capture the eye of a cold one. To capture the eye of the coldest one of all: Mr. McNeil.

She puts the dress down and lies back on the bed. *Now the dress has found me again.* She looks over at the dress. *Begging to be worn, tempting me not to wear it ... knowing I can't resist the power it has over me.* She reconsiders the script running through her head. *If I believe that a dress could hold such power over me, then that would mean I'm powerless to stop what will happen tonight ... or tomorrow. The dress doesn't hold any powers,* she thinks. *It is just a part of the meaning. What is meant to be. What will be. It didn't show up to tempt me; I'm the temptation of it. I choose to wear it, use it, make it a part of my plans.* Jena reaches for the dress. She lays it across her body as she drifts off.

She is on the plane. For the first time, there is a woman sitting in the back, laughing with a man. Their identities are blurry to her eyes. She walks slowly toward them. Their voices get louder and louder until Jena is standing in front of the two of them. The woman and man play no attention to Jena as they laugh and joke with one another. It's like she is invisible to them. Jena watches in surprise and in disappointment. It's her mother laughing with Mr. McNeil like they were lovers. Like they were husband and wife. Jena grows angry.

"Where is my father!" she yells at her mother. Kitty doesn't answer, ignoring her. Jena leans forward, yelling louder. "Mom, where is my father!" Mr. McNeil touches Kitty's face. She kisses him. "Mom, stop!" Jena yells louder. "Stop it! Stop it!" She reaches for Mr. McNeil, but can't touch him. Like she is frozen in time, in a dream she had no control over, Jena realizes she can't be seen or heard. She is left to be tortured by their laughs, their happiness, and she's forbidden to move or stop it. She feels like crying, but can't. Only rage covers her thoughts.

"Painful to watch?" a voice speaks to her. Jena looks around the plane. No one is there. "I know it's very painful to watch, but what can you do?"

Jena thinks to herself, *Where is this voice coming from?*

"You can't do anything," the voice continues to torment her.

"I can do something." Jena screams louder to her, "Mom! Please stop!"

Mrs. Parker looks at her. "I can't, Jena." She smiles at Jena. "I can't stop. I don't want to."

Jena doesn't understand. "What? What are doing? He killed Dad. Why are you sitting here laughing with him? He killed him. He's the cause of all of this."

Mrs. Parker stands up and reaches out to Jena. "I know," she says to her. Jena closes her eyes in disbelief.

She wakes up with real tears running down her face. She sits up quietly, wiping away the tears. Jake is standing over her with a towel wrapped around his waist. She grabs her bag and dress and dashes past him into the bathroom. She stands staring at herself in the mirror. *What the hell was that?* she thinks. *What was my mother doing with Mr. McNeil? He's trying to torture me. He can't get to me in the real world, so now he's going after my mother.*

Jena frantically searches through her bag to find the letter her mother had given her. "Mom," she utters softly. "What's in this letter?" The envelope is slightly dirty, wrinkled from being carried around. She stares at the letter, her tears dripping on it. She lays the letter on the bathroom counter next to the red dress and stares at them both.

Jake knocks on the bathroom door. Jena cries quietly. "Jena, what's up? Let me in." She doesn't answer. "We don't have to go to this party. We could just stay here." She stares at the letter again, reaches for it, and turns it around to open it. "Jena, please talk to me." She puts the letter on the counter.

She wipes the tears completely off her face and opens the door. "I'm going to this party." She closes the door, leaving Jake standing dripping wet with a towel wrapped around his waist.

CHAPTER TWENTY-ONE

J ena walks out of the bathroom and checks Jake out as he dries
off. "You look refreshed."

He smiles at her. "I feel great." He takes off his towel and
catches Jena staring at him. He takes advantage of the moment,
walking around in the nude. "Can you believe that bathroom? It's
phenomenal in there. Marble shower, tub, sink. It has everything—
toothbrushes, body washes for him and her." Jena keeps her eyes on
Jake as he gets dressed.

"Yeah, I think I'll go get ready."

"Jena." She stops. "Where were you?"

She turns around. "I was just roaming around." She walks into
the bathroom again.

Jake stands at the door. "We don't have to go tonight." He
stands, waiting for her to respond.

"I want to go." She turns to look at him. "I know you do too.
Besides, Ken has done us a huge favor, asking his friend if we can
stay here …" Jena smirks, "almost getting killed. I think he'd be
really disappointed if we didn't show up." Jake is silent. "Anyway,
we are wearing costumes. No one is going to know who we are." She
reaches in her bag, searching for her lipstick. "I don't see any reason
for us not to go."

Jake reaches for the door to close it. "Then we'll go," he says in a Dracula voice. "I must go now and get dressed."

Jena yells through the door, "You're not going as Dracula—you're the Phantom of the Opera!"

Jake laughs. "Ha, ha. Just making sure you're paying attention."

Jena listens to Jake's unique laugh. She pictures how his eyes twinkle as he smiles and laughs hard. *He is such a wonderful person. So sweet, so kind, and so loving toward me. Not to mention patient. I wish he wasn't so hell bent to be caught-up in my nightmare, but what would I do without him, without his unconditional love? What friend or lover would stand by a killer? He believes in me, but is he being foolish by denying himself the ultimate feeling in life—freedom?*

Jena stares at herself in the mirror until it grows dark and she zones out in deep thought. *Mirrors foretell so many things about ourselves. What do I see when I look at myself? A young girl with long, reddish hair and blue eyes, tall and slender. Is that all I see? If I look longer into the mirror, I believe I'll see something beyond the human eyes, something deeper, something that once slept but now awakens. It wants to come out, to see the light outside of you. It wants to break free, see the world, learn it, understand how to maneuver its way around, and then take it from you—your life—and make it its own. While you seek to find answers to calm the spirit and ease the soul, it's already taken you. Now you must succumb to it or be ready to battle with it until you or it dies—maybe both.*

She visualizes herself wearing the red dress, walking barefoot in the hot desert, sun beating down on her, feet blistering, mouth dry. She passes many people: the men on the plane, Sam the delivery driver, Principle Ricky, Jake, Ken, Carol, Chance, her mother, her father. She stops in front of Mr. McNeil. He's dressed all in black. She pushes him, but he doesn't move or respond. She picks up a rock and throws it at him; it bounces off. She fights him, but nothing works. He just stands there without moving or responding to her.

Jena turns around and sees that everyone is lined up looking at her all tired out, clothes torn, hot, sweaty, breathing hard. They all turn away from her to walk away like a wounded soldier waving the white flag to end the battle. She is disappointed, sad, feels powerless, and wants to cry, but something inside of her won't let her. She turns to Mr. McNeil, who is still standing there waiting for her. He reaches his hand out to her. She hesitates and then turns to walk away, but he grabs her legs. She screams and kicks, as her body slides farther into the dark sand. Somehow he holds her without even touching her. Her fingers dig deep in the sand while she screams and kicks for help—just screaming without sound. She looks up, and everyone is still walking away, no one helping, no one talking, no one stopping Mr. McNeil.

Then suddenly it stops. He is gone, and so is everyone else … everyone except Jake. He is standing with his hand on hers, pulling her back. *Why couldn't I see him before?* she thinks. *Was he always here?* Jake doesn't look like Jake to her; something is different about him. The way he looks at her is different. It isn't with those loving, dreamy eyes that want her and would never leave her. He is just someone who is helping her, but doesn't love her. She can feel the distance between them the moment he lets go of her hand. Just then, the wind kicks up the dust; his hand is there, and then it is gone. Gone forever. She can see that in his eyes. The emptiness. The coldness. *Why didn't he just let me fall instead of allowing me to see his revulsion with me. Or is that my punishment—for him to help me and then let me see him walk away while I stand here looking like a beast?* She yells for him to come back, but he doesn't. He just keeps on walking and walking until he is out of her sight.

She wipes her dirty hands on her red dress and starts walking. She walks until she comes to the end of the desert, where she can't walk anymore. Falling to her knees, she collapses. She lies still, with no willingness to go on—nothing left to fight for, nothing left to lose. There is nothing, no one; even the sun has retired.

When life's endurance of pain conquers you at the same time that love abandons you, it can cause instant paralyzation of your emotions. Your soul and spirit break free and leave the body there to wait until the dust covers your eyes and your mouth open prays they return to give you one more chance to go on. Even the will to try can slip slowly away while you tell yourself, "This isn't how I want my life to end. I want to live. Oh please, spirit, come back. I want to live. I want Jake."

She focuses back at herself in the mirror. *I can change things,* she thinks. *I can make my life different and make sure that I never lose Jake's love and forever put this dark feeling back where it belongs—as only a reflection in the mirror.*

Jena opens the bathroom door. Jake is in his costume; he stares at her with a dreamy look as she stands in the doorway. *Tonight I'll prove to Jake that I can break free, that I can be the woman he wants and needs. That I love him just as much, if not more, than he loves me. Tonight I'll tell him.* She reflects back to her wearing the dirty red dress, how she felt when Jake let go of her hand and walked away. *I don't want to be alone, just wearing a dirty red dress, lying in the desert, waiting for my soul and spirit to return. I'm alive right now, looking at my heart beating right in front of me—Jake. He's everything a women could want, and I don't want to long for him when he's right where I can feel his strong, muscular body embracing mine; his tender lips pressing against mine, using them to caress my entire body; and his hands wrapped over me, trapping me, so nothing or no one else can even attempt to stop our passion. To watch him walk away from me would tear my entire being into millions of pieces ... and I'd kill anyone who tries to take him away from me.*

"You look beautiful, just stunning," Jake tells her.

"Thank you." Jena picks up the bright-red mask, the color so opposite of what she is feeling. She puts it on. "How do I look now?"

He walks up to her, takes off the mask, and kisses her softly on the lips. "You look beautiful with the mask on or off."

She says to him in a seductive voice, "I bet you prefer off, don't you?"

"I do prefer it off." He takes the bait. He puts the mask down on the bed and squeezes her tightly to him. "I prefer everything on you off." He presses his hands in the middle of her back, pushing her closer to him, and kisses her. He runs his hand down the side of her neck, continuing down to her breasts, and kisses both of them. Looking up at her with those irresistible eyes, he raises her hand to his lips and kisses it up her arm, her neck, and then back to her lips. He whispers in her ear, "I want you right now." Jena is pulled like gravity into the moment. Her emotions are captured like a beautiful butterfly in the jar, and instantly the world outside the room doesn't exist to her; only here is her presence required. "I want to hear you say you love me," he says. "I need to hear you say it. Let's get naked and lie on this bed like there's nothing to bother with in this world." He lifts her in his arms, her feet slightly dangling from the floor as she drapes her arms around his neck, holding on tight as if her life depends on it. He slowly puts her down, rubs his hands down her back, and begins sliding her dress off.

There's a knock at the door. "Open up! Up, up?" Ken's knocking spoils the mood. Jake tidies up Jena's dress and then opens the door with a disappointed look on his face. Ken strolls in. "Hey, hey." He spins around like a showroom model. "So, what do you think?" he says, pointing at himself dressed as a James Bond agent.

Jake closes the door, checks him out. "Not bad. So you bring the Phantom of the Opera suit for me, and you get to be James Bond?"

Ken struts around the room, trying to be cool, one hand in his pocket. He recites a few James Bond movie lines. Jena smiles. He walks over to her. "Oh, my lady." He kisses her hand. "Looks like James Bond is stealing someone's woman tonight," he jokes.

Jena quickly pulls her hand away. "I don't think so."

Jake stands in between them. "That's a negative, dude. The Phantom will kick Bond's ass if he tries to take his girl."

Ken turns around, pointing his finger like a gun. "I'm just kidding, man. Too many ladies will be at this party for me to worry about Jena—although she is looking very beautiful tonight."

Jena grabs her bag and mask. "Let's go." She walks out the door. Moishe is standing in the hallway. He reaches for her coat. She stares at him. "You don't have to carry my coat." She walks off, with Jake and Ken following behind her. Moishe follows them outside.

There is white limo out front. Ken does his James Bond impression. "This is a masquerade party, not the prom," Jena jokes.

"Not my idea, Jena. This car is compliments of Mr. C. A. T. Tyler. Moishe is our limo driver."

Jake walks around the limo. "This is a sweet ride." Ken and Jake act like little kids getting ready to go to the playground.

Moishe holds the door open for Jena. "You're not going to tell me that I can't open the door for you either are you?" She shakes her hand and smiles at him. Jake and Ken get into the limo. Jena starts to step in.

"Wait!" She stops. "I forgot something." She turns around and dashes back into the house; she had left her mother's letter by the bathroom sink. She quickly walks to their room. She hears voices coming from the office where she had earlier spoke with Moishe. Two people are talking. She quickly goes into the bathroom, picks up the letter, and hurries out of the room, but she stops in the hallway when she hears one of the men mention Matt Ross. She turns around, walks slowly to the office door, and stands outside and listens. It's C. A. T. and another person talking.

"Matt Ross owes me a lot of money." C. A. T. is angry.

"He's in jail," the other person says.

C. A. T. looks at him. "Not anymore. I just received word through a third party that the police in Maplesville released him today." C. A. T. strolls around his office. "So that means he's out there roaming around with my money." He points at the other person. "I want my money," C. A. T. pounds his hand on his desk, "tonight!" Jena backs away slowly. "You find Matt Ross—that thief—and you bring him here to me. Tonight. Not tomorrow. Not the next day ... tonight."

Jena quickly hurries out of the house. She doesn't let Moishe open the limo door for her this time. Ken is riding in the front with the limo driver; Jake is in the backseat waiting for her. She sits down with a concerned look on her face and utters a name she thought she'd never say again, "Matt Ross."

CHAPTER TWENTY-TWO

The look on Jena's face worries Jake. "What happened in the house?" Jena looks up and shakes her head. He slides over to her. "What happened, Jena?" He forces her to speak. "Matt Ross," she says sternly.

"Matt Ross?" Jake is confused. "What about him?"

"He's out of jail and most likely is going to be here tonight."

"He is here in town?"

"Maplesville."

He rubs her knee. "So what? He's no one, just some guy we gave a ride to."

Jena stops him from rubbing her. "He's also the guy who tried to make us accessories to a robbery. That's why that Kyler guy is so angry with us. You don't know what Matt told the cops. He probably told them that it was our idea to rob Kyler's. Why is he out of jail?" She ponders. "He is supposedly wanted for multiple robberies and murder, so why would police let him go?"

Jake backs away. "Why do you care, Jena?"

She looks at him strangely. "Why? Because I do, and that's all you need to know right now."

Jake is angry and disappointed. Every time it seems that things are going great with him and Jena, something happens. Something gets in the way. He begins to doubt himself. *Am I ever going to truly make her happy?* Jena pays little attention to him.

A voice speaks over the limo car intercom. "Hello, back there. This is your captain speaking." Neither Jake nor Jena are in the mood for Ken's pranks. "Hello? Come on guys, we're almost at the party."

Jake is angry and so is Jena, both for different reasons. Jake is angry because destiny will not live up to its promise. It keeps teasing him with tidbits of intimate moments with Jena that appear promising, yet end up being a fluke, a dirty trick, like a man who went all-in with his fortune and walked away from the table with nothing. The more he thinks about how horrible the night was going, the more his angry grows, mostly from his disappointment and heartbreak. The prospect of him and Jena sharing another beautiful night tonight seemed dead.

Jena's anger stems from something different. She, too, wishes that everything around her and Jake would just crumble, leaving them there with a piece of earth just big enough for them to stand on. But it isn't that simple for her. Matt Ross represents more than a hitchhiker looking for a ride or a deadbeat thief traveling from town to town. He is her rape, her father's death, the clerk, the doctor on the train … her mother; he is the reminder of it all. And if she is to put it all behind her, she'll have to take on Matt Ross too.

Jena hits her hand on the window. Jake looks over. She's hurt herself. He slides over, takes her hand, and rubs it in his. She can see the rejection in his eyes, just like in her thoughts; he was ready to walk away. "I'm sorry, Jake."

Looking into her eyes melts him. He caves in. He has nowhere to put the love he has for her except in her hands, for her squeeze it, crush it, or even massage it back to life—like she just did. He kisses her wounded hand and reaches for her face. "I don't give a damn about Matt Ross or anyone else right now. I just want tonight to be about us." He kisses her. "I don't want anything to ruin it."

The limo stops. Jake and Jena look outside into another world—a world full of costumed characters. Jena realizes that she can be anybody she wants to be tonight. She doesn't have to walk in those doors fearing that someone will recognize her. She has her mask, her man—the moment is hers if she'll take it … if she can listen to Jake and leave it all behind, at least for tonight, and let the moment take them to places they couldn't without masks. Jena smiles at Jake. "I—"

She's interrupted. The limo doors swing open, and Ken sticks his head in. "Hello, it's your captain." They both laugh at him. "Don't laugh just yet," Ken whispers. "The limo driver just gave me a heads-up that there are uncover cops here tonight. Some of them are from Maplesville, some from Donner's County, and there are local cops here." He looks at Jena. "They're looking for you, Jena. Both of you put your masks on, be careful," he smiles, "and by all means, guys, let's have a rocking, kick-ass time!"

Jena puts her mask on; its fits like it was made for her. "Wait." She grabs Ken's arm. "Where's Chance? Carol?"

Ken takes her arm and helps her out of the limo. "They're here … somewhere." Jena eyes the crowd of college kids dressed up in their fantasy outfits, diamonds and pearls, suits and ties. There are lots of girls wearing similar red dresses. The three of them walk through the crowd, Jake's arms wrapped around Jena's waist, holding her as if their bodies were born together. Ken walks off to flirt with two girls.

Where is Chance? Jena wonders. She eyes the crowd and locks in on a girl. It isn't clear to her where Chance is, but it is obvious where Carol is; she is the girl stalking Ken, watching every move he makes as her anger grows with each smile he shares with another girl. Carol walks up to Ken and argues with him. The two girls he was flirty with stand there and watch, giggling. He blows Carol off. Her face is red, eyes bulging like they are about to explode, and she's breathing hard as she storms away to go inside the university's party room. She is dressed as Cat Woman, and it is apparent that right now she feels like tearing Ken's heart out. *Now I know what Carol is wearing,* she thinks, *but where is Chance?*

Jake guides Jena inside. The place is beautifully decorated with diamond chandeliers, rose petals scattered in various places, waterfalls, tiny elves, and every costume imaginable: Cinderella, Snow White, Dracula, Jason, Michael Myers; some scary and some enchanted, but all pleasing to Jena's eyes. She's in a room full of people who, for one night, want to be someone other than who they are. It's an amazing feeling for Jena, who once again feels a sense of normalcy among her peers. Maybe that's because they are all dressed in costumes and masks, no one really portraying themselves—no one except her. She is the only one who came as she is: a killer.

Jake grabs her, twirls her around on the ballroom floor, bows to her, and then they dance. He pulls her close, and they dance slow, his face pressed closely to hers, eyes slightly closed, his hands braced tightly around her waist. Strolling with the music as if they were dancing on air, dancing in soft wind as gravity collapses, taking them both higher above the crowded dance floor. He spins her around and around, pulling her in close, kissing her, playing with her, caressing her, and then spinning her back out again. Freedom.

"I have to go to the ladies' room," Jena whispers softly.

"I don't want you to leave me." Jake holds on to her.

"I'm not leaving you. I'll be back."

"I'll walk you there."

"I can walk myself," Jena says. Jake holds on to her arm, releasing it slowly while passionately staring at her as she walks away. Jena seductively walks through the crowd. She's alive and free from her past, floating on air, so filled with enthusiasm that she embraces the laughter and happiness of everyone around her. She doesn't feel like an outcast. She feels like a part of it—maybe even, in some way, the reason for it. She passes by Ken dancing with a girl wearing a sparkling blue dress, blue satin gloves, a crown with shiny crystals, and a mask painted like the blue sky with white clouds. *What a beautiful costume,* Jena thinks. *So unique, peaceful, and calm.* Ken plays and flirts with the girl. Jena can't see her face. *Chance?* Jena smiles. Although her last encounter with Chance wasn't pleasant, because of the happiness she feels being with Jake, feeling like a normal person in an enchanted setting, she wanted nothing but happiness for Chance too. She wants her to feel the freedom of being in love with a man who can see past the outer layers of the human soul to the find the black pearl, a treasure that has possessed his heart. She turns around; Jake is still watching. What an incredible feeling to have that man love you back without setting conditions that aren't achievable, even under circumstances such as hers. *Jake is truly the most wonderful and loving man I'll ever meet in my life.* Jena stands still as the motion of the world surrounds her: people drinking, dancing, engaging in intimate kisses. She smiles at Chance and Ken as they dance with a romance-filled life promise that anything is possible if they try.

Jena walks through the crowded room. A tall man watches and then follows her. Jena stops a young girl who is laughing with a friend. "Where's the restroom?" The girl points to two double doors.

The man steps up to the three of them and grabs Jena's arm. "Would you like to dance?" he asks. Jena politely pulls her arm away, shaking her head no.

One of the girls shoves her purse to the other and then grabs the tall man's hand. "I will dance with you." She drags him out onto the dance floor.

Jena uses both her hands to open the double doors leading to the bathrooms. The women's bathroom is on the left, and the men's is on the right. She opens the women's door and steps into the bathroom. The bathroom is large with pink-and-black heart designs over the wall, a marble black-and-white floor, high ceiling, with tiny crystal lights surrounding the entire room. The sinks are gold with pieces of black marble chipped inside, and there is a large mirror that runs almost as high as the ceiling of the room. She walks slowly into the bathroom, taking tiny footsteps with taps that sound like Cinderella slippers brushing the floor. Jena spins around like a princess while watching herself in the mirror, smiling in sheer happiness and excitement. As she stops and stares at herself in the mirror, which suddenly turns dark.

*   *   *

There is crying coming from one of the bathroom stalls. She walks over and tries to gently push the door open, but the person inside stops it. It's Carol, crying and sobbing over Ken. She doesn't reveal herself. "What is wrong?" Carol is silent, sobbing frantically. "Has someone you loved hurt you?"

Carol breathes hard. "Yes," she utters through her tears.

"Is he with someone else?"

"Yes."

"Why don't you just leave him alone? Find someone to love you—someone who deserves you."

"There is no one else," she says in a louder, painful voice. "No one I want. He is everything to me. Have you ever loved someone so much that you can't sleep or think of anything else except his hands all over your body, squeezing you, caressing you until his body feels like it's pierced in yours, mounted together, forever making love in a white room with no sound except your sexual cries of pleasure, known to no one except the two of you?" Carol's voice is louder and strong. "His kiss more powerful than a winter ice storm—never cold, but hot as the sun burns when nakedness is expose to it without fear of time or pain. Don't you tell me that you know anything about that kind of love, because you don't know. You have no idea how still a room can be when you see the man you love holding someone else … kissing her. It's almost like I stood there watching my death."

Carol stands up and opens the door. "You don't know anything." She tries to walk past the woman standing in the doorway.

"Don't I?" The woman pushes Carol. "Don't I know, Carol?" Carol tries to push back, but she shoves Carol up against the bathroom toilet; she hits the wall. The woman drags her out of the bathroom, locks the door, and pushes her up against the wall.

Carol is in shock but she tries to fight back. "Who are you?" Carol screams. The woman throws Carol up against the bathroom sink and begins to choke her. Carol grabs her hands, but her grip is too tight.

"You think you can steal someone's love and make it your own? Pretend to be someone's friend and then backstab and take the only love she ever knew?" The two woman struggle. Carol tries to grab the vase from the bathroom counter. The woman yanks it from her, struggling Carol down to the bathroom floor. "You think you're the only one who's loved someone like that?" She begins strangling her. Carol's face turns red as the life slips from her. "No, you're not." The woman laughs. "I was told that I should let my fire burn," she strangles Carol until there are only seconds of her life left. She removes her mask. It's Chance. She leans down with a mean, angry look on her face and whispers in Carol's ear, "You're my fire." The life slips away from Carol's eyes. She is lift lying on the bathroom floor.

CHAPTER TWENTY-THREE

Chance stands up, unlocks the door, and leaves Carol stiff on the floor with her eyes and mouth wide open.

Jena washes her hands, smiles in the mirror, and leaves the bathroom. A girl dashes past her. "Oh thanks goodness this bathroom isn't locked. The other one down the hall was locked, and I had to go really bad." She pushes past Jena, who is too happy to care if the girl shoved her.

As Chance is putting her mask on, she can see the back of herself standing in the mirror. She sees herself closing the other bathroom door, smiling and laughing. But it isn't a mirror; it is Jena. Jena turns around, and there is Chance staring back at her. The two girls stand face-to-face. Same dress, same hair, same shoes, same mask. Chance stares at her. Jena is shocked.

Chance moves closer to Jena. "You said to find my own fire. Now I have." Chance smiles, puts her mask on, and walks off.

A scream comes from the other bathroom. A girl runs by screaming, "Murder! Someone has been killed in the bathroom!" Other people run to the bathroom. Jena bullies her way through the crowd. She sees Carol lying there dead, lifeless. She rushes back toward Jake while people rush in to see the murdered body lying on the floor.

Jena spots Chance and runs to catch up with her. Chance sees her struggling to get to her. She laughs and manages to push her way through the crowd, leaving Jena stuck. Jena knows she can't scream or say anything without exposing herself.

She bumps into the Ken. He grabs her arms. "What is going on?" he shouts.

"Carol's dead." Jena pushes away from him to find Jake.

Ken rushes off to the bathroom, but he can't get through the crowd. He yells, "Carol! Carol!" The uncover police try to get a handle on the out-of-control crowd.

Jake finds Jena and pulls her to him. "What the hell is going on?" Jena grabs his hand to lead him out of the party.

Moishe is standing out in front of the limo. He sees them coming and opens the back door. Jena and Jake hurry in. Before closing the door, the driver asks, "Are we waiting on Ken?"

"No!" Jena shouts. "Get us out of here!" Moishe rushes to get in and drives off. Jena takes off her mask. She wants to cry, but she can't.

"Jena!" Jake shakes her. "Jena! What's happening?"

Jena's eyes are red. "Chance killed Carol."

Jake gives her a shocked look. "What ... what do you mean, 'Chance killed Carol'?"

"That's what happened, Jake. Chance is dressed up exactly like me. I saw her! She has on the same dress, shoes, even her hair is just like mine."

Jake leans forward and says, "I can't believe that Carol is dead and that Chance killed her."

"She must have planned this all from the beginning," Jena says. "She had to have put my outfit in Ken's car."

Jake leans back in the seat. "This is unbelievable ... I can't believe this is happening."

"Well, it is." Jena looks out the car window. "She looked crazy— probably as crazy as I looked. This is revenge." Jena closes her eyes for a moment. "She wanted revenge on Carol for cheating with Ken … and I guess she wanted revenge on me, and that's why she dressed like me. I'm living in a nightmare within a nightmare. Chance has taken on my darkness and made it her own. I never thought I could feel as happy as I was tonight, or I would never have told her those words."

"What words?" Jake asks.

Jena pauses. "To find her fire. To let her fire burn until it couldn't burn anymore, until she was cold …" she looks over at Jake, "cold-blooded, that is. And I think killing Carol surely proved she is."

"This is unbelievable." Jake puts his head down. His cell phone rings. "Yeah. What's going on? What are the cops saying?"

Ken is upset. "They're looking for a woman wearing a red dress, red shoes, and a mask. That sounds like someone we know, doesn't it?"

"Look, Jena didn't kill Carol. It was Chance."

"Where's the proof?" Ken gets loud. "People are saying that they saw a woman in red leave the bathroom. Jena is in red!"

Jake yells, "So is Chance! She dressed up like that to frame her. She's gone crazy." Jake gets angry. "Crazy over you."

"What?"

"Yeah, man, she's gone nuts. She was heartbroken when she found out you cheated with Carol, her best friend."

Ken is in disbelief. "No, man, that can't be true. Chance and I broke up before we started college. I was kidding around at the restaurant earlier about her being my babes. She was dating someone else."

"Did you ever see her with the other guy?"

"No."

"Then how do you know?"

"Because she told me that she was over me—had forgiven me."

"Well, she lied. Now Carol is dead, and the police, no doubt, are going to try to blame this murder on Jena. I'm not going to let that happen." Jake speaks low, "Ken, you have found Chance before Jena does. Because if she finds Chance first, I think …" Jake pauses, "I think she'll kill her."

"I'll do what I can, but I don't know. She's probably looking for me. She probably wants to kill me next." Ken looks around frantically.

Jake yells. "Don't be a damn coward. Find her!" he slams off the phone.

Jena stares out the window. "Ken doesn't have to find her, because I'll find her. And you're right—I'll kill her."

A pickup that had been following closely behind the limo slams into it. Jake and Jena are kicked forward. Jake hits his head on the window. "What the hell?" Jake looks back. There are two shadows in the truck and a shotgun in the middle of them. The truck slams into the limo again, causing Moishe to swerve into the bushes off the road.

The two men get out of the truck. One grabs the shotgun, walks up holding the gun, and opens the back limo door. "Get out!" He points the shotgun at Jena. Big Papa opens Jake's side and yanks him out to the ground. He cocks the gun. "I said get out!"

It's dark and only the truck light is beaming on them, but the silhouettes reveals who they are: it's Kyler and Big Papa the truck driver. Kyler shoulder is wrapped up in bandages. "I got you now, girl," Kyler says. "No more running, killing people, costing people their businesses. Your time is up. Now give me that bag." Jena hands Kyler her bag.

"Haven't you had enough?" Jena asks.

"Not yet." Kyler points the shotgun with his good arm at her face. "Not until you're dead. You and your boyfriend."

Moishe gets out of the limo, shoots Big Papa, and then points his gun at Kyler. "Give her back her bag." Kyler fires his shotgun at Moishe, but he misses. Jena's bag falls to the ground. She picks it up and ducks as Kyler and Moishe fire back and forth at each other.

She sees Jake lying on the ground, but she can't move because of the gunfire.

"Jake," she calls, but he doesn't move. "Jake!" She crawls through the limo's backseat, keeping her head down. Jake moans; he's hurt. Big Papa stabbed him with his knife before kicking him to the ground. Blood is coming from Jake's upper shoulder. Jena's eyes grow big. "No!" She races over to Jake and sits him up. Moishe and Kyler are still firing it out.

"I'm all right," Jake speaks, and Jena is relieved. She wraps her arms tightly around Jake, his blood draining on her red dress.

I've never felt so helpless, Jena thinks. *I was so scared that he left me here to deal with this world that doesn't understand me and wants nothing more than to make me pay for my crimes—and everyone else's.* If this was it, then this was going to be it! Jena gently lays Jake down. The warm night breeze flows through her hair and ruffles her dress. It dawns on her that she can't change who she was or the past that haunts her. In spite of the romance, the glamour, and the glitz of the night, her destiny had found her. The red dress, the truck, the light, Moishe and Kyler shooting it out in the middle of the road: it was all a part of the entire plan ... and now the plan must be completed.

Jena reaches in her bag, grabs the gun, points it at Kyler, and shoots him. Kyler falls down to the ground, shotgun rising high in the air. Moishe stares at her as she walks toward Kyler. She stands over him and shoots him two more times in the chest. Moishe slowly puts his gun down. Jena stands over Kyler, the warm night breeze blowing, her grip firm on the gun—as if it was made for her to use. Kyler is barely alive, coughing up blood, facing imminent death. Jena kneels down close to his ears. Tears run down his face. She whispers, "Now you go. You go and tell them I'm coming."

Jena's face is the last thing Kyler sees before he closes his eyes. His end had come, and now he was among the rest of them. Mr. McNeil, the hotel clerk, the doctor on the train ...

Jena looked over at Moishe. She puts the gun down by her side, griping it tightly, and then turns and runs to Jake's side. She holds him in her arms, kisses his face, and tries to put him in the limo. Moishe walks over to help. Once Jake is in the limo, Moishe and Jena walk back to Kyler's body. Jake sits up and peeks out the window to watch, pressing on his shoulder to slow down the bleeding.

The warm wind blows as Jena watches Moishe drag Kyler's body to the ditch. Kyler's head slumps over, bleeding, lifeless. Moishe goes back for Big Papa's body, drags it to the ditch, and lays it on top of Kyler's like two sacks of potatoes. He walks back and stands next to Jena. He puts his gun in the back of his pants. Jena watches him. *Such a professional move,* she thinks.

Moishe breaks his silence. "I told you." He looks at Jena, who's still staring at the dead bodies. "Some days I'm the butler, the cook," he looks back the limo, "the limo driver, but today I'm the killer— and so are you." Moishe walks back to the limo, gets in, and puts his hat on. He cranks up the car, turns on the lights, and waits for Jena.

When the moment comes I'll have to answer to all of my sins, but until then I will have to serve out my time living as the person I am. The judge and jury has not yet been formed, so let me prepare them a plate fit for a court, fit for a queen who will soon sit on the throne of death. Matt Ross, I'm coming for you. Soon you'll know what they know: that the dark in the day is no different than the dark at night. Jena gets into the limo. She holds Jake close to her. The thought of losing him sparked alive the part she tries so hard to hide, but she knows that you can't hide behind your own shadow. You have to stand out in front of it, take its hand, and lead it, because you both can't hide from the truth—so why not let both shine? Moishe spins off, leaving only dust on the dead bodies.

CHAPTER TWENTY-FOUR

"You're free to go." Office Reyes hands Matt Ross a bag with all of his belongings in it. He grips the bag tightly, stopping Matt from taking it. "But not for long. We'll be watching you, waiting for you to make your next mistake—and that's when I'll put you away forever. Not even the rats will want you." He lets loose of the bag. Matt grabs his things and walks out. Officer Reyes follows him. "You know you're not going to get away with the crimes you committed." Matt keeps walking. "You hear me?"

Matt turns around to face Officer Reyes. "I understand."

Officer Reyes walks up to him, poking his finger in Matt's chest. "Just what do you understand, creep? Do you understand that I won't rest until I get you back behind bars? Do you understand that I hate punks like you who commit crimes in our society, but somehow get away with it?" Officer Reyes moves in closer to Matt's face. "Do you understand that I'm going to track you down like a dog? Soon as you make another mistake, I'll be there to lock your ass up!"

Matt's looks him straight in the eyes. "I understand." He backs up. "But I also understand that I'm free right now and you're harassing me, officer." Matt turns away and walks out the door.

Officer Reyes walks to door, opens it, and stands staring at Matt as he walks away. He yells for one of his deputies.

"Yes, sir?" Deputy Pauls answers with excitement. "You follow him." He turns to the deputy with an evil look in his eyes. "You find out everything that kid gets himself into and report back to me ASAP! I want him and Jena Parker behind bars for the rest of their lives! You got that?"

"Yes, sir." Deputy Pauls puts on his hat and runs out the door, almost slipping on a rock. He looks back. Officer Reyes is shaking his head. Pauls is embarrassed, so he quickly gets into the police car.

"Idiot," Officer Reyes says as he walks back to his desk.

* * *

Matt is walking around, looking for some action—something to keep him out of trouble, but a way for him to make money or steal it. He walks into a pawn shop. A worker name David is standing behind the counter. Matt walks up.

"What do you need?" David asks as he leans on the counter, eyeing Matt.

Matt wraps his bag around his shoulder. "I need a job."

David stands up. "Work is slow around this town. You'd be better off going up near the university." David smiles. "That's where the jobs are—and the hot chicks."

Matt puts one hand in his pocket, eyeing the cash register. "Well, I don't have a ride. That's why I need a job, you know, to pay the bills." Matt eyes the jewelry lying in the case.

David spots him. "You like jewelry?"

Matt smiles. "If I can afford it, but right now I'm completely busted. So how about helping me out with a job?"

David waves for Matt to move in closer. "Check this out. I hate the owner at this place. He's fired me more than once, but since my old lady is his daughter she makes him hire me back. He claims I've been stealing from him."

"Well, have you?" Matt's curiosity grows.

"Maybe?" David laughs. "But he doesn't have cameras or any type of surveillance, so he don't know shit. He just thinks he knows." David looks around the pawn shop to see if anyone else is listening to him. "Let's step outside." Matt follows him. "Here's the deal." David folds his arms. "I get you a job here, and you help me rob the son of a bitch. What do you say?"

Matt is cautious. "Look, I just got out of jail. I ain't trying to go back. That asshole Officer Reyes ain't going to give me a moment's peace in this town, so I'm just looking for a job for a couple of weeks and then I'm out of this town for good."

David's face grows angry. He unfolds his arms and steps up to glare in Matt's face. "You don't go along with this plan, and I won't give you a moment's peace—and you won't have to worry about leaving this town, because you'll come up missing. So again—are you in or out?"

"I'm in," Matt agrees. "Not because you threatened me, but because I want half of everything." Matt gets close to David's face, showing no fear. "Half of the jewelry. Half of the money." He stares David in the eyes. "Everything. You got that?"

David walks away laughing. "Deal. And, by the way—your hired."

Matt quickly turns around. "So you're the boss?"

"Yes, when that old fart isn't around, I'm the boss—and I just hired you. So put your shit in the back, and let's get to work." Matt follows him. As he's walking in, Deputy Pauls slowly passes the pawn shop staring at him. Matt's not sure how long he's been watching. He politely waves and then walks in behind David.

The pawn shop phones rings. David answers it and then walks to the back. Matt walks around the pawn shop calculating how much money he'd make off the jewelry, TVs, and other items that are worth something. He begins to formulate a plan for how he is going to murder David so he can take his half too.

David hangs up the phone. "That was the old lady. I told her that I hired someone so now her dad can't complain that work isn't getting done and I'd have more time to show her who's boss," David winks, "if you know what I mean."

Matt doesn't turn around; he continues to calculate. "Yeah, man, I know what you mean. Got to keep the ladies satisfied."

David walks over to Matt. "Aye, so you got a lady?"

Matt is silent. "No. Not anymore."

"Oh, drama." David laughs. "Well, I have drama with my woman at times, but all it takes is me going home and laying it on real hard and then she's a happy little baby after I rock that ass to sleep." David gets serious. "Now, enough with small talk. Let's get down to business on how we're gonna pull this job off."

Matt puts his bag down and walks over to David. "So how are we going to do this?"

David rubs his chin. "Well, I got a van out back. That's where most of this stuff will go. I got a friend a few towns over who's willing to buy everything we bring him that's worth something." David continues to plot. "There's a safe in the back that has a lot of cash in it. That old man won't tell me the combination, but I've been watching him and I think I know what it is now. We're going take every cent from that safe and the cash register." David has a devious look on his face. "We're going to rob this place tonight."

Matt's greed grows. "You did say I'm getting half, right?"

"Sure, man, half. It's you and me doing the job—so, yeah, you get half. But if you try to cross me, you'll get more than your fair share."

Matt's not afraid of David's puny threats. He thinks to himself, *I've been up against men far more important than this small town trash, but I'll let him think he's running something until the moments comes when he realizes he's out of his league.*

Matt and David work on cracking the safe open. David tries every combination he can think of, even his girlfriend's birthday, but they are all wrong. He gets frustrated. "Damn it! I thought I had that old man figured out, but he is more clever than I thought." He hits his hand on the wall. "He must have known I was watching him." Matt looks at the safe. "What about his wife?"

"Tory's mother died ten years ago. She barely spoke to her."

Matt eyes the safe. "Yeah, but what about her mother's birthday?" David's eyes grow wide. "Wait." He remembers Tory talking about her mother and how devastated her father had been when she passed away. David tries the safe again. "I don't know when Tory's mother was born," he grins, "but I do know the day she died." He tries the combination on the safe; it unlocks. "Bingo." He opens the door, and coins fall out. There are stacks and stacks of twenty, ten, and hundred dollar bills. David jumps up and down. "Hell, yeah! We hit the jackpot, man. We're rich!" Matt is silent. He lets David enjoy the moment, but he knows all that money will be his before the night is over. David yells, "Grab that bag, man. Let's load it up with all this cash." Matt grabs the bag and helps David load the cash, coins, and jewelry.

Nightfall was all they were waiting on to load the van. David backs the van closer to the pawn shop's back door. He and Matt begin loading up as many items as they can. TVs, camcorders, cameras, DVDs, video games, and everything they thought might be of value. Matt picks up his bag. "Man, I think we got everything." David slaps his hands together. "Hot damn—we did it, man. I'm finally leaving this damn town." David gets emotional while Matt just pretends to care. "I've waited so long to leave this place. It's been hell living in a town where you just can't get nowhere in life. I was a nobody here. No one cared about me." David puts his head down, tearing up. "I thought I'd never see the day when I could leave all of this behind me." David walks up to Matt. "I don't know you, but I'm damn sure grateful you walked in that door."

Matt gives David a blank and uncaring stare. "Me too." He pulls a pocket knife out of his bag, rushes David, and stabs him with it in the stomach.

David turns around to run. "What the hell are you doing?" Matt chases him down and stabs him again and again until he lies still on the floor. Matt picks up a TV. David pleads from the floor, "Please, man. Please don't do it." Matt raises the TV high and drops it over David's face. David's body convulses and then is still.

"I guess you're never leaving this town now," Matt utters. He leaves the TV on David's face, grabs his arms, and drags him to the back of the pawn shop. Reaching into David's jean pocket, Matt grabs the keys, his bag, and the bag of money and jewels. "Sucker," he says as he walks out the back door. Matt gets in the van and hits the main highway leading out of the town.

They had forgotten to lock the pawn shop's front door. Deputy Pauls walks in. "Hello?" he yells out. "David?" He walks around the half empty pawn shop, turns around the counter, and see's David dead body lying in the back with the TV covering his face.

Deputy Pauls makes a call on his radio. "This is Deputy Pauls, come in." He repeats himself, yelling, "This is Deputy Pauls, come in!"

The dispatcher responds, "Go ahead, Deputy Pauls."

"Send backup. There's been a murder at Levy's Pawnshop." He looks around. "There's also been a robbery." He looks out back. "Looks like David's van has been stolen as well. Possible suspect— Matt Ross. Send an ambulance, and put out an APB to all available officers for a roadblock to all main highways. And contact Officer Reyes immediately."

"Deputy Pauls, Officer Reyes was listening in to this dispatch. He's on his way."

Deputy Pauls squeezes his walkie-talkie's talk button. "Copy that."

Officer Reyes doesn't show up on the crime scene. He is too busy racing down the road attempting to track down Matt Ross.

Matt manages to make it to the main highway. He speeds in the van in his effort to get out of town. A black car with black tinted windows is following him close. He tries to speed up; he floors the van. The black car speeds up behind him and bumps the back of the van. Pulling up next to van, someone slightly lowers car the window. A woman's hand, wearing a ruby-red ring, signals for Matt to pull over. He doesn't. He tries to run the car off the road by slamming into it. The car swerves off the highway, but it comes roaring back and slams into the van. Matt runs off the highway, but quickly gets back on. The woman's hand reaches back out the window; this time she is holding a gun. She fires two shots at the van's tires, blowing them out, which causes Matt to run off the highway into a utility pole. The front of the van is completely smashed in. Matt head hits the steering wheel, and he's knocked unconscious.

A man opens the driver's door of the car, and a woman gets out of the back. They both step slowly toward the van. Matt is still unconscious, bleeding from the head. The man grabs Matt, his bag, and the bag of money.

The woman checks out the stolen items in the back of the van. "Nice," she says. She closes the van's back doors and walks over to Matt as he's being dragged out of the van. Matt slowly opens his eyes. His vision is blurred. He tries to focus in on the woman. She smiles at him. "Matt Ross," she says.

Matt's vision clears. "Mary?"

Mary grabs his face. "Yes, Mary." The man picks Matt up and carries him to the car. Mary gets on her cell phone. "We got him … and also, send someone out to Route 45. There's a van out here filled with all sorts of goodies. I'm sure it'll make up for some of our losses." She clicks off the cell phone and jumps in the car's backseat.

Matt is barely conscious. He looks over at Mary and tries to speak, "Mary … why?"

Mary looks over at him. "You know why. And in an hour, you'll have to answer to C. A. T. So go to sleep." Matt completely blacks out. Mary lights up a cigarette as the car spins away.

CHAPTER TWENTY-FIVE

*Y*ou don't really understand the truth about life until your heart experiences its first emotional breakdown. That's when it all becomes clear to you that night and day can both be the same if your heart is broken down, cold, and left in a forest where even you can't find it. Everything gets confused; the truth becomes the lies, the lies become the truth, and in between is nothing to hold onto except your insane rationalizations as to why you feel so empty inside.

Jena holds Jake tight as she struggles with her inner self. The heart is resilient; it can be broken into many, many pieces and somehow still find its way back to total completeness. But this can happen only if you have the courage to let love in, let love prove itself to be true—so that lies and the truth can be obsolete, canceling themselves out to allow the heart to feel true freedom. Jena presses down hard on Jake's bleeding chest while he lies still in her arms. Tears run down her face onto his, tears frozen in the air like mini snowballs that instantly melt the moment they touched his beautiful, warm skin. She never knew she could love someone so much that even the thought of anything ever happening to them would cause her to feel uncontrollable rage—rage that can only be satisfied by death of the person who brought out the ugly force in her. The force she felt when Mr. McNeil killed her father, and the force brought on by that horrible night when she was brutally raped.

Jena knew she loved Jake very much, but she hadn't been sure that the love she felt for him would be stronger than the hate she felt inside. Jena leans down to kiss Jake. He slowly opens his eyes and smiles at her. *I want to give him all of the love I have inside, every ounce of it,* she thinks. She reflects back to when Big Papa stabbed Jake and the anger she felt. When the heart feels threatened it bleeds of sorrow, especially when it comes to someone you love. When the one you love hurts, you hurt. If they feel pain, you feel pain. And if someone tries to harm them—you kill them.

Moishe drives as quickly as he can. He pulls up to the house and then rushes around to help Jena carry Jake into the house. Blood drips from Jake's chest. They manage to get Jake safely in the house. Moishe gives him strong medicine to ease the pain, and then he begins to stitch up the bleeding wound. Jena watches as Jake struggles to keep his eyes opened. Moishe carefully finishes stitching up the knife wound. Jena sits quietly on the bed as Jake falls asleep.

Moishe runs to the car to get Jena's bag. He brings it back, and hands it to her. "Here—you may need this."

Jena looks up at him. "Thank you."

He turns around. "I have something else for you." He hands Jena a gun.

"I have a gun."

"Yes, I know, but a person in your circumstances should have at least two." Jena hesitates. She reaches for the gun and puts it her bag. She looks back at Jake. "He will be fine," Moishe comforts her. "I've had many stab wounds, so I know he will survive." Moishe leaves the room, quietly closing the door behind him.

Jena lies next to Jake, lightly rubbing his body, wishing she could take away his pain. She rests her head on his stomach, listening to his breath flowing in and out. She feels at peace knowing that he is healing, feeling no pain. Hopefully when he awakes, he won't remember the other her, the one who fired a shot without regret ... the one who would do it again. She reaches for his hand and places it into hers, and then she drifts off to sleep with her arms draped around Jake.

*   *   *

Jena is back on the plane, but this time there is no one there except her—no pilot, no passengers, and no Mr. McNeil. *Where has everyone gone?* She thinks. *Why do I feel so alone?* She walked the plane searching each section for something she has lost, but she can't remember where she's put it. She searches and searches, but she can't it find it. She sits down, exhausted from searching and sad that she is alone and that even her worst nightmare, Mr. McNeil, is gone.

There is a light touch on her hand. She looks over and sees the touch came from a little girl, who is sitting next to her brushing a doll's hair. The girl has long, blonde hair and she's wearing a light dress and no shoes. Jena watches her as she quietly brushes the doll's hair.

"Do you know why little girls cry?" The child asks. Jena doesn't say anything, just continues to stare at her. The little girl stops brushing the doll's hair and looks up at Jena. "Here. Take my doll." Jena reaches for the doll, but before she can take it the little girl snatches it back. "I asked you a question, but you didn't answer me. Why do little girls cry!" she shouts.

Jena is shocked. She doesn't know the answer. "I don't know why, little girl. Maybe someone hurt them." Jena looks away.

The little girl stands up on the plane seat. She starts jumping up and down screaming, "No! No! No! That's not why little girls cry."

"Then why?"

The little girl stops jumping and leans close to Jena's face to whisper in her ear. She has a sad look on her face. "They cry because they don't have a mommy or a daddy." She looks behind her and smiles and starts jumping up and down again. Jumping higher and higher.

Jena watches in amazement. "Stop that!" she yells at the girl. "Stop it! You're going to fall." The girl continues to jump higher and higher. Jena tries to reach her, but she can't. "Stop it! Please! You're going to fall and hurt yourself."

She stops jumping, grabs her doll by the hair, and gets down from the chair, giving Jena a mean look. "So?" She walks away with her head down, and then she turns around. "You want to know why else they cry? They cry because Mr. McNeil is behind them." Jena stands up quickly and turns to find Mr. McNeil sitting behind her, grinning.

*   *   *

Jena wakes up breathing hard. She hears loud talking and rumbling going on in the house.

"Shut up! Where's my money!" C. A. T. yells.

"I don't know," a voice mumbles. She hears a punch and then a grunt.

"What do you mean, you don't know? Maybe this will help you remember." Two more punches back to back.

"He says he doesn't know," Mary tries to help Matt. "Besides, here's a bag of money. I mean surely this is enough to make up for what he stole from us."

"Us!" C. A. T. screams. "Us! You mean what he stole from *me*. You were his lover and obviously mine too." Mary points her gun at C. A. T. The driver, Lance, points his gun at Mary. C. A. T. laughs. "Oh, I see, you guys think you're going to have a shoot-out in my house? Take it outside! And take this asshole to the back room and beat him until he talks."

"What about the van C. A. T.?" Mary says as she slowly puts her gun down.

"The money is mine. The hell with the van. It's probably just a bunch of junk."

Lance puts his gun back. "It wasn't junk. It was a lot of good shit."

"Okay then, Lance, you go get it. Take the van from the back, drive it out there, load up all the good shit, and bring it back."

Lance looks stressed. "What!" he yells. "All by myself? Are you crazy, C. A. T.?"

"Yes, I'm crazy—so get the hell out of here. But first take this loser to the back." C. A. T. turns to Mary. "Mary, you watch him. See what information you can get out of him." He walks up to Mary slowly. "I said watch him, not make love to him."

Mary grabs Matt, who's barely standing. She and Lance drag him to the back room. Jena listens as they pass the bedroom door. Lance and Mary tie Matt to a chair. Lance puts his gun to Matt's face and asks, "So where are the millions?" Matt's face droops down, blood oozing from his nose. Lance cocks the gun.

Mary cocks her gun, pointing it straight at Lance. "Leave him," she demands.

Lance points his gun at her. "What? You feel sorry for him? Look at him. Your lover's useless." He puts his gun away and tries to seduce Mary. "I'm a better lover than him any day."

"Yeah, maybe any day but today. Frankly, not ever. I've seen you in action, and I don't think your drill has enough power."

Lance laughs. "Drill. Power. You're funny. That just goes to show just how much you've been lacking a real man. Why would I need a drill," he laughs, "when I can hammer you all night long?"

Mary gets angry. "Don't you have a van to pick up? A lot of shit to carry? I'm sure that will take you—oh, let me think—the rest of night. So get lost." Lance walks out of the room.

Matt tries to speak. "Let me go, Mary."

Mary kneels down. "Where's the millions, Matt? Tell me."

Matt is quiet. "I've gained some consciousness. Mary, why don't you just come with me? We can spend the millions."

"Where is the money, Matt?"

"It's hidden in a place where no one will find it—especially if I'm dead. Just untie me. Let's kill C. A. T. and Lance and get the hell out of here. We can have a beautiful life together. Kids. Lots and lots of money."

Mary steps away. "What about getting married?"

Matt pauses. "Married? Why do we have to get married?"

Mary turns to him. "Because I love you, and if you marry me then I'll know you're ready to commit."

Matt gets angry. "Untie me, Mary." He screams, "Untie me!"

Mary pulls her gun on him. "I'll do no such thing until you say you will marry me and until you tell me where the money is."

Matt laughs. "I'm not getting married."

Mary slaps his face. "Then you're not getting untied, and you'll die in this chair." She shoves the gun really hard into his face. "I'll be one to kill you." She leaves Matt tied to the chair, walks to the door, and turns of the lights. The room is dark with only the moonlight shining in.

Matt pleads, "Mary, don't leave me." She opens the door. "Mary, please don't leave me. You know you love me. You won't kill me." Mary closes the door, leaving Matt tied to the chair.

Matt leans his head back to control the bleeding from his nose. He drifts off, coming in and out of consciousness. The door opens. He can hear a woman's high-heeled footsteps walking behind him. He sits with his eyes closed, grins a little, and starts talking. "Mary, we've been together for a long time, and I do love you. You know that. I just wasn't the kind of guy that wanted to get married, but I thought about it, and well … if I was to marry anyone, it would be you. I love you, Mary." A woman's soft hands untie the ropes from his hands and legs. He leans forward. The woman puts a gun on the table, walks to the window, and looks out at the moonlight. Matt stands up and manages to turn on the lamp on the desk. There's a gun in front of him and a woman wearing a red dress standing in front of the window. He stares at her, but he's not sure who she is. "Mary?" Matt picks up the gun. He grips it tightly in his hand. "Mary?"

She walks slowly around the room. "Do you know why little girls cry?" She talks with her back to Matt. Matt is silent. "I asked you a question."

"I don't!" Matt hesitates to answer. Jena cocks her gun. Matt hears it and points his gun at her back.

She slowly turns around. "Little girls cry because they don't have a mommy or a daddy."

"Who are you?" Matt asks, holding the gun firmly. Jena walks slowly toward him with only the moonlight shining slightly off her face. Her shadow moves in closer to Matt. "Don't come any closer, or I'll shoot you." Matt walks backward. He turns on the room light. Jena is pointing her gun at him, and he points his at her. They both circle the room, eyeing each other. "Jena Parker," he utters.

"Matt Ross," she utters. "I've been waiting for you." Jena walks a little closer.

Matt licks his lips. "Yeah."

Jena smiles. "Oh, yeah. I knew when I saw the moon shining bright that this would be the night I'd kill you."

Matt laughs. "I don't think that's going to happen." He mocks her. "Not tonight. Not ever."

Jena fixates on Matt. "Do you know what it's like to feel hot stones sunk in your belly? To get so angry and frustrated that all of your good emotions shut down and all that's left is a cold shell covered by skin, barely attached, not sharing any particular connection yet occupying space together?" Jena moves closer to Matt. "I feel that same anger and frustration when I look at you."

Matt tries to seduce her. "Jena, you're a beautiful girl. I felt something for you the first time we met out there on the highway. I know you felt it too. You felt the sensation of two heroic individuals with the same common interest—to rebuild our lives, separate from the pain that was forced on us. You want the same things I want. You want to conquer. You want to make them pay for the life you have to live now. I'm sure every one of them deserved to die." Jena stares at Matt. "You and I can run this world that we've created. We can walk it together, side by side. No one would be able to stop us." Matt grins. "Hell, they can't even catch us."

"Do you know why little girls cry, Matt?"

Matt laughs. "Jena, you've already given me the answer—because they don't have a mother or a father."

Her eyes are cold. "No, not always. Because sometimes when they are crying inside, they are really laughing." She shoots Matt in the chest. "And that's why you have to die." Jena watches while Matt's body falls limp to the floor. His eyes focus on Jena as he falls. Jena leans down near him. "Do you feel it? That cold feeling that runs through your body when it knows the end is close? Now coldness meets coldness." She smiles. "How ironic is that? But the difference is you're leaving and I'm staying." Matt tries to speak as tears run from his face. She whispers to him, "Now you go. You go and tell them that I'm coming." Jena stands up, stares down at Matt as he lies stiff on the floor.

The room door flies open. Mary stands in the doorway in shock as she witnesses the death of the man she loves. She instantly falls to her knees, crying over Matt. "Matt!" She shakes him, but his body flops with no life. She looks up at Jena in rage and then down at the gun Jena is holding in her hand—the gun that killed her love. She stands up, points her gun at Jena, and screams through her tears, "You bitch!"

CHAPTER TWENTY-SIX

Mary points her gun at Jena, hands shaking, tears running down her face. C. A. T. yells for backup and runs down the hallway into the room. Moishe is behind him.

C. A. T. sees Matt bleeding from the chest and yells out. "What the—"

Mary turns and shoots him in the head. He falls backward into the hallway wall. She starts firing at Moishe. "Stay out of here, Moishe," she yells. She points her gun back at Jena. Jena just stands and stares at her. Mary's need for revenge is far past just firing a gun at the woman who killed the love of her life; she wants to kickass. Mary throws the gun down, steps over Matt's body, and rushes toward Jena. She jumps on Jena, hitting her as hard as she can with her fist. The gun drops out of Jena's hand to floor. Jena punches her in the stomach. They both fight like two boxers in the ring. Jena punches Mary in the face. Mary hits back by punching her in the stomach. Jena grabs ahold of Mary and throws her down to the floor. She punches her several times in the face. Mary tries to hold her off and manages to flip Jena over. She grabs Jena's neck. Mary's face and eyes are red as fire as she chokes Jena. Jena's eyes roll back. Jena thinks back to the night Mr. McNeil shot her father. How she felt when she saw her mother on her knees with her father's blood on her hands, crying in total despair. She thinks back to the night she was raped, her face beaten, and her innocence taken. Her rage grows more and more as Mary grips her neck tightly. Jena manages to lift her hands and place them on Mary's face. She inches her fingers over to Mary's eyes, and she starts scratching Mary's eyes so deeply that blood begins to flow from them. She pushes Mary over, picks her up, and throws her up against the bookshelf. Several books fall, including Franklin's book, *Cold Reda Jones*. Jena stares down at the book and then drags Mary's exhausted body to the window and throws her out of it.

Mary lies on the ground, unable to move and bleeding from some of the window glass that pierced her skin. Mary's eyes are bleeding, her face and body battered and bruised. She stares up at Jena, still alive but barely conscious. She bats her eyes slowly, staring at Jena, begging through her eyes for her to stop. Jena sits on the windowsill, dress torn, staring at Mary's terrified face. The warm breeze runs through her hair and her red dress. Mary's breathing is shallow. She looks away from Jena's face in shame, sorrow, and pain from the loss of her love, Matt.

Moishe walks up behind Jena holding his gun in his hand. Jena stands up and continues to look down at Mary. The wind blowing with the sudden sense of calmness, Jena stares at Mary. She remembers that somber look of loneliness and hopelessness. It is the same look she saw on her mother's face when her father was killed. Mary lies on the ground like a child who is lost in the forest. Someone who had been abandoned by everyone, even the man she loved. Although he was killed by another, Mary still blamed him for his actions leading her down a road of regrets of ever being in love with him at all. Mary looks up at Jena, who is staring at her with a pitiful look on her face. The two of them lock eyes in the understanding that, although they bare different reasons for the pain caused in their lives, they knew that a life without the loves that kept them sane—Matt and Jake—would be a life of death.

Mary screams out loud as she cries, "Oh, Matt. Matthew, please come back." She digs her fingernails in the dirt and shouts. "Kill me! Kill me! Oh, Matt. He's gone. You took him away. He's gone."

Moishe points his gun at Mary. He can't take anymore of her self-pity, but he hesitates to shoot. Jena grabs Moishe's hand with his finger resting on the trigger, and she forces him to shoot Mary. She removes her hand before he can react to stop it. Moishe gives her a long stare.

Jena stares back at him without fear. "I took her life away. Matt's dead. So now, I just gave it back to her. When a person is that torn inside, the pain just grows until all that is left is a silent person. A person who will never view life the same again. Never speak to her daughter or see a husband smile at her." She walks away, leaving Moishe standing over Mary's body. Moishe watches as she walks away.

Jena walks back to the room. Jake is still sound asleep. She walks to the mirror and looks at her beaten, dirty face and her torn dress, an outward expression of her tortured soul. "Who am I?" she asks out loud. "The more I think I know, the less I understand." She looks at Jake. Questions run through her mind: *What do I tell him when he awakes? Do I tell him I've committed more crimes? That I've vindicated our love by defending it? Will he understand, or will he finally see me as that creature in the night—the person I fear when I look in the mirror?* She walks over to Jake and sits on the bedside next to him. "Why do you love me so much?" She caresses his wounded chest. "Don't you see me? Don't you see who I am?"

Jake slightly opens his eyes, reaches for her hand, and squeezes it. He looks into her eyes. "Yes. I know who you are, my beautiful Jena," he utters. "You are the woman I love very, very much." He struggles to sit up and then brushes his hand gently on her face and pulls her in closer to him. He whispers, "I'll never leave you." He rubs the back of her head. "Never." He lies back down, smiles at her, and places her hand on his heart. "Do you believe me?"

She tears up. "Yes. I do believe you. Why you do is a mystery to me, but I believe you." She chokes up. Jake shapes his hand like a cup, places it under her face to catch her teardrops, slowly takes the handkerchief out his costume's coat pocket, places her teardrops in it, folds it, and puts it back in his coat pocket. Jena burst in tears.

He rubs her arm. "I'll carry you as long as I can, my sweetheart. My love. I told you there's nothing else but you."

"Jake, everyone …" She wipes her face and continues, "C. A. T.'s dead, and Mary's dead too."

Jake is silent. "Call my brother. Tell him we're coming back to Maplesville, and we need his help." He reaches in his coat jacket, grabs his phone, and hands it to Jena.

Jena dials Jake's house phone. Ted answers. "Ted."

"Jena?"

"Yes, it's me. Can you talk?"

"Yes. Mom's at the hospital."

"Jake's been hurt."

"What?"

"He's been stabbed, but he's all right." Ted is quiet. "We need your help. We're coming back to Maplesville, and we need somewhere to hide."

"Ask him about Dad," Jake says in the background.

"Jake wants to know how your father is doing."

Ted laughs. "He's recovered. He's awake."

Jena smiles and turns to Jake. "He's awake." Jake sighs in relief.

"That's great news, Ted!"

"When are you guys coming?"

"We're leaving tonight. I will drive." She stops. "I will drive to my house."

Jena, that's dangerous. "I know, but I want to go home. I want to go to my house. See my Mother's and Father's pictures. I need to be home, Ted!" she screams. Jake sits up.

"It's okay," Ted says. "We'll find a way. Just meet me down the street from my house, and I'll take you to your house."

Jena starts crying. "I don't know, Ted."

"It's okay. Drive safely. Get my brother back home. I can't wait to see you two."

"Me too, Ted. Good-bye."

"Good-bye."

Jena hands Jake the phone. "I'll get washed up, and then we'll go." She kisses Jake on the forehead. "I …"

Jake listens with an eager look on his. *Please say it, Jena,* he thinks.

"I'll be back soon to pack up everything."

I know she will say it, he thinks. *I know she feels the deep, unbreakable connection between us. I don't need her to say she loves me, because I know she does.* Jake grunts as he tries to sit up in the bed. The room door opens. Moishe is standing in the doorway with his gun in his hand. "Get out!" Jake shouts.

Moishe puts his gun away. "I'm not here to hurt you or her." He walks closer. "I'm here to help." He reaches to help Jake up. "What do you need me to do?"

"We need to get to Maplesville." Jake looks at the bathroom door. "Jena is in no condition to drive, and I'm not either. Can you drive us?"

"Yes. I will. First, let me help you get to the car. Then I will come back to help Jena pack. We'll pack everything we can take from this house—including the money that's in the living room."

"Money?"

"Yes, a bagful that Matt Ross brought."

"Matt Ross is here?"

"He was, but now he's dead."

Jake is confused. "Dead? How?"

"Jena killed him. She killed him, she and Mary fought, Mary killed C. A. T., and—well, I guess you can say I killed Mary."

Moishe puts his arms around Jake's waist. "No need to be sad or upset. They were all crooks. Con men who robbed, cheated, and killed people. Many of them." He walks slowly with Jake. "So have I." Moishe opens Ted's car door and eases Jake onto the backseat. He starts to close the car door, but Jake stops him, giving Moishe a look. "Don't worry—I won't hurt her. She's a lot like me. She doesn't want to do it, but something inside of her can't stop. We are simple people, kind in unimaginable ways," Moishe thinks back to Jena and him standing together over Mary's body. "But if we are pushed, whoever is doing the pushing will see a side of us that no men or women will ever recover from. Matt saw it tonight. Mary saw it too." Moishe looks down before closing the car door. "There will be many more who will see it." He smiles at Jake. "It is good she has you to bring balance into her life. I once had my balance, but they killed her." He closes the car door and walks back into the house.

Jena is just coming out of the shower. She panics when she sees that Jake is gone. "Jake!" she yells.

Moishe walks into the room. "It's okay. He's in the car waiting for us."

"For us?"

"Yes, us. He asked me to drive you to Maplesville, and I said yes."

"Why?"

"Because I believe that you have a destiny to fulfill." Moishe grabs Jake's and Jena's bags. "I'll take these out and come back for more things, including the money, which we will need." Moishe steps to the room doorway then stops. "I think you still have a chance to change ..." his voice turns melancholy, "unlike me. I will go on this journey with you ... because I may see that miracle that I wished so much would have happened for me and my Maria." His eyes tear up. "I see my Maria in you." He walks out of the room.

CHAPTER TWENTY-SEVEN

Moishe remains quiet for the first half of the drive. Jena is in the front seat, while Jake is lying down in the back. Jake wakes in severe pain. Jena can hear him moaning. She looks back. "Are you okay?" Jake doesn't speak. He moans again. "He's in pain. Did you bring anything?" Jena asks Moishe.

"Check the bag on the floor. I'm sure I put some medicine in it." Jena reaches in the bag. She flashes back to the doctor's medicine bag on the train. Moishe catches her drifting off. "It's on the side." Jena reaches in on the side of the bag, pulls out the pain pills, and hands one to Jake. Jake takes it and instantly falls back to sleep.

"He fell asleep quick. Was that medicine safe?"

"Yes. It is strong medicine, but it will not kill him. He will not feel any pain for quite a while." It's dark out. Moishe drives with caution. "You love him, don't you?" he asks.

Jena pauses. "Yes, I do. I love him very much, but I haven't told him."

"What are you waiting for?"

"I don't know. Every time I try, I just can't get the words out. It' like I feel like I don't deserve him ... or his love."

"Don't you think that he should be the one to make that determination? You can't stop someone from loving you, no matter how much you wish they didn't."

"Where are you from, Moishe?"

"I'm from a place far away from here."

"Where?"

"A small village in a poor country."

"So you don't want to tell me."

Moishe pause. "I don't tell people a lot about myself."

"Why are you helping us?"

"I told you, I want to see you change. I believe you can. Do you believe you can?"

"I don't know. There are times when I think this is all over—that Jake and I can live a normal life. But then tonight I realized that I'm never going to have a normal life. Now that this angry beast within me has been let out, I can't seem to find a way to stop it. He shouldn't be dragged down with me. He is too wonderful, kind … he's the only person in the world I'd die for."

Moishe opens up. "Her name was Maria … Maria Flotino, and I loved her very much." Jena listens. "She lived in an orphanage, just like me." Moishe flashes back to his life. "Her father beat her mother almost every day, and where we were from no one cared. Men were allowed to beat their wives. She watched her mother cry from the bruises her father left. Her body black and blue, face swollen, eyes bloody. Her mother had an emotional breakdown. Maria was fifteen. She came home from school and saw her father lying on the floor, facedown with a knife in his back. Her mother was in her room crying … afraid that they would take Maria away from her, and she'd be killed. Maria helped her mother hide the body. But as the days past, people started to notice that her father was missing. Soon the police came and took her mother away, and that's when Maria was placed in an orphan home. I was already there. My mother had abandoned me when I was baby. I was sixteen when Maria arrived. I remember the first time I saw her. She looked afraid and alone. I love her the moment I saw her. Her beautiful smile. The way she moved, the smell of lavender in her hair. She didn't know the hidden secrets of the orphanage." Moishe voice hardens. "She didn't know that she had come from one hell to another. Girls were being raped … so were the boys. They barely fed us. Some of us didn't take baths for days, and the water was contaminated with dirt and filth. She and I would meet and pray together. Pray that we'd find a way out of that place—a way to be together. One night we saw an opportunity to escape, and we did. We both ran as fast as we could, but we didn't get far before a tall man caught us. He threatened to take us back, but he said he wouldn't if we'd come freely with him. We both agreed and went with him. He was the leader of an assassin unit. They train both me and Maria—gave us weapons, taught us how to defend ourselves."

He looked over at Jena. "They taught us how to be killers. Maria and I would be given assignments. We'd find ways to see each other … make love. Then she was given an assignment that she didn't want. The assignment was to kill her mother. Her mother had been released from jail, and over the years she'd become an activist against the government. Maria was being sent to kill her. I begged Romli to give me the assignment. He refused, said Maria had no family and it was her duty to kill her mother. Maria left, but she couldn't do it. Romli sent out another assassin to kill her and her mother—he sent me. He told me if I didn't do it, that he would kill all three of us. He sent another assassin with me just so he could witness that I'd done it. We tracked them both down, but I couldn't kill her or her mother. I knew that before I'd even left. I'd just agreed to take the job because I knew he'd find someone else to do it, and I wanted so badly to see Maria. Maria had escaped the town with her mother. With her skills, she managed to hide them both out in the jungle. I could not find them, but Romli had tricked us. He sent out more than one assassin with me. He sent many out to find her. By the time I found her, Maria and her mother had both been executed. Romli wanted me to find them. He wanted me to feel unbearable pain. I held her in my arms for hours, hoping that she'd awaken and just hold me one last time. Kiss me, touch my body, and make love to me one last time. I buried her out in the jungle while the other assassin hid and watched me, waiting to make his move to kill me. But I killed him. I was Romli's best man. He had taught me skills that he'd hidden from the other trainees. He taught me how to smell the scent of all of the other assassins. I trained like a dog. He told me he wanted at least one person to know this trade. He trusted me. It was his trust that saved my life and allowed me to track the other person down. I hung him from a tree so Romli and his men would find him easily. Then I escaped to here, to this town where no one knew me. C. A. T. offered me job. It was safe, and I never told him my true past."

Jena remind silent. Moishe continued, "So you see, I understand the life you lead now, when circumstances lead you down the path of uncertainty. You and I both were calm and peaceful people until the darkness found us, and now we are trapped and trying to find a way back to that calm and peaceful place we once knew. For me, my life has been one hell after another—but finding Maria was my peace. It was my chance to live and love. Now she is gone forever, and I'm just a shell waiting for the sun to go down."

Jena feels sorrow for Moishe. "How many people have you killed?" she cautiously asks.

"I've killed hundreds. I've been on assignment since I was eighteen years old. I'm now fifty-five. I've killed many people—some who deserved it, and some who have not. Now tell me about you. How many people have you killed?"

"I've killed at least six, counting Mary and Matt."

"You didn't really kill Mary."

"I helped pull the trigger, so I killed her."

"You mentioned seeing the way she was. What did you mean?"

"I just knew that she wasn't ever going to be the same again. That's what happens when someone you love dies." Moishe doesn't push. "I know you want to ask me who I loved who died? Don't you?"

"I'm not that kind of person. I don't ask questions that don't want to be answered. If you want to tell me, then you can. If you don't, then you don't have too. I'm not here to judge you. I'm here because I want to be—because I can see the extension of me and Maria in you and Jake. You two still have the opportunity to see your horizon together."

"I hope so."

Moishe pulls into a gas station. "I need to get gas before we all are walking." He leaves his wallet in the car. Jena picks it up, opens it, and looks at his license. It doesn't say Moishe; it says Rick Patrick. Jena looked around in Moishe's wallet. She finds a card that has Officer Reyes's name and phone number on it. Jena looks back at Moishe as he pumps the gas. *Is he lying? Who is Moishe? And who is Rick Patrick?* She smiles at Moishe. *Why is Moishe in contact with Officer Reyes?* Moishe gets back into the car and drives back on the road.

Jena is suspicious. "Who are you?"

"What do you mean?"

She yells, "Who are you, and who is Rick Patrick?"

Moishe speeds up. "Why were you snooping in my wallet?"

"Because that's what I wanted to do. How do you know Officer Reyes?"

"You ask too many questions."

"Really? You sat here and spoon-fed me this unbelievably sad story about you and Maria, and now I find out that your name isn't Moishe, that you're someone named Rick Patrick."

Moishe drives faster. "Jena, you have to trust me. If you don't trust me, then I can't help you."

"Why should I trust you when you can't even tell me the truth."

"I told you the truth, but there are many truths. There is the truth that you want to hear, and the one that you don't."

"What is that supposed to mean?" Jena is angry.

"It means that I knew who you were when I first met you. It means that I was working with the police. But after I saw the love between you and Jake, I couldn't turn you in—not even with their threat of sending me back to my country. They found out who I am. I've been spying on C. A. T. in exchange for the police keeping their silence, but I don't care anymore. There's nothing left of me."

The cell phone rings. It's Ted. "Where are you?"

"We're close," Jena tells him.

"How close?"

"We are about twenty minutes from Maplesville."

"Okay. Meet me at the garage near my house."

"All right." Jena clicks off the cell phone and turns back to Moishe. "I'm sorry for not trusting you."

"I could have captured or killed you and Jake when I drove you to the party, but I looked at you two in the backseat—the way you looked at each other, the way Jake loves you—and I saw my Maria. I saw the beauty of love, passion, and the length that a man and a woman would go through to be with one other. I cannot bring Maria back, but I can help save you from self-destruction. Help you to understand and control the anger that rises when you are tested beyond your means. If I can somehow save the love between you and Jake, then when I leave to see my Maria we too will bask in the passion and glory of love."

Jena feels hopeful for the first time. "I want so much to put the past behind me. To give the man I love children. To feel his touch without fear bearing over my shoulders."

Moishe reaches for Jena's hand. "You can ... and I will help you."

And like the calm right before a storm, they both feel like they're reaching the top of the mountain after a tough climb—that maybe there can be a light at the end of the tunnel. Moishe rolls down his window. The wind blows as he drives, while he and Jena talk and laugh along the way. Jena turns to look at Jake, the wind blowing through her hair. She reaches to touch him and smiles at him as he sleeps quietly and peacefully in the backseat.

CHAPTER TWENTY-EIGHT

J ena has her head down, reading a book.

"Is your name Jena Parker?"

She slowly looks up. "Yes," she says shyly.

He holds his hand out. "My name is Rick Johnson." Jena squints, trying to place the name. "We went to Maple High School together."

She nods her head. "Oh, okay." She starts reading again.

Rick sits down. Her eyes zoom up from the book. "I knew you didn't remember me." He laughs. "You may not remember me, because I was somewhat of a nerd—a loner. That's why you probably didn't see me when you came into the library." He grins. "I was in the back ... kind of hiding ... out of sight, you know." He looks at Jena's book. "Already studying, and it's just our first day of college." Jena is quiet; she's not sure how to react to Rick's friendliness. Rick feels her uneasiness. He stands up. "Well, I'll let you get back to what you were doing." Jena stares off at the library doorway. She sees a boy standing in the shadow of the door, wearing a hoodie. Rick turns around. "Something wrong?" Rick appears to be concerned. Jena stares at the library doorway, blinks, and the boy is gone. She stands up with fear in her eyes. Rick grabs her arm. "Do you need help?"

"No, I just thought I saw someone staring at me, but I'm tired so I'm sure I was just seeing things." Jena sits down.

Rick shrugs his shoulders, smiles, and walks off. "I'll see you around."

The librarian taps her on the shoulder ...

*   *   *

She suddenly tunes back into Moishe as he talks about his life and Maria. Moishe notices the look of concern on Jena's face. "What's going on? Why do you look afraid?"

"I had flash of a memory that I'd forgotten." Jena pauses. "Someone I didn't even remember speaking to, but there he was ... I guess I blocked it or something."

Moishe thinks hard, *What is Jena hiding?*

Jena leans back in her seat. The laughter and great moment she was sharing with Moishe instantly fades away. She is left in a state of solitude. Sometimes you try to run, but you can't move; sometimes you try to speak, but the words just won't come out; and sometimes you try to forget the painful truth, but it finds you no matter how hard you try to bury it with love and laughter. *It won't let me forget, and now it's coming back to make me face it, to make me swallow its spoiled food, dirt, and filthy water.*

"We're almost there." Moishe tries to bring her back.

"Okay. Thanks." Jena spots the garage. "Turn here. Park. I'm sure Ted will be here shortly."

Moishe parks the car in the garage. They both sit quietly waiting for Ted. Moishe finally says, "Something is bothering you, Jena. What is it? We all have a past. I've told you mine. I hope you know that you can trust me to tell me yours. I've seen it all, Jena, so there's nothing you can tell me that will frighten or surprise me."

Jena breaks her silence. "I was ..." Moishe listens closely. "I was ..." She begins to cry.

Ted knocks on the driver's window. Moishe rolls down the window. "Hello, my name is Ted." Ted shakes Moishe's hand. "Jena, are you all right?"

"Yes, Ted, I'm fine."

Ted opens the back door. He shakes Jake. "Hey there."

Jake slowly opens his eyes. He's happy to see Ted. "What's up, man?"

Ted helps sit Jake up. "Oh, man, it's good to see your ugly face." They both laugh.

"Yeah, I bet. It looks like you had a rough night."

Ted looks around the car. "It looks like *you* had a rough night. Ken called the house. He's worried about you guys. He told me about Carol and Chance—wow, can you believe that she'd do something so horrible?"

Jena looks away. "I can believe it," she answers abruptly. "Ted, I want to go to my house." She turns around. "So what's the plan?"

"Well, I borrowed a friend of mine's car." He points. "It's parked right over there. I figure I'd drive you guys down the street, get close enough so you can walk, and hopefully none of us will get caught."

Jena gets out of the car. "Ted, no one's looking for you." Ted and Moishe help Jake walk to Ted's friend's car.

Jena stops Moishe from getting into the car. "Moishe, you don't have to come. I truly appreciate all of the help you've given us, but I don't want to drag you any further into this dreadful situation."

"You're not dragging me into anything. I want to be here, so let me." Moishe opens the back door for her. Jena sits next to Jake in the backseat.

He holds her hand. "I've been out for long time, huh?"

"Yeah, but I'm glad you're doing better."

He kisses her hand. "Me too."

Moishe hops in the front seat. Ted puts the car in reverse, backs out, and drives toward Jena's house.

Jake is cautious. "Are you sure you want to do this?"

"Yes, I'm sure, Jake. I want to go back. I believe this will help me face my fears—what I've been hiding from. I can't run anymore. The time has come for me to start from the beginning. I know this is the only way. Please trust me."

"I do, Jena." Jake kisses her hand. Ted peeks at them through the rearview mirror. His eyes blaze with curiosity of the love Jake and Jena share. Jake catches him. "You like to watch?" He laughs at Ted.

Ted is embarrassed. "No. I just think you two are very lucky to have each other."

"Thanks, bro. I'm sure one day you'll find someone you love just as much as I love Jena." Ted stares at Jena. She stares back at him. *Something strange about him today*, she thinks. *Maybe he's just lonely, worried about his mother and father.*

Jake is happy. Ted stares back at Jake in the rearview mirror. Moishe watches as his eyes move back and forth. He makes conversation with Ted. "You are a strange one, huh?"

"No. I'm just quiet. I don't have many friends, except for my brother and one or two more." Ted drives slowly through Jena's neighborhood. The streets are empty, quiet, and dark. He stops the car. Jena gets out.

"Wait," Jake yells.

"Why?" She closes the door and walks around to his side. "Can you walk on your own?"

"Yes."

She reaches for his hand and peeks into Ted's window. "Ted, take Moishe to your house to eat and get cleaned up, and then bring him back." Ted nods his head.

Moishe holds his hands out and looks at them. "I guess I could use some cleaning up." He wipes the dirt from his hand onto his pants. He touches Jena's hand, waves to Jake, and then they drive away.

*   *   *

The car is quiet. Ted feels uncomfortable being with Moishe, but he trusts that Jena and Jake wouldn't allow him to be with a maniac. He makes conversation. "So you helped my brother and Jena?"

"Yes."

"That's great, man. I really love my brother and, well, Jena's always been like a sister to us." *Well that is until my brother fell in love with her, so now I guess they are an item,* Ted thinks to himself.

Moishe spies him from the corner of his eye. "Jena is a beautiful girl," Moishe says. "I could see anyone finding her attractive—would do anything for her."

Ted smiles. "Yes, she is. I once had a crush on her myself, but she never really found any interest in me. My brother seems to get all the girls."

"Does that bother you?" Moishe looks at Ted.

Ted shakes his head, playing it off. "No, of course not. I'm not jealous of my brother. He can't help being better looking than me."

Moishe is suspicious of Ted. "So do you have a girlfriend? Someone you love?"

Ted flashes back to a girl standing out in the school yard. Her face is blurred out. She waves, and he waves back at her. "Yes, there was a time when I loved this girl so very much that I'd do anything to get her to notice me. When we were kids, I used to stare at her all the time. She caught me a few times, but I pretended I was looking at something else." He smiles to himself thinking of her. "I wish I could have been more to her, but I guess she didn't see in me what I saw in her."

Moishe listens. "Hmm … why didn't you tell her you loved her?"

Ted thinks, starts driving faster, and a mean look comes over his face. "I didn't tell her, because it wouldn't have mattered anyway. I wasn't the popular guy. I wasn't a jock. I didn't know how to speak to girls." He raises his voice at Moishe, "Could we talk about something else? I mean, I barely know you—and I hardly want to expose my love life to a complete stranger." Ted pulls into his driveway, gets out the car, and leans in Moishe's window. "My mom's not home, so we should be able to get in and out without any problems. You're welcome to use our bathroom, and there's plenty of food in the fridge." Moishe gets out of the car. Ted walks up to him. "Look, I wasn't trying to be rude. My dad's in the hospital. My mom's been worried. Jake has been stabbed. So I hope you understand I'm a little on edge."

Moishe just stares at Ted. He looks him in the eye. He can see the lies, feel Ted's uneasiness. He's hiding something. "Sure," Moishe says and starts walking. "Just take me inside and show me where things are."

Ted opens the house's front door. Moishe walks inside, checking out the house. Ted points to the bathroom. "There are some clean towels in there." Moishe walks into the bathroom without saying anything to Ted. Ted flops down on the living room couch. He leans over, rips his fingers through his hair, and stomps the floor. "Why was he asking so many questions? Who the hell does he think he is?" Ted talks to himself. "Let him ask me one more thing. I'll show him." He stands up and walks quickly back and forth around the room. "Piece of shit, question asking." He looks back at the bathroom door, continuing to pace back and forth and talk to himself. "It's none of his business." He goes into the kitchen, opens a drawer, and grabs a knife. "I'll stab him. He better not ask me anymore question, or I'll really stab him." He grips the knife tightly in his hand, walks toward the bathroom door, and puts his hand on the doorknob. There's a knock at the front door. He looks back, walks toward the door, and quickly places the knife underneath the couch pillow before opening it. He tries to turn on the porch light, but it won't work. He opens the door. There's a girl with a red jacket with the hood thrown over her head standing in the doorway. Ted tries to close the door quickly, but she pulls a gun on him.

CHAPTER TWENTY-NINE

Both of them stand in the doorway in the dark. The girl moves farther through the doorway. Her face is revealed: it's Chance. She holds the gun on Ted. He's frightened and starts to shake.

"What the hell are you doing, Chance?" She sticks the gun closer to his face. "What do you want?" Ted asks.

"I want you to come with me."

"What? Come with you where?"

Chance starts to slowly back up with the gun in one hand, pulling on Ted with the other. "To my car." She backs Ted all the way out the door into the dark driveway. Her car is parked behind his. "Now, turn around," she demands.

Ted pleads. "Come on, Chance. You don't want to do this."

"I said turn around." Ted slowly turns around. His face is sweating. "Now start walking to my car." Ted moves slow. Chance pushes him. "I said start walking, not crawling like a turtle."

Ted breathes hard. "Okay. Okay. Chance, please don't kill me like you killed Carol."

She screams, "Shut up and walk." She stops Ted when they reach the back of the car and hands him her keys. "Open the trunk!" She dangles the keys in front of Ted. "Take it! Open the trunk!" Ted grabs the keys and wiggles the first one in the trunk keyhole. His hands are sweaty and shaky. The keys drop to the ground. "Pick them up!" She points the gun down at him. Ted quickly picks up the car keys. He manages to open the trunk of the car. There's a still body lying in the trunk with a sheet over the head. The hands and feet are tied.

Ted starts crying. "Who the hell is this? Chance, please. Please. Don't do it!" Ted turns around. Tears of fear run down one cheek. "I'll do anything, but please don't kill me." He looks back down at the body and then turns back to plead with her. "What did I do to you? Huh? I've always been a good friend to you."

Chance pulls down the hood of her jacket from her head. "Shut up, turn around, and remove the sheet from the head of that body."

Ted stands with his hands in the air. He shakes with the rumbling thunder of Chance's voice. "I don't want to see. Please."

Chance rushes closer to him. "I said do it!" Ted carefully takes the sheet off the body in the trunk. It's dark, and he can't see the face. The person still isn't moving. Chance keeps the gun on Ted as she moves over to the end of the trunk. She shakes the person's feet. "Wake up, sleepy head." A male voice tries to talk through the mouth tie.

Ted moves in closer to the body. He leans down. "Ken? Man, is that you?" Ken tries to talk and wiggle out of the rope. Ted turns around. "Chance, why is Ken in the trunk of your car?"

Chance points the gun while she walks closer to Ted to make him back up a little. She reaches for the mouth tie, talking to Ken, "I'm going to take this tie off your mouth, and if you scream or so much as say one single word I'll shoot you and I'll shoot Ted." Ken's eyes grow big. Even in the dark his eyes glow from fear. Chance removes the tie. Ken remains quiet. She grabs Ted by his shirt. "You want to know why he's in my trunk?" Ted nods his head. "He's in my trunk because I put him there and because he cheated on me in high school, he's a jerk, he's womanizer ..." She points the gun at Ted. "Do you want me to go on?" Ted shakes his head and hands to signal no. "Okay then." She puts the tie back on Ken's mouth. Ken tussles, trying to stop her from putting it back on. He quickly speaks, "Chance, no—please. Ted, help me. Help me, man. She's crazy."

Chance smacks Ken with her hand. "Shut up! Shut! Up!" She puts the tie back on, closes the trunk down, and then roughs Ted up some more. "You bring Jena and Jake to me, or I'll kill Ken and I'll track you down and kill you too." Ted is silent with fear. "Are you clear on what I am saying to you?"

Ted can barely speak. "Yes, I'm clear."

"Good. That's a good boy." She hands Ted a small piece of paper. "Take this and put it in your pocket." Ted snatches the paper, quickly putting it in his pocket. "On that paper is my cell phone number. You call me in an hour, and I'll let you know what to do next." Ted nods. "In the meantime, you get Jena and Jake. I don't care how you do it, but you get them and bring them to me." Chance puts her hood back on. "Don't make me look for you." She gets into the car and spins off.

Ted stares at the car as it spins off. He runs into the house, slamming the door behind him. "Oh shit. Oh shit," He mumbles walking around the room. "Oh shit. Oh shit. She's crazy. Chance has gone completely crazy." He picks up the house phone to dial his cell to warn Jake. The cell phone rings with no answer. His voice mail comes on, and he leaves a quick message. "Jake, Chance was here." His voice sounds scared. "She had a gun on me. She's got Ken tied up in the back of her trunk, man." He pauses. "She's gone crazy. Look, she wants me to bring you and Jena to her. She said if I don't, she'll kill Ken and find me and kill me! Call me back, man. I don't know what to do. We've got to find this maniac to rescue Ken. Man, he's lying in the trunk all tied up." He tries to calm himself. "Call me ... Call me." He hangs up the phone. Pacing around the room, he looks for a weapon to use. He stops in front of the couch and remembers the knife he'd stuffed under the pillow. He grabs the knife just as Moishe opens the bathroom door.

Moishe pulls out his gun. "What are planning on doing with that?" Moishe walks slowly toward Ted, pointing his gun like an expert shooter.

Ted holds the knife loosely in his hand. "Umm ..." He's in shock and doesn't know what to say. "Wait. You have no idea what just happened to me."

Moishe aims at him like a sniper ready to hit his target. "Really? What happened?"

Ted tries to explain, "Chance was here. She had a gun." Ted sits down on the couch. "She has Ken tied up in her car's trunk."

Moishe keeps the gun aimed, not sure if he should trust Ted. "Yeah, go on."

"She wants me to bring Jena and Jake to a location."

"What location?"

"She just gave me her cell number and told me to call her and she'd tell me."

Moishe reaches out his hand. "Give me the number." Ted just stares at him. "You heard me. Give me the number." Ted reaches in his pocket, pulls out the crumpled piece of paper, and gets up to hand it to Moishe. Moishe opens the paper. "There's no number here. It's just letters." Moishe thinks back to his espionage days. "Ah, I see. She used letters instead of numbers." Moishe stares at the knife in Ted's hand. "And just what were you going to do with that?"

Ted looks at the knife, remembering it was originally to deal with Moishe. He lies. "I ... I picked it up to take with me." He walks around the room. "I needed something to fight against Chance."

Moishe raises his chin. He doesn't believe Ted. "She had a gun?"

Ted stops, looks around the room being careful with his answer. "Yes, she did."

Umm, Moishe thinks. "So you were going to take her out with a knife? While she has a gun."

Ted's eyes move quickly. He turns around. "Yeah. I don't have anything else."

Moishe eases his gun down, though he still doesn't trust Ted. "Well, I do, and we are going to go find her, rescue Ken, and I'll deal with Chance."

Ted grips the knife. "She said to bring Jena and Jake. If we go without them, she'll kill Ken, me, and you."

Moishe laughs. "She'll probably kill you, but she won't kill me. Now let's get out of here." Ted doesn't move. Moishe walks up to him. "What's wrong? Are you afraid?"

Ted just stands there. "I'm not afraid ... I've just never been in this kind of situation."

"Really? You've never done anything you wish you hadn't?" Moishe stares Ted square in the eyes.

"What are you trying to say?"

"I'm not *trying* to say anything. I'm telling you. You've got a dark side. I can see it in your eyes. You can't hide it from me. I've seen too many men—or in your case, boys—who try to hide their monsters, but you can't hide a monster from a monster." Moishe walks to the door, and opens it. "Let's go." He stands in the doorway. "I will deal with Chance." He stands with his back facing Ted and slightly turns around. "And then later, I will deal with you." Ted is angry. He rushes toward Moishe. Moishe quickly turns around, leans down, and has the gun pointed at Ted's stomach. Ted stands up, knife in one hand, with both hands in the air. "Don't push me. You don't have my skills."

Ted stands humiliated with his hands in the air. "You think you know me, but you don't."

Moishe leans up. "Oh, but I do—and there's a time and a place for everything. This isn't the time," he looks around the house, "or the place. If you are not who I think you are, then we will not have any more problems. But if you are ..." Moishe walks out of the house without finishing his sentence, leaving Ted to ponder what his words would have been.

Ted doesn't want to push Moishe. He follows him out the door and gets in the car. Moishe sits in the backseat. Ted gets in the car and gives him a strange look. "Why are you sitting in the backseat?"

Moishe crosses his legs, one over the other. "Simply because I don't trust you."

Ted gets in the car, adjusting his rearview mirror so he can keep an eye on Moishe. "I have to say I'm uncomfortable with you sitting in the backseat."

"You should be. Now call the number."

"You have the paper." Moishe hands Ted the paper. He dials the letters. The phone rings.

Chance answers and speaks before Ted can say a word. "Meet at the old mill. Park, and I'll find you." She hangs up the phone.

"What did she say?"

"She said to meet her at the old mill, that she'd find me there."

"Okay then, let's go. As we get closer I will get out, and then we will handle this situation so we may get back to Jake and Jena."

Ted doesn't reply. He drives until he gets to a dirt road littered with scattered rocks and tree branches. He stops, sighs. "How am I going to drive over this mess?"

Moishe opens the car door and gets out. He peeks in Ted's window. "I don't know, but do it. I'll get out here." He taps on the back door to get Ted's attention. "Keep your eyes and ears open." Moishe disappears in the grass alongside the road. Ted continues to drive slowly and cautiously down the road.

CHAPTER THIRTY

Chance is standing in front of Ken. He's tied to a chair. She removes his mouth tie and laughs at him. "It's kind of funny seeing you tied to that chair, begging for your life. I wish I had a mirror right now to let you see your face as you beg, cry, and plead. You'd probably laugh at your own self."

Ken's face is red. "Untie me, Chance. Let me go."

"No. That is definitely something I'm not going to do. So ask me to do something else."

"Like what?"

"Oh, I don't know—maybe ask me to take off my clothes."

Ken turns his face away. "Why would I want to see you naked?"

She grabs Ken's face really hard. "Because that's the kind of person you are. That's what you wanted from me before, so why not ask for it now?" Ken avoids looking in her eyes. "Look at me." She tries to force his face to look at her with her hands. She screams, "I said look at me! Look at my beauty. Ah—you see it now, don't you? My beautiful face, my eyes," she stands up and rubs her hand over her body, "my body. You like that, don't you?" She continues to caress her body all over.

Ken is angry, but he's also aroused. "I'm sorry I hurt you."

Chance takes off her shirt. "Are you?" She takes off her bra and starts to slowly caress her breasts, playing with herself. Ken tries to look away, but he can't. She slides down her pants, sits on his lap, and starts kissing him. He tries to resist, but he can't. "Oh, the passion between us. We had so much sex." She bites Ken's ear. He squirms. "Oh, why squirm? You used to like it when I'd bite you." She squeezes his balls. "Yeah—now that's a man's balls." She looks down at Ken. "You've got big balls, don't you?" She squeezes them really hard.

Ken yells. "Stop it!"

"Oh, am I hurting you?" She toys with him.

He squints his eyes. "You're crazy, Chance. You need help."

Chance stands up and slaps him. "I need help! Who are you to tell me that I need help? What I need is to kill you! That's my help." Ken's just stares at her with a crazed look. She gets back on his lap and starts playing with his hair. Ken feels helpless and trapped in her insane world. "Do you remember the first time you asked me out? We were in the ninth grade, and I was quite surprised because I really didn't think you liked me." She nibbles on his ear, smiles. "Even back then I thought you liked Carol. You always flirted with her and never paid me much attention, so I was quite shocked when you chose me." She sits back to look at Ken. "Why did you choose me?" She ponders her thought. "Well, Carol was somewhat of a slut back then—easy breezy—and I was the shy girl. The virgin. That's why you chose me, right? Because Carol was easy. She wasn't a challenge. Heck you could have gotten her anytime, so you prayed on me. You wanted to take away my control. Make me one of your stories you tell when you get around your friends—laugh about how you had me over and over again. In all those different positions. How I moaned and screamed as you took my virginity. Ruined me. Ripped my insides out, and then turned me into your slave. That was your whole, entire plan. To strip me down until I'm bare minded, simple, until I only function enough for you to play with my emotions without me even knowing it." She gets up and starts redressing. "All the while, you were screwing my best friend. The other girls at school, laughing while I was crying floods and floods of tears. Worthless tears over you ... You," she shouts out loud, "you're nothing. Look at you, sitting all tied up by a little bitty girl. Somehow, now you look small to me." She picks up the gun from the floor, holds it loosely in her hand, plays with it, looks at it. "It's not because of this gun that I feel power." She looks at Ken sitting in the chair trying to hold back his feelings of fear, regret, and pain. "It's not the gun. It's me. I feel powerful because of me. I took back the power you stole from me. I took it back from you, and now I have it. Now I have your power too. Now you know how it feels to have someone break you down." She looks over. Ken has his head down. "How does it feel?"

He raises his head up. "I feel like shit, Chance. I'm sorry I hurt you. I'm sorry that I'm a user, but you didn't ..." He starts to sob. "You didn't have to kill her ... You could have ..." He stops.

"I could have what!"

"You could have been free of me without killing her. Now she's dead."

Chance gets angry. "Wow!" She waves the gun around. "Wow! Wow! Wow! You're tied up in a chair, about the be killed, and you are worried about a girl who's already dead. And you call me insane. Wow!"

"Chance," Ken calls out her name.

She stops him. "Just shut up! Don't speak anymore! I don't want to hear anything else you have to say! You're weak, powerless—so shut up." She hears the mill door open. "Shush, be quiet. I hear something." She yells out, "Who's there?"

Ted comes walking out. "It's me. Ted."

Ken starts moving around in the chair, yelling, "Help me, man! Get me out of this damn chair!"

Chance points the gun back and forth between Ken and Ted. "Shut up!" she yells at Ken. Pointing the gun at Ted, she tells him, "Pick up that tie, and put it back on his mouth."

Ken panics, pleading as Ted walks over to do what she said, "Please, man, don't. Just grab her ... wrestle her down ... get the gun ... do something!"

"Man, I'm sorry," he tells Ken as he ties his mouth.

"Where's Jena? Jake? I told you that I wanted them here."

Ted holds up his hands. "I couldn't get ahold of them."

"Liar!" Chance screams. Ken starts moving around in his chair.

"Chance, I left a message. Jake has my cell, but we took them Jena's mother's."

"Her mother's? Why? That house is abandoned."

"I know, but that's where she wanted to go." Ted tries to talks his way out of being killed. "I'm sure he'll call me as soon as he checks the message, and when he does I'll tell him to meet here."

Chance eyes him. "Yeah, I know you will." She shoots down at Ted's feet. Ken jumps up and down in his chair. Ted runs back. "Come on, don't shoot me. I did what you wanted. It's not my fault that he didn't answer the phone."

Chance turns the gun on Ken. "You're right. It's not your fault—it's his." Ken tries to yell through his mouth, but only a muffling sound comes out. Ted is terrified. Chance cocks the gun. She shoots Ken in one leg. Ted runs. Ken screams in pain. Two gun fires are heard. Chance looks around, but she doesn't see anyone. She starts firing her gun aimlessly around the mill. "You want some?" she yells as she shoots around. "You want some of me? Well come get it." Moishe shoots down at her feet. Chance spies around the mill. "I'm not afraid of you, asshole."

"Put down the gun, little girl," Moishe voice echoes through the mill.

"I'm not a little girl," Chance says, "and I'm not putting down the gun." Moishe walks out of the shadows.

Chance is surprised. "Who are you?"

"That's not important right now." He looks over at Ken's bleeding leg. Ken pleads for help with his eyes.

"Yes it is important, because I want to know the name of the man that I'm about to shoot."

"I do not exchange names with strangers. Now put it down!" Moishe tries to keep his temper cool.

"No. Why don't you go after your coward friend, Ted. This is my problem, not yours."

Moishe's eyes grow big. "If it deals with Jena, then it's my problem now."

"Ah, I see." Chance flexes. "I remember seeing you as you pulled up to the party. Yes, you were the driver. Hmm, well I guess Jena wins again. She manages to charm every man she meets, even old ones."

"I don't want to shoot you, but I will. So I'm telling you again— put down the gun and walk away while you can." Hard stepping and then running is heard coming from the back of the mill. Ted is running fast to try to tackle Chance. When he gets halfway to her, she turns and shoots at him. She barely misses. Moishe is able to get close enough to her to take away her gun. Ted stands up. He's not hurt, suffering only a scuff to his knees.

Chance pushes Moishe; his gun drops. She grabs her gun back and points to fire at him. Ted sees the scuffle, gets up, and tackles her to stop her from shooting Moishe. She falls down, but then she manages to get back up and start running. Moishe is also knocked down to the floor. He quickly gets up, grabs his gun, but it's too late—she's gone.

Moishe is stunned at Chance's quick maneuver. He gives Ted a thankful look. He stands, breathing hard from the excitement. "Thank you." Moishe puts his hand out to Ted. Ted graciously accepts his handshake. His eyes gleam with a sense of pride and happiness that Moishe would want to shake his hand. The two of them lock eyes for a second, and then they race over to help Ken, who's bleeding from the leg pretty badly. "Left his leg," Moishe tells Ted. "We must stop the bleeding." Moishe rips off his shirt to use it as a tourniquet around Ken's leg. Ted holds Ken's leg firmly so Moishe can tie it. "Now untie him so we can get him to a hospital." Ted stops. "Why are you stopping?"

"We can't take him to a hospital. It would raise too many questions. The police are looking for Jena. Ken's shooting would only raise the police's suspicion that Jena is possibly in Maplesville." Ted unties Ken. "We just can't risk her and my brother getting caught."

Moishe thinks. "Okay, we'll take him back to Jena's. We'll all hide. But we must stop by a drug store so I can get supplies to fix the wound. If we don't hurry, he could bleed out and die. We must go now."

Ted and Moishe carry Ken to the car. All of the tires are flat. "Damn it, Chance," Ted says. They drag Ken into the car. Ted pulls his fingers through his hair, looking at Moishe. "What are we going to do?"

Moishe gets in the driver's side. "Get in. We're going to drive this car on all rims." Ted hops into the car. Moishe puts the car in gear. "Hold on, because this is going to be a hell of a ride." Moishe drives the car as fast as he can without causing sparks from the rims.

Ted is frustrated. "We're not going to make it. Ken's going to die. Look at him, he's barely holding on."

Moishe drives. He keeps his cool. "I've seen men shot five and six times and make it. We will make it."

An old black truck is coming down the road. It's driven by a man in his sixties wearing a country straw hat, toothpick in his mouth, smoking a cigarette. Moishe stops and the man stops, looking at the flat tires and at Ken in the back. He takes his toothpick out, but leaves the cigarette in. "Looks like trouble," the man says.

Moishe opens the car door and walks up to the truck. "It is trouble. We need your truck."

The old man gripes, "My truck? Old Annie here? I can't do that."

Moishe opens the truck door. "You can, and you will old man."

The man reaches for his shotgun. "I can use this thing."

Moishe puts his hand on his gun, which is tucked outside his shirt in clear view. "Not before I use this. Now get out of the truck. We need it. Our friend is shot."

The old man grabs his shotgun, gets out of the truck, and peeks in the car at Ken. "Oh, he's about to die." Ted picks up Ken, and Moishe helps get him onto the bed of the truck. Moishe gets in, backs up, turns around, sticks his head out the truck window, and says, "I'll get it back to you." He drives off, leaving a burst of dust in the old man's face.

He throws his shotgun down and then pulls a cell phone out of his dirty jeans. "Earl, come get me. 'Cause someone stole my truck. I don't know who, just come get me at the old mill. We got a car here—tires flat, but it looks new. Get down here now." The old man puts the cell phone back in his pocket, picks up the shotgun, and walks to the mill.

Chance comes out the woods and pulls a gun on him. "Who did you call?"

The old man drops the shotgun. He can't speak. "Ah … I called …"

Chance yells, "You called who?"

"I called Earl."

"Give me your cell." The old man reaches in his pocket, takes out the phone, and gives it to Chance. "Now, when Earl gets here you're going to tell him that this is my car and you're helping me."

The old man has his dirty hands raised in the air. "Why would I do that?"

Chance brings the gun around to the front of him. "Because if you don't, I'll blow you and your dirty, dusty jeans away."

CHAPTER THIRTY-ONE

Moishe drives as fast as he can, dust misting from the truck as it spins down the dirt road onto the highway. Ted checks on Ken—pale face, chilly body. Ken passes out. Ted is afraid. He yells to Moishe, "Pull over!"

"What?"

"Pull over. I think he's dead."

Moishe pulls over. He jumps in the back of the truck and feels Ken's pulse. He sighs. "He's not dead, but he won't make it unless we get him to a hospital."

Ted holds his head down. "The hospital is five miles from here." Moishe jumps in the truck, quickly gets situated, and puts his foot all the way down on the petal. Minutes later, he pulls into the St. Mary's hospital emergency room entrance.

Ted goes inside and yells for help. Nurse Louis comes running out. "We need help." She runs to the truck, sees Ken, and then runs inside to get a stretcher, two more nurses, and a doctor. They all help get Ken into the bed, and then they race him the emergency room. Moishe and Ted rush in with them. Nurse Louis stands at the counter, letting the other two nurses and doctor take over. "What's his name?"

Ted looks at her. "Umm … Ken."

"Ken *who*, sir?"

Ted gets nervous. "I don't know his last name. Just his first. His name is Ken."

"Okay. Do you know his parents?"

"Umm. No, I don't."

"Sir, in order for us to properly treat this patient, we have to have more information."

Moishe walks to the counter. "If this is a matter of money, I'll pay for everything. He reaches in his pocket. In cash."

Nurse Louis starts typing. "Okay then, we list him as John Doe. Please go around the corner to arrange payment."

Moishe walks to the payment counter. "I'd like to pay for this emergency visit for … John Doe."

The clerk looks up the name John Doe. "Sir, he has just been admitted for five minutes. We have no idea how much this visit will be. I will need a copy of your driver's license and for you to fill out some papers so we may contact you when a bill is ready."

"I can't do that."

The clerk frowns. "And why not, sir?"

"Look, I'm not from this country. This is a friend of mine who I'm trying to help. I will come back tomorrow to check with you on the amount of this visit. Please take care of my friend." Moishe walks away.

Ted meets him outside. "What happened? Did they call the cops?"

"Not yet, but I'm sure that woman will. Let's go." Moishe walks to the truck. Ted follows. "We must get back to Jena and Jake before Chance finds them."

Ted looks over at Moishe. "What makes you think she'll find them?"

"Because I overheard you tell her that they were at Jena's house. If she is looking for them, then that's where she will go."

"I have to go home first."

"Why? We don't have time to stop by your house."

"We have too."

They get into the truck. It's quickly blocked by a police car. A police officer walks up to the truck. "Is this your truck, sir?"

Moishe answers, "Yes. Is there a problem, officer?"

The officer walks around the truck, writes down the license plates. He walks back to the window. "I'll be back." He goes to run the license plates.

Ted look behind them. "Back out, man. He's going to find out this truck is stolen."

Moishe looks back. "If I back out, then we have cop problems."

Ted gets mad, but he lowers his voice down to a whisper. "We've got cop problems whether you back out or not. We've got to get the hell out of here, or we're going to be arrested."

"We will wait."

"What? I'm not going to jail." Ted reaches for the door to make a run for it.

The officer comes back. "Okay, your good. This truck isn't the truck we're looking for. We're looking for a truck that was stolen and is associated with the burning of a house and a murder."

Moishe tries to get more information. "A murder?"

"Yes, a murder. Possible suspect—Jena Parker. But this is your lucky day, because this isn't the truck." The officer gets into his vehicle and drives off. Moishe follows him out.

Ted is relieved. "Man, you're one cool cat. My heart was about to pound out of my chest."

Moishe is quiet. He looks around as he drives to Ted's house. "Such a little town. Little towns are always filled with mysteries," he turns, "and murder. I want to apologize for what I said to you earlier. You know, about me not trusting you. You saved my life back there at the mill, so I owe you a lot of gratitude."

Ted smiles; he feels honored. "Thanks." Ted plays with the truck's glove box. "This is an old truck."

"Yes, but this old truck saved Ken's life." Moishe looks in the rearview mirror and notices someone is following him.

"What are you looking at?"

"Someone's following us. I'll turn here to make sure." Moishe turns into the gas station. The car follows him in. It's a woman driving a blue car with black tinted windows. Moishe pulls in and then out again. The car follows him. Ted looks out the back window.

"Don't look back!" Moishe yells.

"Sorry. Do you think it's, Chance?"

"I don't know. Could be her. Could be a cop, or could be a coincidence. We just don't know yet." Moishe turns down Ted's street. He parks in the driveway. The blue car follows him. They sit in the car. The blue car parks; no one gets out. Moishe reaches for his gun. "You wait here." He opens the door. "If they start shooting, you run." Moishe gets out and walks to the blue car. He stands glaring at himself in the shiny, tinted window. The window slowly moves down. He points his gun.

An old woman with gray hair wearing sunglasses stares back at him, a gun resting in her lap. "Who are you?" she asks Moishe.

"Who are you? And why are you following me?"

The old woman takes off her shades. "You're driving my old man's truck. I was following you because I thought you was him, heading over to another woman's house." Moishe puts his gun down. The woman puts her shades back on and returns her gun to the glove box. "I was about bust a cap in someone's ass, but he got lucky today." She starts pulling out of the driveway. "If you see him, you tell him I'm looking for him." Moishe is quite surprised.

Ted gets out of the truck. "Who was that?"

"Some gangster old lady looking for her old man. How long do you need?"

"Just an hour, maybe only a half hour. Come inside. Relax a little. I'm sure my brother will appreciate every free moment he has with Jena." Moishe walks inside with Ted. Both of them seem relaxed. Moishe flops down on the couch. He lies his head back and closes his eyes. "You got anything cold."

"You mean a beer?" Ted goes to the refrigerator. "Here you go. My dad keeps a few in the fridge."

Moishe pops open the beer. He takes a sip. "You don't drink?"

"Yeah, I do—but not like my dad. He drinks a lot." A sad feeling comes over Ted. "So does my mother. But Jake and I, we aren't big drinkers ... although we did get drunk one night. It was his first day at college, and they had a party. So I went up there to hang out." Ted sits down next to Moishe. "We had the time of our lives. Jake was a little bummed out that Jena didn't want to go to the party, but Ken and I cheered him up. Got him drunk." Moishe stares at Ted, takes a big gulp of the beer. Ted puts his hands behind his head as he remembers about that night.

Moishe takes another sip of beer. "So you guys had a wild night, huh?"

"Yeah, it was wild. I mean, beer and alcohol and—oh man—the girls. I'm not very popular in high school, but I was popular that night." Ted laughs. "There were so many beautiful girls there, and my brother couldn't even enjoy his night." Ted stands up.

Moishe finishes his beer. "Why, because of Jena?"

"Yeah, because of Jena. He just couldn't get her off his mind. Every time a girl would approach him, he'd open his wallet to look at the photo of Jena." Ted puts his head down. "Every time he'd open his wallet, Ken and I would laugh our asses off." Ted just stops talking midstory.

Moishe gets a strange look on his face. "Ted?" Ted zones out. "Ted?"

Ted looks at Moishe. "You want another beer, man?"

"Sure." Ted gets Moishe another beer. "You want to talk about something? You seem strange all of a sudden."

"No, I'm just worn out from today. It's been a very wild and crazy day. I wonder where Chance is. Think she'll come here looking for us?"

Moishe drinks down the beer. "I don't think so. I think she's had enough for today. She's quite a disturbed young lady."

"She wasn't always like that. She was once a very sane person. Beautiful, nice, and kind. I used to talk to her every day at school. We'd eat lunch together. If you knew the Chance I knew, you would have never thought she was the same person you saw today. It's strange how you think you know someone, but you really don't." Ted walk off to his room. "I'll be back. You can help yourself to anything in the fridge or in my brother's bathroom in his room." Ted leaves the room.

Moishe goes to the refrigerator and pulls out the entire case of beer. He turns on the TV and drinks at least five more beers. He starts laughing at a funny show on TV. Moishe gets tired, but he fights sleep. He looks at his watch and realizes that at least two hours has passed since Ted left to go to his room. Moishe stumbles to the refrigerator to get more beer and then heads back to the couch. Ted is taking a long time in his room. Moishe's laugh fades as he tries to keep his eyes open. His head bobs back and forth as he drifts off to sleep. He shakes his head to try to wake himself up. He looks at his watch. He has spent three hours on the couch. He gets up and calls for Ted. "Ted." His vision is blurred, and the room is dark except for the light from the TV. "Ted. What are you doing?" He slides open Ted's room door. There's a small night lamp on, the bed's empty, and his room window is open. Moishe opens the door wider. "Ted?" He's barely able to stand, but he slowly looks around the room. Suddenly he feels a thump on his head. He falls on the bed. His hearing is limited, and he has double vision. He can feel his body being dragged across the floor. He tries to speak and see who's dragging him. It's someone wearing a hoodie, but their faced is a blur to him. "What's going on?" His voice drags. "What are doing?" Moishe feels another thump on his head and totally blacks out.

CHAPTER THIRTY-TWO

Jake holds Jena's hand as they walk in the dark to the rear entrance of her house. Jena stands back as he tries to push open the door. He presses his body as he hard as he can into the door. His wounded shoulder is injured further. Jena touches him. "Are you all right?" She touches him all over. "I'm sorry, I know you're in pain. Let me try."

Jake stands between her and the door. "No, I want to." Jena stands back while Jake pushes as hard as can he on the door. The door pops open. He stands back, holding his shoulder. Jena stands in the dark doorway. Her feet are frozen. Jake lightly runs his fingertips through her hair, rubs her shoulder. "It's all right," He comforts her. "I'm here with you."

She steps one foot inside the house. "It's dark and cold in here."

Jakes whispers, "Turn on the lights."

"We can't. If we do, someone will know we're here." Jena steps completely through the doorway. "My father has flashlights in the kitchen. We'll use them." Jake follows her inside. "Besides, the moon is bright tonight." She reaches for Jake's hand. "We'll pull back the curtains, let it shine through." Jake leads her into the kitchen. "That's funny."

"What?"

"You know my house better than I do."

He reaches for the flashlights under the kitchen cabinet. "Here." He hands her one, picks up another, and turns it on.

"Keep it low, Jake."

He places his flashlight on the living room floor. Jena flashes the other around the house, staring at the pictures on the wall, the furniture, the mantle where the antique vase her grandmother gave her mother sat. Everything looks the same to her, even in the dark. Jake sits down on the floor near the flashlight, holding his shoulder. Jena kneels down near him. "You're in pain? I'll find something to help you."

She begins to stand up; he grabs her arm. "No." He gently pulls her close to him. "Just come sit next to me."

Jena turns her flashlight off and cuddles next to Jake. "You're warm."

He grins. "Yeah, well I guess I'm just a hot-blooded person."

"Hot blooded, huh?"

"Yeah." They both laugh.

"Thank you for coming with me. I really wanted to be home."

Jake reaches over to touch her face. "I'd do anything for you."

"I know." Jena kisses him. "I'll do anything for you too." Words Jake has been waiting to hear. Jena rubs his chest, moves her hand down to his bulging pants, starts rubbing him. He leans his head back and breathes out softly.

"Jena, let me find the heater to turn it on."

"No. We can make our own heat." She starts kissing Jake's neck and face and then takes the tip of her tongue and lightly traces it over his lips. She moves over to sit on top of him. He breathes hard. "I'm not hurting you, am I?"

"Not at all—and even if you were, I could give a shit right now." Jena starts the motion of her body on his. He claws his fingers into her back, squeezing her as she plays with him. She unbuttons Jake's belt, zips down his jeans, and reaches for his jock.

"I'm so ready for you," she whispers.

"Show me," he whispers back. He unbuttons her blouse, pulls her bra halfway down, and licks her hard nipples. He pulls down on her as she braces herself on him. "Awe …" They both moan. Jena digs her fingers into his good shoulder and leans back. She pants and moans in the delight. He clenches on to her harder. "Oh, Jena," he cries out. "Jena." He whispers, "I love you. I love you so much."

Jena leans forward bringing her face next to his. "Tell me again."

"I love you."

"Again, scream it."

"I love you, baby. Oh … I love you," he says it over and over again.

She nibbles on his ear, whispers, "Please don't ever stop."

"I won't. I won't ever stop."

She lies still next to him. Both of their hearts beating together, creating one beat. "You are my hope," she whispers softly to him.

Jake holds her tightly, but then moans a little. Jena kisses his wounded shoulder. "I'm sorry. It's okay, really. I just have to man up."

She slides to the side of him. "I know my father had some pain medication. I'll get you some, turn on the heat, and find us some blankets.

Jake sits up. "Turn on the heat? Wasn't I hot enough for you?" He snuggles her face with his. "Didn't I light you on fire?" They both laugh.

"Yes, you did, but now I'm cold." She grabs a flashlight and puts it up to her face, giving her a creepy look, and says, "I'll be back."

Jena walks into the kitchen and searches through the drawers to find the pain medicines. She finds the bottle, walks to the thermostat, turns the heat on, and grabs a few blankets out of the downstairs closet. *It's only been two weeks, but I feel like I have been gone forever*, she thinks as she flashes the light through the house. *Everything is the same, but it's not. Nothing is the same.* She holds the blanket close to her chest and shines the flashlight up the stairs, capturing each stair, one by one, until the light reaches the top. She shines the light on the very spot where she would sit listening to her parents talk, laugh, and dance to their favorite song. Her father's whispers in her mother's ears. Her mother's high-pitched giggles. How they swayed together as he romanced her with his smooth dance moves.

"Kitty," her dad whispers. "You're my little Kitty." Her mother laughs. "Purr for me, Kitty."

"Stop it, John. You know I don't purr like a kitty cat." He picks her up.

She softly screams, "Put me down." He swings her around the room, Kitty smiling down at him, and then he'd slowly slides her down and kiss her.

Jena remembers when her father landed the most romantic kiss on her mother's lips, and then he picked her up again, like a princess, and carried her to the couch. Jena took that as her cue to leave them alone. *I always dreamed of having such a love as my parents had.* She stares at Jake as she walks toward him. *And now I do.* Laying the blanket on him, she says, "Here's a soft blanket for you."

"Thanks, my love."

She holds her hand out. "Here are some meds too."

Jake takes the bottle. "What is it?"

"Umm, not sure, but I do remember my dad taking them for his back." She sits down next to Jake. "They make you a little sleepy." She plays with his hair.

"I don't want to go to sleep. I want to sit up all night and stare at you," he jokes.

"Take them, Jake. It'll help you with your pain." She slides the blanket over them both. "And if it will make you feel better, I'll go to sleep with you." Jake takes two pills. They both cuddle close. Jena kisses him on the nose. "See, doesn't this feel great."

Jake starts getting drowsy. He's beginning to drift off, but he replies, "Yeah, it does feel real groovy."

"Groovy?" Jena laughs. "Oh, the pills are starting to take effect."

Jake slowly fades out. "Yeah."

"Yeah?" Jena plays with him. "So how many of me do you see?"

Jake slightly grins. "Just one." He pulls her close. "I don't care what drugs I take, there's only one Jena ever." Jake falls asleep.

Jena holds him. She whispers, "You're my king, and I'm your princess." Jena stares around the dark room, her eyes focusing in on every corner of the living room. She sees a light. A force pulls her. She tries to resist, but her body gets light like a feather. She can feel it floating away, and in moments she is looking down on herself and Jake. She turns and walks slowly toward the light. Her body movement feels robotic. An unseen force calls for her. She walks and walks toward the bright light and finds herself in an open field with twelve black doors—all open, waiting for her to walk through. She doesn't know which door to go to, so she walks to let her spiritual body guide her. She closes her eyes and walks to the door of its choice. She walks through it, and discovers little children playing. Parents walking around and talking. School buses. Jena stares at it until it's all out of sight. She walks barefooted in the cool, white sand. It's a playground with seesaws, swings, and a place to play in the sand. She sees a little girl on the swings, laughing as her father swings her back and forth. She walks toward them. The little girl has a bright red bow in her hair, a white dress, and blue shoes. The girl holds on tightly to the swing. Jena can see only the back of the head of her father, but she somehow knows he is smiling and talking to the little girl. Jena feels happiness. She feels like she knows where she is. *It's me … That little girl is me.* Jena smiles. The little girl's laughter gives her joy and a sense of comfort. *If that's me, then that is Dad. That's Dad swinging me.* She looks up and sees her mother standing next to the swing, bent down with her hands on her lap, smiling at the little girl and the father. "Mom," she utters as she reaches out for her. A gust of wind blows; Jena's hair swings back, her body pushed backward … The father runs to the little girl, picks her up, and holds her. Her mother is standing with one hand on her face with tears of joy seeping from her eyes. Jena wants to be a part of that moment. She walks slowly up to the father. Her mother stares at her with a dreadful face, the little girl screams, and then the father turns around, but his face is melting …

Jena suddenly awakens. She looks around the room and then at Jake and realizes that it was just a horrible dream. "I hate him," she utters to herself. *Why is he still here? Why is he still in my mind?* She pulls the blanket off of her, slides up her pants and buttons them, picks up a flashlight, and walks toward the stairs. She shines the flashlight up the stairs. "Mom …," she says as she walks slowly up the steps. The flashlights catches her shadow on the wall, the stairs make a cracking sound with every step she takes. At the top of the stairs, she flashes the light on every room door until it finally reaches her mother's room. She walks toward it. Opening the door, she shines the light on the dresser, the window, her mom's closest, and then the bed—where she last saw her.

CHAPTER THIRTY-THREE

What have I done? She closes her eyes as they begin to tear up. *If there was ever a time I regret my own doings, this would be it. My mother, my precious mother is gone.* She slides her fingers over the covers and remembers her mother's face right before she drank the milk—her sunk-in eyes, her drooping face, the gray in her hair, and the bags under her eyes. It seemed that she aged overnight from a woman in her forties to an old woman. *My mother's body was occupied by a stranger and kept alive so she could relive the death of my father every single day of her life. A woman whose spirit had left her behind to wander the earth in torment of why it had abandoned her without its beautiful presence.* She stares at her mother's empty bed and flashes back to that night, walking up the stairs with the milk in hand. Just hours before, she had taken the life of a doctor on the train who merely asked her name.

"What's your name?"

"Jena Pa ... Jena Gray."

He, too, dead with a cold, stricken look on his face, as if he had seen something that scared his skin lily white. He didn't see a ghost. He saw a girl who had been broken in many pieces until her light had flickered out, blown away to the stars, hiding out somewhere in the universe.

I want so much for my light to return. She looks at her mother's pillow and stands up. *But do I even deserve it? I've taken away my mother's darkness, hoping that would bring her light—but what if it didn't? What if she's just out there, afraid, crying, waiting for my father to come? Sitting in a dark room alone, staring at the door, waiting for him to come to dance with her. She could very well be no more free than I am.*

Jena hears a noise. She flashes the light throughout the room and then walks toward the door. She shines the light down and sees shoes, shines it farther up and sees pants, and then shines it right into a face. Ted is standing, staring at her. She shines the light closely at his face. "What are you doing here?" He just stares. "What? Is something wrong with your father?"

Ted steps closer to her. "No, there's nothing wrong. I just wanted to come check on you and Jake."

Jena moves around the room, keeping the flashlight on Ted's face. "Jake is fine. He's asleep."

"I know. I saw him downstairs." Ted steps around the room in the dark. Jena follows him with the flashlight. "Jena, do you remember when we were kids playing at the playground, how I always put sand in your hair?" Jena listens. "You ever wonder why I did that?" Ted continues to walks around the room; Jena follows him. "You know when we were both in high school, I would wish we'd have every class together," he chuckles, "because I knew it would make Jake jealous. Ken too."

"What's wrong with you, Ted?"

He shouts, "Nothing's wrong with me. Why does something have to be wrong with me?" He walks closer to Jena.

"Because you're acting strange. You're here in the dark, telling stories. I … I just don't understand."

He walks close to the light. His face sets off a dark shadow. "What don't you understand? You don't understand why I always put sand in your hair? Why I always wanted to play with you when your mom brought you over? Why I always watch you when you're not looking or when you're too busy smiling with my brother? Or … maybe it's something else you don't understand. Maybe you don't understand what happened to you that night."

"What night?" she shouts.

He grins. "Oh, that night. I know you remember … or maybe you don't want to remember." Ted turns around and steps toward the window. He's wearing a hooded jacket. His silhouette in the window sets off a memory for Jena. She flashes back to the library, when she thought she saw someone standing in the library window door wearing a similar jacket.

She slowly walks behind him. "Ted, do you know what happened to me that night?" The room is dark, but for Jena it gets darker as her anger grows. "I asked you a question," she says in a forceful voice. "Do you know what happened to me that night?" she yells.

Ted tells the story. "We were all at the party. You had just told Jake that you didn't want to go. I know this because I was watching you and him. I saw the angry, disappointed look on his face after you said you were going to the library. Jake, Ken, and I all met up at the party." Ted flashes back. "The music was awesome. Girls everywhere. We started drinking. I'm excited to be hanging out with the college kids, drinking with my bro, Ken, and all of the rest of the gang. Chance and Carol were there too. It was the party of all parties, but my brother wasn't in a party mood. That's because his beloved Jena wasn't there. Do you know every time a girl would come over and try to talk to him, he'd pull out his wallet to stare at your picture? Man, I'd never seen someone so in love with a girl … someone besides me. You see, Jena, I loved you too. But you …" he smirks, "but you didn't notice me. I was invisible to you. All of the signs I gave you from when we were kids, grade school, high school … nothing. You saw *nothing!*"

Jena's voice starts to shake. "What happened, Ted? What happened!"

Ted pauses. "Jake wanted to leave the party and, well, so did I.

Ken didn't. He was having the time of his life. We were all pretty damn toasted, but we managed to walk out of the party. Jake was the drunkest of us. He was stumbling all over the place, but somehow he remembered you were at the library. I knew it, but I was hoping he would just leave with another girl. But he just couldn't ... He just couldn't let me have you. I left with a red cup full of alcohol—and yeah, I had some roofies in my jacket. I told Jake and Ken I'd go inside to get you, and I did, but you were chatting with some nerd. That made me so mad. You saw me, and I raised the cup up, signaling for you come. That's when the librarian tapped you on the shoulder, telling you it was time to go. You met me at the door with a smile—the most beautiful smile in the world. It was the first time you had smiled at me that way. You were like an angel that just came down from heaven. I knew that this was my only chance to be with you. Jake and Ken were so drunk. I knew that this was our time. Yours and mine, Jena. I showed you the red cup and told you to drink it, that it was good. You said no. No. I didn't want to talk, but I played with you. Made you laugh. You trusted me, so you took a sip. I could see the roofies taking effect right away. You leaned on me. That really turned me on, so I took you out back. Jake and Ken were out front, probably passed out. You were so zoned. You didn't know what was going on. It was dark out there, cold ... cold as ice, but I never felt so much warmth as I did being close to you. I started kissing you. I could tell you were still coming in and out from the drug, because you called me Jake and then you thought I was Ken ... and then you saw me and you started to scream. I couldn't have that, so I started hitting you in the face. I felt so horrible. I didn't want to hit you, but you were starting to get too loud. If Jake heard you, I knew he'd come running. Your voice faded once the drug took full effect, and I had my way with you. You were even willing at times. When I was finished, I looked down at you and realized what I had done. I was sorry, but ... there was a part of me that was so happy I finally had gotten to be with you. That you finally saw me."

The flashlight is beaming on Ted's jacket. Jena is close to Ted's back. She whispers in his ear, "I'm going to fucking kill you." She throws the flashlight down and slams Ted up against the window. His face slams into it. She grabs him and slams his face against it again and again. Her strength is twice his. Ted tries to fight back, but Jena starts beating on him. Ted pulls the knife out from his pocket, nicks her with it. She stands back like a raging bull ready to charge him. He stands with the knife tightly gripped in his hand, nose and face bleeding, hood still on his head.

He shouts, "You wanted the truth. Well, now you've got it." They both circle each other. Jena's face glowing red, even in the dark. Ted wipes the blood from his nose, holding the knife in his hand. "I don't know why you're so damn mad. We could have had the best life together. Better than you and Jake, better than anything."

Jena breathes hard. "The only life you're going to have is a life six feet under." She charges Ted and pushes him up against the window. The glass break outs. Ted drops the knife as he slips out the window. Holding on to the sill with one hand, he begs Jena to pull him in. She just stands there and watches while his hand slips.

"Jena, please. You don't want to do this."

"Yes, I do. I want to watch you beg, watch your hand slowly slip, and then I'm gonna watch as you fall to your death. You're wrong. I do want you to die." Ted tries to pull himself up, but he slips.

"Jake—my brother—he'll never forgive you."

Jake walks out from the shadows and pushes Jena out of the way. "Yes, I will." He releases Ted's hand and watches as he screams, falling to his death. Jake stares at his brother lying on the ground, body crooked.

Jena walks up beside him. "What did you hear?" she asks in a concerned voice.

Jake puts one hand on his wounded shoulder, walks toward the door, and stops. "Everything." He walks out of the room.

CHAPTER THIRTY-FOUR

Jena stands in the window with her arms crossed. She looks down at Ted's dead body with a cold and uncaring expression. *Destiny. Oh how it will find you, even when you aren't looking for it. Somehow it knows when to rear its ugly little head. When you feel safe, secure, that's when it wants to reveal itself—claim itself as the winner. That's until it meets me.*

She walks away from the window and goes down the stairs. Jake is sitting on the couch. He is in shock that his brother was responsible for hurting Jena and that he just killed him. Jena stands in front of him. "I know that was hard."

"He hurt you, Jena."

"He did, but he was still your brother."

He looks up at her. "Was he? He wasn't the brother I knew." He stands up and faces her. "Anyone who hurts you or tries to hurt you will not be a part of me." He walks to the back door of the house. "I have to bring Ted's body inside before someone finds him."

"I'll help you." Jena walks toward him.

"No. I'll do it alone. We'll have to put him somewhere until we can figure out what to do with him." Jake walks out and comes back dragging Ted's body inside and upstairs to the hall bathroom tub.

Jena stares off out the living room window to the McNeil's

house across the street. The moon is shining bright on the roof of the house. She thinks back to when she saw Mr. McNeil hiding next to his house holding a shovel, his dark figure glaring over at her house. *All the while plotting to kill his own wife and unknowingly becoming the man I grew to hate.*

Jake slowly walks downstairs. "We should get some sleep." He lies down on the floor without saying another word to Jena.

Jena lies down next to him, facing the opposite way. It is the first time in a long time that Jena has felt Jake distance himself from her. She knows that he is hurting from Ted's death. But she also knows that if anyone deserved to die, it was Ted. She is not glad he is dead; she is glad he is among the likes of Mr. McNeil. Two undeserving souls, trapped out there together with nothing and no one but themselves and other selfish yokes like them.

She closes her eyes and, just like magic, when she opens them the living room is lit up like a Christmas tree. The sun is blaring through the front window, casting sparkles off the dust that hangs in the air. Jena first thinks it is a dream, but she knows it isn't because of how she felt when her eyes opened. She leans over. Jake is lying shirtless under the blanket, sound asleep. The patch on his wounded shoulder is bloody. Jena touches it, his arm, and his chest. "You're my hero," she whispers as he sleeps. She looks around the living room as if she is seeing her own house for the first time. The antique vase her grandmother gave her mother shines like it never has before. Her parents' photo sits next to it on the mantle. Jena picks the photo up, wipes off the dust, and kisses it. She holds it close to her heart. She gently puts the photo down and walks to kitchen. She remembers when her mother cut her hand, how she helped her, and how her dad complained about having no meatloaf for dinner. She smiled. Her father's voice echoed in the kitchen. She remembers coming home from school when she was ten and discovering her father was in the kitchen trying to cook.

*   *   *

"Jena, honey, open the cabinet and hand your old man two cans of sweet peas." Jena opens the cabinet, reaches in for the cans, and hands them to her father, who is having a hard time keeping the pots on the stove from boiling over. She laughs at him. "Oh, you this is funny?" he says.

"Yes, Dad. You don't know how to cook."

"Well, your mother does all the cooking, but she is sick."

She goes over to give her dad a hug. "Do you want me to help?" He looks at her with desperate eyes. Jena starts helping him.

He kisses Jena on the forehead. "You're the best daughter ever."

"You're the best Dad ever." They both talk and laugh in the kitchen.

*　　*　　*

She walks back over to the living room, looks down at her bag, reaches in, and pulls out the letter her mother wrote her. Holding the letter in her hands, she walks upstairs to her mother's room. She sits on her bed. She could hear her mother's voice. "Jena … Jena, get up. It's time for school." She closes her eyes and she smells breakfast coming from downstairs. *How I miss you, Mom,* she thinks. Her mom would get up every morning to cook her breakfast. Jena could feel the tears brewing up inside of her as she held the letter in her hand. Her mother's lovely face flashes in her head—the sound of her sweet voice. *How much I took you for granted, Mom. I'm so sorry.* She slowly tears open the letter and unfolds it. She closes her eyes, but she knows this is long overdue. It's time for her to read it.

My dearest Jena,

There is so much I want to say to you, my darling daughter. I'm so very proud of you. The day that your father and I have been waiting for has finally arrived. I want you to know that I'm very proud of you. You have grown up to be such a beautiful, caring young lady. I couldn't have asked for a better daughter, a more wonderful, smart, and understanding person than you.

I'm so sorry that I have been so distant, but the death of your father crushed me in an unimaginable way that can't be described in any words on the earth. His death ripped my heart out. I knew I was never going to be the same after that night when I saw your father lying there dead on the floor, killed in cold blood. I wanted to die with him.

I did die, Jena. My mind took me with him, and I'm so sorry that I left you alone to deal with your own pain. It is unbearable for me to be in this house without him—to lie in that bed without his warm body beside mine. I've wanted to kill myself so many times, but every time I'd try I'd see your face—your little girl face, your eyes, your smile when you were a baby—and I couldn't do it. But, my sweetheart, the time has come for me to tell you the truth. A truth that may make you hate me in a way a daughter should never a hate a mother. There are things you don't know. Things that I've hidden from you. I now realize, though, that your obsession with Miles could lead you down a path of destruction and that I have to do everything in my power to stop that destruction from happening—even if it means I may lose you forever.

Your father and I fell in love in high school—but, my darling, he wasn't my first love. I was in love with Miles until he lied and cheated on me. That's when I broke off the relationship, and I started dating your father. Eventually your father and I got married. It was always our dream to have a beautiful daughter like you. We tried and tried, but it never happened. I felt so depressed, so lonely, and so desperate that one night I confided in Miles—a night that seems so long ago. Yet the blood on my hands from your father's death wasn't just from the bullet. It was my own doing ... Jena, Miles is your father. Miles McNeil is your father.

I know you must hate me. I hated myself for so long, until I saw your beautiful face the day you were born and the happiness that it brought your father. You were everything to him. His world. He loved you so much. I could never have told him the truth. I didn't have too; he knew and had forgiven me. He held me like he'd always held me, and loved me like he'd always loved me. The bond between your father and I was strong.

I had one weak moment that caused Miles to become obsessed with you—not because he was some dirty old man, but because he was your father. Miles wanted to build a relationship with you, but I had forbidden it. Your father hated when Miles was around you.. He didn't want you to know the truth.

Please never doubt the love I feel for you. It is so painful for me to have to tell you this. You're everything to me. When you are much older, you'll find that life isn't always so simple. The choices we make can lead us down a path of darkness, but we must forgive ourselves so others can find us in the light. True love can guide you and bring you out of any storm. The love I shared with your father is beyond this universe. He and I are one. We are one with each other, and we are one with you. Please don't destroy your life.

One day, my sweetheart, you will find a love so intense, so far beyond what this world will ever reveal. You will be in this world, but with him you will feel like you're in heaven. Every time your father held me in his arms, I was in heaven. I know that I will see your father again. We will sing, dance, and laugh again, and he will hold me so tight as he whispers in my ear, "I love you, Kitty. You're my light."

I love you, my sweet daughter. You are my heart, and you're my light. Please find it in your heart to forgive me.

Love you always,
Mom

The tears run down Jena's face like never before. She huffs and tries to catch her breath, but she feels the room closing in on her. The sun has risen. She has been born again—born back into the world. She chokes up with tears. Her emotions are out of control. She stands up, looks around the room, and runs downstairs.

Jake is standing in the living room. She stops and looks at him. He can see the letter in her hand. She opens the front door and runs—runs so fast. Jake calls for her. He runs behind her. She runs and runs until she is standing in front of her mother's grave. Tears stream down her face. She falls to the ground. Her knees cave in the dirt. "Mom!" she yells. Jake reaches for her; she folds her hands. "Don't." She screams even louder, "Mom. Mommy!" She lies down near the grave. "Mommy, please. I'm so sorry. I'm so sorry, Mommy." Jake's heart is breaking for her. Her pain is his. Her tears drop from her eyes onto her mother's grave." Mom! I'd do anything—anything—to bring you back! To have you here! Now! I ... I ... I can't go on like this. I can't be this person ..." Jena stands. "I won't be this person anymore." The wind blows through her hair. She puts her hand on her mother's tombstone. "You are the most wonderful person I could have ever asked to have as a mother." She breaks down again. "I will not, Mother ... I will not be like this anymore!" She turns around and starts running. Jake grabs her. She screams, "Let me go! Leave me alone!"

"Jena, stop!"

"No! I won't be this person, Jake. Not anymore!" She runs ... runs as fast as she can.

Jake follows her, calling her name behind her, "Jena! Jena!"

She doesn't stop until she gets to the police station's parking lot. Police officers are walking around. No one notices her. She breathes out and walks in the door. Officer Reyes is behind the counter. He looks up at her. Her face is red, her hair wild. She is breathing hard, with the letter gripped in her hand. He stands up.

"My name is Jena Parker, and I'm turning myself in."

Jake flings open the police door as Officer Reyes is handcuffing Jena. "You have the right to remain silent," Officer Reyes says.

Jake screams, "No! Stop!" Other officers grab hold of Jake. "Jena, don't!" She looks at him.

Officer Reyes holds Jena's arm. "Do you understand these rights?" Jena nods her head yes.

"No! It was me," Jake yells out.

Officer Reyes looks at him. "Were you there?"

Jake pauses. "Where?"

"When she was—"

Jena cuts off Officer Reyes. "No. He wasn't there. It was just me."

An officer comes running in the door. "We found a dead body in the tub at the Parker's house." He takes off his hat. "It has been identified at Ted Paterson."

Officer Reyes lets out an angry sigh. He grabs Jena's arm to take her away for booking. Jake fights to try to get loose from the officers. "Calm down or we are going to arrest you."

"Arrest me," he screams. "I don't care."

Officer Reyes is frustrated with Jake. "Lock him up until he cools down." Five police officers struggle to hold Jake down and take him to a jail cell. They push him in a cell, close the door behind him, and lock him in.

He braces on tightly to the jail bars and yells, "Don't arrest her! Jena!"

A criminal in the next cell yells back, "Give it up, man, she's done!"

He yells back, "Shut up!"

"Hey, I'm just trying to give you the real, hard facts."

Jake beats his hands on the bars, holds his head down, and tries to control his tears and anger. He sits on the bed to think what do next. He runs back to the bars and screams out. "I want my phone call! I want my phone call!"

A police officer walks up to him. "What are you screaming about?"

"I want my phone call. I'm supposed to get at least one phone call, and I want it."

The officer frowns. "If you attack me when I open the cell, I'm going to shoot you dead on the spot." He reaches in his pocket for the keys. "You got that, son?"

"I got it. Now let me out."

He opens the door, handcuffs Jake, and walks him to a pay phone. "Here's a quarter. Now make your damn call." The police officer stands right next to him.

Jake gives him an angry look. "Is there such a thing as privacy?"

Officer Tuck gives Jake a dirty look, crosses his arm, and backs up just a little. Raising his eyebrows, he waits for Jake to proceed with his call.

CHAPTER THIRTY-FIVE

"Turn forward." *Snap.* "Turn to the left." *Snap.* "Now turn to the right." Jena turns to the right as Officer Smith takes her photo. She is escorted to a jail cell. Walking the jail hall, a few women recognize her and start screaming her name.

"Jena! Jena!" Soon that entire area of the jail is chanting her name. "Jena Parker! Jena Parker!"

Officer Smith yells at them, "Shut up!"

One of the woman scream out, "You shut up. She's our hero! Jena! Jena!"

Jena looks at the women. Some were hookers. Others look like young girls like her, moms, and even a woman with a black eye and busted nose stares at her as she passes them. Officer Smith opens the cell door, takes off Jena's handcuffs, pushes Jena into the cell, and closes the door behind her. He whispers to her. "Now you're famous."

Jena backs away from the bars, turns, and faces the wall. The women continue to chant her name.

*   *   *

Jake calls his mother. She doesn't answer. "Mom, I'm jail." He hangs up the phone. The officers grabs his arm, takes him back to his cell, slams the door, and then walks away.

Jena and Jake both sit in their cells. Jena stares off thinking about her mother, her father, and the road that brought her to this lonely jail cell.

Jake's only thoughts are of Jena. *What is happening to her? Are they hurting her? Is she all right?* He can't think of anything else. The police guard brings him his food tray. He looked over. "I'm not hungry."

The guard sets the tray inside Jake's cell. "We don't care." He walks off, leaving the tray.

Jake looks at the tray, but he doesn't move. He stares at the ceiling, desperately hoping that he can find some way to help Jena get out of jail and avoid going to jail for the rest of her life. The thought of never seeing or touching her again is driving him insane. Jake begins to cry, breaking down in tears. *Jena, damn it, I let you down. I'm so sorry, babe. I'll find a way to get you out of here.* He lets the tears run down his face.

*   *   *

Jena sits in her cell with her head down. Her mind finally lands on Jake. She feels guilty for dragging him into her insane world—for letting him fall in love with her, knowing that she is trapped to live a life of revenge and despair. She lies on the bed, stares up at the top bunk, close her eyes, and asks the Lord to forgive her. "Forgive me, Father, for I have sinned." She puts the covers over her body and head to block out the light. The guard stands watches her, gives her a long stare, reaches for the covers, hesitates, sets the food tray down instead, and locks the cell. He stands outside the cell and watches her to see if she'll move, if he can get a glimpse of the famous Jena Parker.

Jena doesn't move. She can hear the guard's heavy breathing. She waits until he leaves to remove the blankets from her head. She peeks over at the food, puts the blankets back on her face, and closes her eyes. *I'm truly afraid of tomorrow, but even so it will come. And when it does, I'll have to embrace it. This is only way I will survive.*

*   *   *

Jake doesn't sleep a wink. He watches the ceiling of the cell most of the night. At times he gets up, stands against the wall, and then lies down again. It is the most restless, loneliest night of his life.

The guard opens Jake's cell. "You're free to leave. You're mother has bailed you out."

Jake gets up. "I didn't know I was arrested."

"Well, now you do." He cuffs Jake and pushes him out of the cell.

Mrs. Paterson is waiting up front, depressed and sad. Her eyes are red, her face looks worn out from depression. She runs up to Jake after the handcuffs are removed. "Ted. He's gone."

Jake doesn't move. "Sorry, Mom."

"Jake, let's get out of here."

"Mom, I can't leave."

"What do you mean, 'you can't leave'?"

Jake can't bear to hurt his mother in the police station. He leaves with her and reluctantly gets in the car. Jake seems aggravated. He doesn't speak.

Mrs. Paterson is nervous. "Jena killed your brother, didn't she? She murdered him."

Jake tries to remain silent.

"She's a cold-hearted killer, and I hope she rots in jail." Jake gets angry, but he lets his mother vent. "What did poor Ted do to her to make her hate him so?" She starts crying. "He was such a nice, peaceful kid. And now he's dead. My son is dead!" she screams. "He didn't deserve it!"

Jake loses it. "Yes, he did!"

Mrs. Paterson is in shock. "What are you talking about?"

"Jena didn't kill Ted. I did."

"What!" she yells in shock.

"I killed him."

"Why would you kill your own brother! For that slut!"

"She's not a slut, and he deserved to die for what he did to her."

She slams on the brakes. "He did not deserve to die!"

"Mom, Ted raped Jena! He raped her and beat her!"

Mrs. Paterson stops and stares off into the distance. "Get out, Jake." Mrs. Paterson says in settled voice.

Jake sits for a moment. "Mom," he calls.

She yells, out of control, "Get out of my car now!" Jake gets out. He looks back at his mom. Her eyes are bulging out, her face as red as a beet. "Don't you ever speak to me or your father again." She spins out.

Jake watches as she spins away, the car wiggling out of control. Jake walks down the road. He has nowhere to go. No money. No family. No Jena. He's lonely and lost. A white car pulls up next to him. A girl sticks her head out. "Get in."

He looks. It's Chance. "I'm not getting into your car."

"Jake, you need help. You have nowhere to go. You may not like me, but let's face it—I'm all you've got right now."

Jake isn't thinking straight. If he has to use Chance to somehow free Jena, then that's what he is going to do. He gets in the car. Chance drives toward her home. "Just how are you going to explain to your parents why I'm in your house?"

Chance smiles. "My parent are away, so they'll never know."

"Where are they?"

Chance hesitates. "They're out of the country, like they always are. You can sleep in my older sister's room. It's a comfortable room—has a bathroom and everything." Chance reaches for Jake's hand. He pushes her away. "I'm just trying to be friendly. To comfort you," she says in a sly voice. "I know how hard this for you—to know Jena has been arrested ... that you may never see her again."

"Oh, I'll see her."

"Jake, you have to be realistic. Jena has killed multiple people. There's no doubt she's going to go to jail for life. Probably even the electric chair."

Jake gets angry with her. "Chance, you killed Carol—you should be in jail."

Chance is silent. "Well, I'm not. And those bastards don't know that I killed Carol." She looks over at Jake. "Are you going to tell them?"

"I'll do whatever it takes to get Jena out of jail, even if it means turning you in."

"Well you can tell them I killed her, but they won't believe you. Jena is the one they want. They don't want me."

"Please, can we not talk about this anymore? I have to find a way to break her free."

Chance says in a rude voice, "Maybe she's already free. Have you ever thought about that?"

Jake snaps at her. "She loves me, Chance. I know she doesn't want to be apart from me. And right now, the way I feel, I'd kill for her freedom." He looks over at her. She remains quiet.

CHAPTER THIRTY-SIX

Jena sits in her jail cell. She doesn't want to eat. She doesn't want to think about the world outside.

The guard opens her cell door. There's a man standing next to him wearing a blue suit, a red tie, and carrying a briefcase. He walks up to Jena and stands in front of her. "I'm your lawyer." Jena is silent. "My name is Josh Pillars, and I'm a court-appointed attorney sent here to represent you."

"I don't want your representation."

"Oh, but you should think about it. I'm one of the best attorneys in this little town. I know I can get you back your freedom."

"I don't want to be free."

He sets his briefcase down, walks around the cell, stares out the tiny cell window. "So you want to be locked in a hellhole cell like this for the rest of your life?"

"This is what I deserve."

He claps his hands, applauding her. "So you deserve this?" He turns around. "What about the ones who you hurt you? What do they deserve?"

"They got what they deserved."

The lawyer tries to get into her head. "So are you telling me that there is no one worth it for you to get out of here?" Jena thinks. "Ah, yes—there is someone, right? Someone you care deeply about."

She thinks of Jake. "That's none of your business."

"Maybe not, but you can let it be my business. Let me represent you."

Jena stares up at the lawyer. "I'm not innocent."

He laughs. "You're not guilty until the court says so, and even then we can still fight it." He whispers to her, "Don't throw your life away. What's done is already done."

Jena smirks. "You're a slick lawyer. Why do you really want to represent me?"

"Because I believe I can get an innocence verdict from the jurors. I believe I can get them to set you free." He comes closer to her. "So you can be free forever. You won't have to look over your shoulder or worry about the cops chasing you down. You'd be free to go out into the world as you please. Free to love ... Jake."

She looks at the lawyer. "You don't know him."

"No, not personally, but I've heard you two are inseparable. That you have a love so passionate that you'd sacrifice yourself, claiming a murder he committed."

"What are you talking about?"

"I'm talking about his brother, Ted."

"Ted's death wasn't his fault."

"Really? I believe the district attorney will find otherwise. It's only a matter of time. They will go after him, and I know you don't want that."

"No ... I don't."

"Jena, let me be your lawyer. Let's distract them with our case. Your case is indeed very, very enticing to this town. To the police department. To the world."

"No one cares about me."

"You see, that's where you're wrong. Your story is unlike any other. People in town crave more news about you. The press is going crazy trying to find out every detail about you. Heck, there are at least twenty lawyers lined up outside to come represent you." The lawyer holds his hand out. "You don't believe me? Come see. Come look out the window."

Jena walks slowly to the small window in her cell. Jena looks out the barred window. There are people everywhere. News reporters from all the television channels. Reporters from different states, fighting over who will stand in the closest spot near the jailhouse. Little children, families, people with signs supporting Jena: "Free Jena Parker," "Jena Parker is innocent," "Jena Parker was a victim herself, so why is she in jail?" There are hundreds of people outside the jailhouse. Jena stares in amazement. Her eyes scan the crowd. She sees a man holding a big sign: "Free Reda Jones." It's Franklin.

"See, I told you. Look, you're famous."

Jena walks away from the window. She thinks about Jake. The love they share. All of the sacrifices he's made for her. His beautiful eyes, his smile, and his hands as they wrap around her body, handling her gently like a precious jewel. "Why should I trust you instead of one of the other lawyers?"

"Because some of them were hired by the district attorney to convict you. Others have their own personal reasons for wanting this case—I guess you can say, the eye of greed."

"What about you?"

"Well, I see a case that restarts my career."

"So you have a motive too."

"Yes I do, but my motive is no good if I lose. I want to win! In doing that, I not only get you back your freedom and give you back your love, but I also redeem myself. We have to give and take—that's the way of the world—but it doesn't have to be bad. We can take this extraordinary moment to tell your story in a way it will never been told if you don't let me help you."

Jena stares out the cell bars. "I will never see Jake again if I don't fight to get out of here. I know him. He won't rest until he gets me out, in turn, leading his life down a road of nothingness. And we still won't see other." She turns around. "I don't have any money."

The lawyer puts on a bright smile. "You don't need any. The court supplies me, and we'll use that to our advantage." The lawyer holds his hand out to Jena again. "This time, it's to seal the deal." Jena shakes it. "Welcome to my world."

The lawyer calls for the guard and looks back at Jena. "Don't worry, we're going to win this. Our first hearing is tomorrow morning. Be ready." The lawyer leaves Jena's cell.

She walks back over to the window. The guard comes back in to bring her breakfast. He sits it down. "Looking out the window to find freedom?" he asks.

"No. I'm just looking out the window."

The guard comes closer. "Good, because freedom isn't outside this window. Freedom is in your heart, and that's only place you're going to find it." Jena's a bit surprised to hear those words come from a jail guard. He closes the cell door. "Don't hide from yourself. Face it. Understand why things are the way they are. Seek, and you shall find."

But what will she find? She thinks, *When I pull back the curtains, will I find the Jena Parker ... or Jena Gray?*

The day goes by quickly for her. The many, many people who crowd around the jailhouse keep Jena fascinated by their curiosity of her life. Franklin seems like her biggest advocate. She sees him talking to people and showing them his sign, chanting and cheering with people, raising his hands up in the air. Jena can feel Franklin's emotions for her.

*   *   *

"Time to wake up, Jena Parker. You have a busy day ahead." The guard taps on the bars with his stick.

Her lawyer stands behind him. He walks in the cell with a smile on his face. "Are you ready?"

"Yes."

"Well, let's go." The guard handcuffs Jena and then walks her out of the cell, down the hall, into the courtroom. News reporters are all lined up in the hall, trying to talk to police officers, lawyers, anyone they can get information from. The court is packed, with people standing and fighting to get in the doorway.

The judge already seems frustrated. "Bailiff, get these people out of my courtroom!"

"Yes, Your Honor." The bailiff starts pushing people out. "Move people. We can't hold all of you." News reporters and lawyer attempt to hand him money. They'll try everything to remain in the courtroom. Bailiff Charles Thomas frowns at the money. "You take me for a fool? Get out of here!" He yells at the young reporter. "Hmm … twenty dollars. Man must be crazy."

The judge screams, "Order!" She slams down her gavel. "Order! I want order in my court!" Jena stands in the back doorway. Franklin peeks in the main doorway, sees her, and screams, "Jena! Hey, Jena!" Bailiff Thomas slams the door. Jena walks in the room behind her lawyer.

"State your case," the judge says.

"Your Honor, we are here today to set bail for Jena Parker," Jena's lawyer says. "This young lady hasn't been a threat to society. All the charges that the district attorney has submitted to the court can be debunked. No one has seen Jena Parker kill. Everything they have is just hearsay. Your Honor, we believe that Jena Parker is innocent, and she deserves a chance to prove her innocence in a court of jurors—not by the district attorney's office."

District Attorney Al Adams stands up. "Your Honor, how are you?"

"I'm just fine, Al. Now proceed."

"Your Honor, this young lady," he points at Jena, "may look innocent, but she has committed multiple crimes in Maplesville, New York, and other counties. We can't let her go free to roam around our nice town and to kill more people. You're an honorable judge, and I know you don't want to have a murderer running lose—"

Attorney Pillars interrupts. "Your Honor, there's is no evidence that Jena is a going to kill anyone."

Adams outshouts him. "Your Honor, I don't want to disgrace this court, but this young girl," he puts his head down, "well, she killed own mother."

Everyone in court starts talking among themselves. News reporters take notes. Everyone eyes Jena. Jena puts her head down.

Pillars touches Jena's shoulder. He walks up closer to the judge, turns around, and stares at Adams. "Your Honor, we all can see that the DA just wants a grand show, but the fact remains that they don't have any proof that Jena killed anyone. Do they have pictures? Do they have witnesses? The question is do they have the appropriate evidence to stop bail for this young girl?"

The judge stares around the room. Everyone sits in silence, waiting for her to make a decision. "Attorney Pillars, please go back to your seat. I have reviewed some of the information in the case. I can see that Jena Parker hasn't had any past conformations with the law or the court. But there are still some concerns about these murders that were committed coupled with the fact that she couldn't be accounted for. Even after she was accused, she still could not be accounted for. Therefore, I believe I have a duty to this court, to this town, and to the judicial law process to deny bail for Ms. Parker."

People stand up. Reporters start talking, and DA Adams smiles. The judge yells, "Order in the court." The judge looks at Jena. "Ms. Parker, you're denied bail, and you are to remain in jail until your court case. At that time, the DA and your attorney will provide me with more evidence so I may make an appropriate decision on whether you will be charged. Do you understand?"

Jena nods her head. "Yes, Your Honor, I do."

"Good. Court is adjourned."

"All rise," the bailiff says, releasing the court.

CHAPTER THIRTY-SEVEN

Attorney Pillars begins putting all of his paperwork back in his bag. The court guard comes to get Jena. "Jena, this isn't over." Jena nods her head and leaves with the guard.

Adams tugs up on his pants while walking over to Pillars. "You're taking a hefty case." He laughs. "You're in a little over your head, aren't you?"

"That's what you seem to think." Pillars grabs his briefcase and walks away out the courtroom.

Adams talks as he follows behind him, "Pillars, you don't have a chance. This girl is going down." Pillars keeps walking as Adams screams behind him, "Your career is already blown, why take another chance?" Pillars walks out of the courthouse building.

News reporters swamp him with questions. A reporter asks, "Is Jena Parker going to prison? Did she kill her mother, Mr. McNeil, and the man on train?"

Pillars stops. "I have no answers to give you right now."

A reporter gets angry and yells out, "Oh, yeah you do! So tell us what we want to hear!"

"Yeah," another screams out. "We've been waiting out here all night! All day! We want answers."

Pillars muscles his way through the crowd. "Well, you aren't going to get any today." He gets into his car and drives off.

DA Adams comes out. The reporters all swamp him with questions as well.

"Is Jena Parker guilty?" one reporter asks.

Adams has no problem answering. "Yes, she is, and we're going to make sure she spends every day of her miserable life in jail."

Another yells out, "What if she's found not guilty."

Adams turns around and gets in the reporter's face. "She won't."

The reporter gets cocky. "Well, you don't know that for sure, do you? You're just trying to convict this young lady."

Adams pokes his finger in the reporter's face; suddenly, he becomes the news. "What I'm trying to do is make sure a killer is put behind bars. You got that!" Adams pushes his way through the news crowd. Adams leaves. The reporters scramble back around the jailhouse.

*   *   *

Jake wakes up. Chance is staring at him. "Are you hungry?" she asks.

"It's early, Chance."

"I know. That's why I'm up. I'd like to make you breakfast."

"You don't have to do that."

"Yes, I do. You're a guest in my house, and I want you to feel at home."

"This isn't home, Chance."

"It's home for now." She stands up and Jake realizes she is wearing nothing but G-string red lace panties.

He looks away. "I suppose you plan on making breakfast in your underwear?"

She snaps the string of the underwear. "Oh, this old thing. It is kind of sexy, don't you think?"

Jake removes the covers, keeping his eyes focused away from her. "I'd like to get up now so I can go see Jena."

Chance stands in the doorway. "Well, I don't think you're going to get to see her today."

"Why not?"

"Because I just heard that the DA managed to stop her bail, at least until the next court hearing."

Jake jumps out of bed. He's just wearing briefs. Chance glares at him. "Get out, Chance." She stares for moment and then walks out and closes the door. Jake walks to the window. *Damn. I have to do something—but what?* Jake moves the curtain back. There are nails in the window. He tries to open it, but he can't. He looks for something in the room to use to break the window, but there isn't anything. He runs to the door and tries to open it, but it's locked. "Chance!" he screams. "Open this door."

Chance is standing outside the door, smiling. "Not until you say you love me."

"Are you nuts?"

She plays with her hair. "Maybe."

"Open the damn door now!"

"No. Like I said, you have to tell me you love me."

"I'm never telling you that."

"Then I'm never opening this door. Oh, I hear my parents calling me."

"You said your parents were out of town."

"Got to go. I'll be back with breakfast, and hopefully you'll have some very nice words to say to me." She leaves him banging on the door.

"Open this door! Open it!" He puts on his clothes, muttering, "I'm going to kill that girl." *Don't worry, Jena, I'll get out of here somehow.*

* * *

Jena is led back to her cell. The guard walks behind her. "Not good, huh?"

"No. Not at all."

"Well, you shouldn't be down about it. Most people don't get bail. Some people get bail, but it's too high for them to make it, and they end up right back in this place called jail."

Jena turns around quickly. "What do you want from me? Why are you talking to me?"

"Calm down, little lady. I'm just a very sociable person."

"Really? Is that what it is? You're just being nice to me?"

"Turn around, and keep walking," the guard says.

Jena turns around and starts walking. "It must be something for you to have to see criminals come in here, day in and day out." She tries to get inside the guard's head. "You've probably seen it all. Killers, robbers ... woman who have been raped, beaten, or both."

"I've certainly seen enough." He opens Jena's cell door, takes off the cuffs, and then steps out and closes the door. "My mother went to jail when she was seventeen. She was charged with murder." Jena stares at the guard. "You're not going to ask me who she murdered?"

Jena turns around. "No, I'm not."

"She murdered her father for raping her. She was sentenced to life in prison. But back then they were a little more sympathetic toward women, so she got released early for good behavior. That's when she met my father, Leroy. She and my father fell in love, had a baby—me."

Jena turns around. "Why are telling me this story?"

"Well, maybe I feel a little sympathetic toward you. I've heard the stories about what happened to you up at that college. Can't help but think about my own mother and what hell she went through being in jail just for killing an asshole. Young girls like you shouldn't have to go through such pain and humiliation. My mother died three years ago. She was a good mother. Gave me everything she could, despite her horrible past. The only way she got through it all is that she never gave in to this world's letdowns. She served her time. Forgave her Father. Regained her spirit—took it back from the darkness—allowed herself to love and be loved. Most woman probably wouldn't want to have a baby after what she went through, but she did everything she could to have me. So I'm telling you, don't give in to the darkness. Fight it! That boy, Jake, he loves you, and I can tell you love him too. Life comes with the good and the bad. It's unfortunate that you've seen so much of the bad at such an early age, but those challenges you can overcome." The guard walks away, leaving Jena with a lot to think about.

Jena realizes that she isn't the only woman to face such challenges—to have done something that society deemed wicked. She walks back to her cell window. *There are still hundreds of people standing outside with signs—some nice, some not so nice—all out there because of me*, she thinks. *I wasn't born to be this way.*

Jena thinks back to when she was that simple girl living a simple life. She and Jake would walk down the halls of the school, talking and laughing. How they'd sit at the lake and talk for hours. How she'd always known that Jake loved her, but their friendship was so precious to her that she never wanted him to confess to it—because if he confessed, than she would have to too. That's her fear: she doesn't want to lose the one person who she knows can give her a life of unconditional love—the same kind of love her parents shared.

She remembers the dance she and Jake shared. Looking into his eyes was like looking into the doors of all her inner desires. She could she them getting married. Her standing in a beautiful lace wedding dress. Him with a sky-blue tuxedo. Just them and the minister out in the middle of nowhere, standing on top of an ice mountain, blue skies, and beautiful white doves flying around them. She could see their house and children running around playing. Jumping up and down on the couches. Jake coming inside to play with them. A handsome boy and two beautiful little girls—twins. All that shined in Jake's eyes as they danced and laughed together. *Why can't I have that?* She thinks. *Why can't I just live a simple life of eternal love with Jake?*

The guard comes back with Jena's food tray. He walks inside, sets it down. "You might want to eat. Keep your strength up."

"Thank you."

The guard walks out. "Remember what I said earlier. Don't give up."

Jena eats for the first time since she was arrested. A sense of confidence comes over her. She wants to see Jake so badly, and she hopes tomorrow she will.

*　　*　　*

The night falls quickly. Jake is still trapped in the room. All day he refused to eat or say what Chance wanted him to say. Chance stands outside the door. "I know you're hungry." Jake is angry and doesn't respond to her. "I'm not a cruel person, Jake. I don't want to treat you this way."

He yells out, "Then don't! Let me go!"

"I can't do that."

"Why not? I don't love you, Chance, and I never will. I don't even understand why you're doing this. We barely spoke in high school, and now you want me to tell you I love you?"

Chance's voice is sad. "I just want someone to love me. Someone to just want me for me." Jake sighs. "Everyone wanted Carol or Jena, but what about me? Why doesn't anyone just want to hold me in their arms." She wraps her arms around herself.

"Chance, your parents can't be happy about you locking me in this room." Chance is silent. "Chance? Are you still there?"

"Jake, my parents are dead. I killed them both. They're upstairs lying in bed, all dressed up like dolls. That's what they were to me—just dolls. They never spent any time with me. They were always out of town, going somewhere, seeing the world without me. Well, I guess now they're permanently out of town."

"You're better than this, Chance."

"Am I? You love Jena, and she's a murderer. Why can't you love me?"

"Because I can't, so let me go."

"No. I won't." Jake bangs on the door.

Chance screams, "Jake, you can bang all you want, but I ain't opening this door. I won't let her have you." She lowers her voice and says, "There are candy bars behind the stuffed animals. That's all you'll get until you love me. Until you make love to me."

Jake bangs on the door harder. She jumps. "You get this straight: I'll never love you, I'll never make love to you, and when I get out of this room—and I will get out of this room—I'm going to make you pay for every moment you kept me away from Jena." He kicks the door. "You got that!"

CHAPTER THIRTY-EIGHT

Several weeks have passed since Jena's arrest. Jake is still trapped at Chance's house, and Jena is still trapped in her cell.

Attorney Pillars pays Jena a visit. "Sorry I haven't been able to come as often as I hoped, but I have other clients." He sits down next to Jena. "We have court in a week, so we must prepare for it. Jena, I have some bad news. The DA has found some evidence. They have photos of you entering the hotel where Mr. McNeil was allegedly murdered—photos of you walking in with him, and leaving with Jake. Now, I don't believe that their case is strong. However, they have you on camera, and that sends a strong opinion to the judge. The thing is, they don't have the murder weapon, and they can't prove without doubt that you murdered him. The other murders— the doctor on the train, the clerk, Ted," his speech slows, "and your mother—they can't be proven at this time. But the DA will still try to link you to all of those murders. I'm prepared to fight against any allegations they bring up in court. I want you to know that I'm on your side, and I will bring forth an innocent verdict."

Jena stands up. "I want to see Jake."

Attorney Pillars stands. "Jena, the police haven't been able to find Jake since you were arrested."

"What!"

"He's missing, Jena. They can't say for sure if he's dead or if he's alive. They just don't know. They have been searching for him to ask him questions, so have I, but we can't—"

Jena is hysterical. "What do you mean, you can't?" She grabs Attorney Pillars' suit jacket. "You look here—you better find him, or I'll be that creature in the night."

He gently removes Jena's hands. "I know you're upset, but you can't lose it now. We're too close. The DA is looking for every inch of doubt he can present to the judge. I'm sure Jake is all right, but if you get convicted, you'll never know!" He grabs his briefcase and calls for the guard. "I'll be back in four days, the day before our next hearing. We will win this, so pull yourself together." He walks away.

Jena's emotions come to a standstill. She feels frozen in time. All the magic she felt, her hopes, her dreams, they all lifted from her body the moment Pillars gave her the news about Jake. She falls to her knees and bursts out in a whirlwind of tears. Lying on the floor face up, her hands pinned to the floor, every fear she'd had, love, sadness, and anger all disappear from her. She feels lifeless, as if millions of people walked up to her and, one by one, each took a piece of her soul, leaving her alone to bare the truth of the madness she created—that the truth of her world is more harsh than she had imagined, much more unbearable than her heart can withstand. She can see the horizon up ahead, feel the cool breeze of freedom, but the further she walks without her soul, the less she can feel the breeze and the further the horizon seems.

Then the darkness comes, and all of the people around her are gone. Her arms lift in the air, back to the wind as it strips her of every piece of clothing, leaving her bare naked for her self-shame to judge her and for her wickedness to laugh at her. Nowhere to run. Nowhere to hide. The ugly truth has found her, taken everything from her, and left her to live out the rest of life to never forget it. She'll walk the earth naked, shamed, and forever without love or even hate … nothing.

The tears run down her face to the floor. Jena has finally reached that breaking point, the end of her cold raindrops. "Jake," she utters as she lies in a pool of her own tears. She is exhausted from the emotional breakdown. Lying on the floor, she slips away to the only place that ever truly made sense to her. Her dreams.

*   *   *

A bus horn blows as people are crossing a crowded street. The bus driver yells, "Come on, people, get out of the street. Move it!" Jena can feel she's in her body, but she can't see herself. There's a tall man standing next to her. She sees him smiling at her. He's talking to her, but she can't see his face or remember what he's saying. He's wearing a black trench coat, dark sunglasses, and a scarf around his neck. He's carrying a briefcase and a gun. She walks next to him across the street. She is sharp and poised. People are walking around every corner. Jena and the man stand in front of a tall glass building. Her eyes follow his up to read the sign: Airport. The man opens the door for her, and they begin walking through the airport like secret agents. Jena can read his lips as he talks. "We have to check in now," he says. He speaks in code words that only she can understand. They walk through crowds of people at the airport. A little boy eating ice creams smiles as he passes with his mother. They all seem like they're in a rush to get somewhere. The man begins talking to one of the ticket attendants, who is standing around giving out information and directions. He taps Jena on the shoulder to signal it is time to go. They begin walking and then step on the airport escalator. There are mirrors on both sides. Jena looks at herself. She can finally see herself clearly. She isn't the young Jena anymore. Her hair is shorter and colored black, and she is wearing black shades, black boots, and a red leather trench coat with a gun at her side. She looks at herself quickly and smirks, and then she looks forward.

Jena is shocked to see herself. She wants the older Jena to look back at the mirror, but she never does. She sees the man and her walking, their backs facing her in the dream. They give the flight attendant their tickets. He gestures for her to walk in front of him. He follows her in as they board the plane. Jena can't see beyond this point, and she feels her body drifting away from the attendant, away from the crowded airport, and away from her dream.

*   *   *

She suddenly opens her eyes. The cell room is dark. She finds herself splattered in wet tears on the floor. She gets up, wipes herself off, and stands by the bars. Looking out down the hall, she sees it's empty. No guards. The other inmates asleep. She lies back on her cot, drapes the blankets around her body, and tries to recall the dream. The man, the airport, the mirror, me … that was me. She ponders the dream until the morning sun shines in her window. The dream stimulated something inside her. She realizes that she isn't going to be a young girl forever, that she is going to become a woman one day—a woman like the guard's mother. *Will I be free?* she thinks. Days go by quickly, and soon the day comes for her to return back to court.

*   *   *

Jake is still trapped in Chance's house, surviving off of only candy bars, water from the bathroom sink, and his own anger.

Chance comes to the door. "Aren't you tired of being caged up like an animal?"

Jake is quiet. His anger has overcome him, and he's done speaking to Chance. His only reason for living is Jena, and now he knows the time has come; he has to break free from Chance's insane institution to rescue the woman he loves.

She yells, "So you're not going to speak to me? Well, you can just die in there!" She walks away, out of the house, gets in her car, and speeds off.

*　　*　　*

The guard opens Jena's cell. She leaves to conduct her daily hygiene and then returns to her cell to eat. She'll be left there until it's time for her to go to court. The guard comes to her cell. "You have a visitor."

"I thought I'm not supposed to get to see any visitors."

"Well, we're not supposed to allow it, but seeing as you are going to court today I'm going to let you. She says she's your aunt Denise."

Jena stands up. "My aunt? Really?"

"Yeah. She looks kind of young to be an aunt, but she sure seems eager to see you before you go to court. Now, I'm going to sneak you in a room. You'll have five minutes—that's all." The guard walks Jena to the room, lets her in, and closes the door.

The chair turns around. "Hello, Jena," Chance says.

"So I see you're not only trying to pass yourself off as me, but also as my aunt?"

"I just wanted to come by to say hello."

"Well, that's quite odd—since the last time I saw you I wanted to rip you to pieces. You think if you can dress up like me, look like me, that you'll be me?"

Chance stands. "No, but I do understand why you love Jake. He's a handsome one, especially when he sleeps."

"Where is he?"

"Oh, in my bedroom."

Jena runs up to her. "You better be glad I'm still in these handcuffs, because I'd really be convicted for murder if I wasn't."

Chance laughs. "You're going to jail anyway, and I'm going to have Jake all to myself. He's a little reluctant right now, but when you're locked up and he's horny, I'm going to be the one to satisfy him." Jena and Chance continue to confront each other.

*　　*　　*

Jake tries to pull the door open. He walks around the room trying to figure out a way to get out. Throwing the bed over, he takes the bed frame and slams it up against the wall until it crumbles apart. He takes a piece of the wood and uses it to break the window out. He grabs his things and jumps out the window.

He sees a woman walking down the street on her cell. "Ma'am." The woman gives him a crazy look. "Ma'am, please—I need to call the police." She hands him the phone; he dials 911. An operator answers and asks for the reason for the call. "Yes, there's been a murder at 115 Lowtowers Road. Hurry. The Killer is Chance Middleton. She's killed her mother and father." Jake hands the phone back to the woman, who's in shock and instantly calls back to tell the person she'd been on the phone with that there's been another murder in town.

Jake hitches a ride to the courthouse. The traffic leading there is backed up. "What's going on, man?" he asks the driver.

"Where you been? That mass murderer Jena Parker's trial is today. Today we'll find out if she's going to jail for life or going to be set free to kill more people. We're only a few minutes away, but it looks like we're going to be here for hours." Jake gets out of the car and runs like he's never ran before. People stare at him as he passes.

Jake walks through the jailhouse doors. The office is empty, since all of the police officers are out manning the traffic, taking interviews from the press, and standing guard for possible riots at the courthouse. The jail guard walks out and discovers Jake.

"I know you."

"Sir ... out of breath. I really need to see Jena before she goes to trial."

"You're the kid that loves her, right?"

"Yes, sir. I love her. Please help."

"Well, she's in with a relative right now." He looks around. "Come on."

Just then an APB comes over his walkie-talkie. "Ten-four, go head." He listens as he walks Jake to the room.

"There've been two more murders on Lowtowers Road. Everyone be on the lookout for a young lady about five feet five, red hair. She's Chance Middleton, possible suspect in the murder of her parents."

The guard and Jake walk quickly to the visitation room. "Man, what's going on in this town?" the guard says as he opens the door. They look in and see that Chance has pulled a knife on Jena and is about to stab her.

Jake yells out, "That's her! That's Chance."

The guard pulls out his gun. "Put the knife down!"

"Put it down, Chance!" Jake yells out. Jena just stares Chance in the eyes.

Two more cops walk in the room. They pull out their guns and circle Chance. "Put it down!" one yells out.

Chance is trapped. She surrenders, dropping the knife. The cops grab her. "Chance Middleton, you're under arrest for the murders of your parents and the attempted murder of an inmate."

The guard runs to Jena and holds her close to him. Chance gives Jena a dirty look. Jena smiles at her. "Well, you wanted to be my twin—now you are." The police officers walk Chance out.

Jake stares at Jena. The guard walks Jena to the door, but he feels bad for Jake. "Look, you two have ten seconds. Make it count." He steps outside the door.

Jake grabs her, holds her in his arms, and kisses her face all over. "I love you. I love you, Jena."

The guard grabs Jena's arm and takes her back to her cell.

CHAPTER THIRTY-NINE

Attorney Pillars is searching for his client. He goes to Jena's cell, sees she is missing, and yells for the guard. He sees the guard walking behind Jena down the hall. "Where have you been, guard? It's time for court. Please bring Ms. Parker along now." Pillars walks swiftly to the courtroom.

The circus has already begun. News reporters are everywhere, some fighting each other to get in the courtroom. Hundreds of people stand outside the courthouse waiting for the verdict. People scream Jena's name. "Jena! Jena! Jena!"

The DA walks into the courtroom with confidence, smiles at Pillars, and winks. Pillars is nervous.

"All rise. Here is the Honorable Judge Mary Cliffersom. You may be seated."

DA Adams begins. "Your Honor, I've provided supporting evidence that Jena Parker was on the hotel surveillance tape, which I believe puts her at the scene of the crime at the time of the murder. She was seen leaving a New York club with the victim as well. Ms. Parker was checked in at the hotel where the clerk was murdered. She also purchased a ticket for the train where the doctor was murdered. We also believe that she is responsible for the murders of her mother, Kathleen Parker; her neighbor's wife, Mrs. McNeil;

and Ted Paterson. Your Honor, the evidence is clear that this young lady," he points as he shouts, "killed all of these people. Do not let this murderer run free in our town! In our society! It is simply ludicrous! She's a dangerous individual, and she should be locked up behind bars."

"Okay, District Attorney Adams, thank you. Attorney Pillars, please state your case."

Pillars looks at Jena. "Your Honor, has the DA provided you the murder weapon? I believe that answer is no. Has the DA provided any other evidence beside hearsay that Jena Parker murdered these people in cold blood? I believe that answer is also no. Your Honor, how could this court convict a young girl for murders based on this evidence? It may put her or someone who looks like her at these scenes, but it doesn't mean she murdered these people. Your Honor, my heart truly goes out to the murder victims and their families, but to send a young girl to jail for these crimes when there is no murder weapon—well, I find that to be ludicrous."

The judge says, "I will review the case, and the jurors will make their decision. Court will adjourn for one hour."

The bailiff says, "All rise." Everyone leaves the courtroom.

Pillars feels confident about his plea to free Jena. Adams grabs his coat and walks out of the courthouse. Pillars smiles at Jena as the guard takes her back to her cell to wait for court to come back in session.

An hour has passed. Everyone is back in the courtroom. "All rise."

The judge sits down. All twelve jurors take their seats. "District Attorney Adams and Attorney Pillars, now would be the time for you to present your closing arguments."

Adams goes first. He walks up to the twelve jurors and smiles at them. "Do you see my smile? It's nice, right? I look like a nice guy—someone who would never, ever hurt any of you. But you know that I'm here in court today fighting for the safety of the great people of this town. You know that I'm smiling because I want to convict a murderer today, a murderer who smiles and whose face may appear innocent. But just like my motives to sway you to believe my case against Jena Parker," he turns around, "her attorney, Attorney Pillars, is here to smile at you to make you believe that an innocent, young girl couldn't have possibly committed these crimes. That somehow she could be in all of these places where these people were murdered and not be the murderer—I find that to be the biggest smile of all. I would tell you jurors to ask yourselves this: if you knew that a person was at ten stores with ten murders," he stares them all in the face, "what's the possibility that this person didn't commit the crimes? Thank you." DA Adams looks over at Attorney Pillars and Jena, lifts his eyebrow, and sits down.

Attorney Pillars is concentrating in his chair. He looks over at Jena, back at the spectators and reporters in the room, and then he walks up to the jurors. "Good afternoon to you all. I know that you're all exhausted and ready to get home to your families, so I'm not going to keep you long. I'm going to keep you only long enough, in hopes that you leave this courtroom with a clear conscious that you didn't convict the wrong person. You see, I'm not smiling. I'm not smiling, because this is a serious situation." DA Adams frowns. "Yes, very serious. So there's no need for smiling as the DA suggest. Jena Parker is just like your daughters or your granddaughters. She's just a teenage girl who had to witness her father being murdered and bare her mother's withdrawal from her. Yet this young lady managed to graduate high school and get accepted into college—just so she could have her innocence taken from her there. Now you ask yourself this, would you be disappointed? Would you be sad? Probably yes. I'd say twelve out of twelve of you would be. Having those emotions doesn't make her a murderer. That wouldn't make any of us murderers. And just because I am at the store, doesn't mean I stole the milk. The DA doesn't have any murder weapons to prove this young lady killed anyone. Therefore, her life is in your hands.

I hope that you think about that when look at all of the evidence. Thank you." Pillars sits down.

"The court will adjourn until the jurors have made a decision," the judge says. She hammers down with her gavel.

"All rise." Everyone leaves the courtroom. Jena gives Pillars a proud smile.

He pats her on the shoulder. "See, I told you everything will be all right." He smiles at her as the guard takes her back to her cell.

The guard is happy, which makes Jena feel more confident. "I think you've got a shot at winning this."

Jena feels hopeful. "Maybe." He closes the cell door. "Thank you so much," she says just before he walks away. "Seeing Jake was all the hope I needed. No matter what happens today to me, knowing that he's alive is my victory."

The guard nods his head, his eyes gleam with glory that he could bring two people who love each other together. "I'm a sucker for love," he says as he walks away.

The twelve jurors weigh the information from the case: the photos of the victims; the video from when Jena walked into the hotel room with Mr. McNeil and out with Jake; the records showing that she was at the hotel the night the clerk was murdered; the train slip showing that she had purchased a ticket on the same train as the doctor.

One of the jurors, a doctor, reviews the medicine found in her mother's system after the autopsy. He says, "This medicine is rarely given to patients without a doctor's prescription." They all look over the evidence over and over again, trying to agree on a verdict.

"That doesn't mean she murdered the doctor," another juror yells out.

"Well, it could tie her to both murders, because how did the doctor's medication get into her mother's system?" another juror says. They all look at each other.

An angry juror stands up. "Look, I'm not convicting this young teenager of all these murders just because some of you want to play detective. We're not here for that. We're here to review all of the evidence to determine that there isn't a responsible doubt that she could commit these crimes—and right now I have reasonable doubts." He flops down in his chair.

They begin arguing over the evidence. Hours pass, and they still don't have a verdict. Two more hours pass. The bailiff alerts the judge that there's been a verdict reached. All the jurors are escorted back into the courtroom. The court is let back into session. DA Adams, Attorney Pillars, and Jena are back at their tables.

The bailiff takes a piece of paper from one of jurors and hands it to the judge. She opens it, reads it, and then looks at Jena and the court.

"Jena Parker, please stand," the judge says. "I'm about to read the verdict that the jurors have decided in this case. I want everyone in this courtroom to remain seated and maintain a sense of respect for this court once I read this decision."

Jena stands up slowly. DA Adams has an intense look on his face. He plays with his tie, jerking it back and forth. Attorney Pillars grips his briefcase, sweat pouring down his face. People in the courtroom are on the edge of their seats, eyes wide. The reporters are locked in on the judge, DA, Pillars, and Jena.

The judge hesitates before she speaks. She looks over at the jurors one last time. "Jurors, is this decision final?"

The juror on the end stands up. "Yes, Your Honor."

"Jena Parker, you have been found guilty of murder and are hereby sentenced to life in prison without parole." The court crowd gets rowdy.

"Order!" the bailiff yells out. "Order in the court."

The judge finishes. "You will serve out your sentence in the Luttonville County Penitentiary. Court is adjourned."

"All rise!" The courtroom crowd goes crazy. Some people start throwing chairs. News reporters are on their phones and in front of cameras reporting the verdict. Pillars loses it and starts arguing with DA Adams, accusing him of submitting false evidence. Jena begins to cry. The guard cries too as he escorts her back to her cell. Jake is outside the courthouse when he hears the news. He falls to his knees and starts crying, as people who were for Jena and against her begin to argue and fight.

CHAPTER FORTY

I had a dream once that I was lying naked in a mud puddle in the middle of the forest. I could hear birds flying above, small animals running around, and trees blowing swiftly with the wind. I lay in the mud as if I was sleeping in my bed, imagining warms blankets and soft pillows—all those things that comfort the mind. This mud didn't smell horrible or disgusting like most mud. It smelled of beautiful lavender and roses. The smell was so inviting that I began smoothing the mud all over my face and body, as if it was lotion. I covered my entire body and then walked through the forest, breathing in the beautiful, crisp air, touching the bark of the trees, watching the animals play. I allowed myself to absorb the wonders and mysteries of my surroundings—the beauty of nature when it's not corrupt by misfortunes or temptations. I felt as though I was a part of a hidden secret nestled in the forest. Forbidden to be found. A safe haven to protect my spirit ... my soul.

I feel a rupture in the earth. The trees shake, and leaves fall everywhere. The animals scatter, trying to find a hiding place. Suddenly the forest grows dark, and the mud begins to ripen of an odor. People with their faces covered ride on horses down the road toward me. There is a black horse, a white, and a brown. With every step of the horses, the earth shakes harder. The men ride up to me, pointing at me with shame, and then they ride away. There's always a reason why secrets are hidden.

They are hidden deep in our hearts, disguised as pleasant-smelling mud, only for us to discover they were just covered under layers of lies.

Jena stands near the door with her hands and feet shackled in chains. She stands with several women who have also been sentenced to prison. They all stand waiting to see the light from the outside, knowing the light that shines in when the doors open is only an illusion of freedom and the beginning of a life of pure hell. Outside the doors are hundreds of the same people waiting to see, waiting to judge, wanting to look into each of their eyes to see if they can capture a gasp of sorrow or laughter.

Jake is among those people, and Jena can't help but to look at him as she passes. *One last look at my dying love. Of the love that once was, is, but never will be.* Several police officers stand next to Jake. They fear he will run wild and attempt to free her, but the look in his eyes when she sees him is a still look of hope and love. He gently smiles at her with just a few teardrops falling. He's cried so much that his well feels dry, yet he couldn't have loved her more than he does at that moment. And even though she is leaving, he knows he is leaving with her—for wherever she is, he is, and that will always be their story.

Jena and the other women get on the bus. People cheer her name: "Jena! Jena!" But they are just voices in the distance to her, because the only words she can hear are the words soaring from Jake's eyes. A glimmer blazes from them, circling her and shooting straight into her heart. All of her desires, fears, and love are embodied in his eyes. No words need to be spoken. The magic of the moment isn't the people cheering, the police walking around touting their might, or the dramatic view of her in chains and orange clothing. It is Jake and her. When he smiles and she smiles back. Two friends, lovers— unshaken by distance or by circumstances. They will weather it all, knowing that their love is beyond a life sentence. That the world can't hold it back when the passion two people share lives above the clouds, the world, deep in the universe. Those are the only words that matter to her.

They watch each other until the bus is out of sight. She knows that she will see him again, touch him, and make love to him, because love has no chains. Jena gazes out the bus window not knowing what might lie ahead, but knowing she is ready to face it.

Alongside the dusty road is a man holding up a sign: "Reda Jones Will Return!" It is definitely Franklin, and although the trial is over, his determination to keep his Reda alive is unstoppable.

Jena is placed in a cell with another woman. The woman is quiet when Jena enters. There are pieces of paper and pencil on the top bunk. Jena looks around and then climbs up top.

"I put that there for you," the woman says. "That paper and pencil. Use it to write down your feelings or to tell someone you love them." Jena is quiet as her cellmate speaks. "I know that being locked up can be lonely at first, so maybe writing will help you. It's helped me. By the way, my name is Paula Johnston. I've been in jail for five years. I have a daughter. Her name is Amy, and I hope to one day see her again."

Jena picks up the paper and pencil and writes down Jake's name. "My name is Jena Parker. Thank you for the stuff."

Weeks go by. Every day Jena tries to write down her feelings, but she can't put the right words together. Getting used to prison took some time for her, but after a while things became routine and she became routine with it. Word comes down that Chance had been convicted of the murder of her parents and was also sent to the prison, but their paths haven't crossed yet.

Jena hears keys jingling. There's a guard standing in the door. "Jena Parker," A prison guard calls her name as he opens the cell door. "Come with me." Paula peeks open one eye. Jena jumps down from her bunk and walks with the prison guard. He puts her in an all-white room and sits her down in a chair. He nods at the other two prison guards in the room, who stand wearing black prison guard uniforms, black guns, and brown sticks by their sides. He closes the door. Jena sits and waits.

The door opens, and Warden Peters, Attorney Pillars, Detective Martin, and Officer Reyes all walk into the room. Attorney Pillars smiles at her. Officer Reyes stands behind her, and Detective Martin leans against the wall. Pillars says, "Jena, there's been a new discovery involving your case. We have someone who is asking to see you before any final decisions are made. Warden Peters has agreed to this meeting. Officer Reyes and Detective Martin are also in agreement." Jena has a confused look on her face. "This individual has asked to speak to you alone, without us sitting in and without us videotaping this meeting." Jena is quiet. "Do you understand?" Pillars asks.

"Yes," she replies.

"Bring him in," the warden yells to the guards. The guards go out and bring in a man. It's Moishe. Jena's eyes grow big. She'd thought Moishe had been killed or had abandoned her. Everyone begins to leave the room. Officer Reyes and Warden Peters stand in front of Moishe, giving him a dirty look. Moishe walks in between them and then sits down in front of Jena. Warden Peters's and Officer Reyes's eyes follow Moishe. Officer Reyes is extremely angry. He puts his hand on his gun.

Warden Peters stops him. "Not here." Officer Reyes storms out of the room. Warden Peters follows.

Attorney Pillars is the last to leave. He pats Jena on the shoulder as he walks out. "You two have fifteen minutes," he says before the guard closes the door.

Jena has a surprised and happy look on her face. "Moishe, what are you doing here? What happened to you?"

Moishe just smiles. "A lot. It's good to see you, Jena." He looks around the room. "Not in here, but still it's good to see you."

Jena blinks her eyes, stares at Moishe. "What's going on?"

He stares deeply into her eyes. "Jena Parker. What a magnificent person you are. You bit the bullet. You're courageous act to take responsibility for your life proves that you are worthy of your freedom."

Jena looks away. "I deserve to be here."

Moishe taps his fingers on the table. "Maybe. Even so, you have braved it all. It must be hard being in here knowing that you will never be able to touch the one you love again."

Jena lifts her chin up. "I will see him again."

Moishe leans back in his chair. "Yes, but you won't touch or feel the warmth of his hand, or he the softness of your skin."

"He's in my heart and mind forever."

"It's not the same, Jena." Moishe says as he leans forward, folding his hand. Jena is quiet. "So Ted is dead?" Moishe asks as he smiles.

Jena gives him a mean look. "He deserved to die."

"I must agree with you. The creep knocked me out, obviously to get to you. Luckily, I have friends, friends in high places, whom I'd told that they must find me if they were without contact from me in twenty-four hours. And they did. Unfortunately, I was in the hospital and couldn't get to you until now." Moishe rubs his head. "Remember the assassin group I told you about?"

"Yes."

"Well, I still have friends from that group, and we have formed another group."

Jena gets a little nervous. "Moishe, they can hear us."

"They can't, because I have a device to ensure they can't. Even though they said they wouldn't listen in, I don't believe them. So I made sure that this conversation will remain strictly between you and me. I have a good friend named Pulue. He's helped me and called on many, many favors for me. Or should I say, for you."

"For me? What kind of favors?"

"Favors that you call in when you want to get a young girl free."

Jena doesn't believe Moishe. "That's impossible."

"Is it? Have you ever heard of corruption?"

"Yes."

"Well, there is a lot of corruption in this society. People who pretend to be something they're not. Now it's time for me to cash in on those corruptions, and Officer Reyes and Warden Peters have answered my call. Police brutality should be called criminal hospitality. Isn't it something when you can't distinguish between a man of the law and a man of crimes? Officer Reyes is a man of crime and a man of falsehood, as he imposes his law-binding attitude to lock up criminals who are innocent. Over half of the inmates in this jail are innocent of their crimes."

Jena looks in his eyes. "I'm not innocent."

"No, you're not, but neither is Reyes or Warden Peters. Those two men are vicious criminals who are paid out of the deep pockets of other free criminals and corrupt politicians. They are both involved in the cover-up of the murder of the mayor's wife and his two daughters—an investigation that is still ongoing, with no intentions of being solved."

Jena has a shocked look on her face. "How do you know this?" she asks.

Moishe looks at her and slightly smiles. "I know this because I was the man for hire." He has an ashamed look on his face. "I was supposed to turn you in the night of the party. But when you shot Kyler to protect the man you love, I saw something in you that reminded me of my Maria. I saw a powerful young girl and a courageous young man in Jake, two people willing to sacrifice it all—not only for love, but for the right to love. You two aren't in the world; the world is in you, in the love you share. I thought of my Maria and all of the promises that will be broken because our love was allowed to fade away in the wind when she was killed. You two don't have to fade away in the wind. Jena, you're free."

"What do you mean?"

"I mean after this conversation, you will be set free from this place."

"But the murders?" She shudders. "They have evidence."

"Yes, they do, but it doesn't point to you anymore." He stares at her. "All of the evidence now points to me."

"Moishe, you can't do this—"

"I can … and I have. All of the murders—the hotel clerk, the doctor on the train, Carol, Ted, Mr. McNeil, and … your mother— all now are my murders."

Jena has a shocked look on her face. "How?"

"Easy—I call in favors, and they deliver. The assassin group is much more powerful than you can imagine. I worked for an evil man years ago, but now they have reestablished the group, reorganized everything. We have high technologies, the best in the espionage business. We are located all over the world, even in places you have never heard of."

"How did you do all of this, Moishe. You weren't at these places."

"Yes, I was. My name is in the book at the hotel from the night you were there. The train system's records have my name as one of the passengers on the train the same day you traveled. I was at the party when Carol was murdered."

"And Mr. McNeil?" Jena asks curiously.

"The surveillance tapes? Yes, I'm on them. I'm on the tape, showing that I also entered Mr. McNeil's hotel room. I can be linked to Ted. I was seen with him. I have also arranged it that I was in Maplesville the night your mother died. Everything has been arranged. Everything leads back to me. I confessed to the murders, and I'm now going to take your place."

Jena gets out of her seat. "I won't let you do this."

Moishe stands up. "Jena, it's already done. They have the murder weapons with my prints on them: the knife that killed the doctor, the medicine that killed your mother, the gun that killed Mr. McNeil and I killed the hotel clerk. My prints are even on the window Ted was pushed out of. They will officially arrest me after this conversation is over. I told them that I would confess to all of it if they would let me talk to you first. Now you can see Jake, now you can be free again—or you can make another choice. You can come be a part of our group."

"An assassin?"

"Yes. We could train you. Enhance the skills you already possess."

"Is that why you're doing this? To make me an assassin?"

"No. I'm doing this to give you back your life, but you must think about your beginning. Why do you think you are different? You saw the dark side in yourself and how quickly you mastered the skills of being a killer. You have it in you. It's up to you to choose."

She closes her eyes. "But Jake?"

"You will see Jake after you have gained your skills. Do you think you can control your anger? Will you strike again if someone provokes you? Take the darkness that you have, and transform it into the lighter darkness. One that kills people who steal from others, create crimes, take from the poor. People like Officer Reyes, Warden Peters, or the slimy creeps like Ted."

Jena quickly looks up at Moishe. "I will not see you, Moishe."

"Yes, you will."

"How? You will be in jail."

Moishe softly laughs. "A part of every deal is always another deal. I will not be in jail long. This is just a smoke screen to get you out. Officer Reyes and Warden Peters couldn't just let you walk out. There has to be some reason for you being released, and I'm your reason. Besides, my friends will rescue me in a few days with a little help with my escape from Officer Reyes. They will be looking for me, and not for you. Just like the mayor's family murder, the search for me will never be solved. So go to Jake and be his Maria, and then come fulfill your destiny. They will be coming back in here to arrest me in a few seconds, so now we must pretend. Let them hear what they want to hear."

The room door opens, and Moishe begins to put on a show—mostly for the sake of the guards and Attorney Pillars. Everyone stands in the room, watching as Moishe starts his show.

"Jena Parker, I apologize for committing these crimes that you were unfortunately blamed for, and I appreciate Officer Reyes," Moishe says as he stares at him, "and Warden Peters allowing me to confess and personally apologize to you."

Jena is quiet but catches on quickly. "Thank you for coming forward to reveal the truth." The guards stand Jena up. She takes one last look at Moishe before they handcuff him and take him away. Jena stops to thank Attorney Pillars. He smiles at her.

"I'll be taking care of all the paperwork today, and you will be out of here by tomorrow." Jena nods her head as she takes one more look at Moishe and then stares over at Officer Reyes, who is eyeing her closely. The two lock eyes. Jena remembers the dream where he arrested her in the desert and the day he handcuffed her when she turned herself in. She knew from the look in his eyes that they would see each other again, and the next time it would be all-out war.

The guard holds on to her arm as he leads her back to her cell. Walking the prison halls, Jena thinks of Jake and everything that has happened up until this very moment. She feels empowered as she passes all the other cells while the inmates yell and scream for freedom and for justice. The guard opens the door.

Paula is asleep. Jena tries to be quiet as she climbs back up to the top bunk. She picks up the paper and pencil Paula had given her and thinks back to when she was a child, a teenager walking the halls with Jake, the smiles, the tears, the laughter, the horrible night her father died, the night that changed everything—but did it? *Was I always heading down this road?* she thinks. She thinks about her father and her mother. She imagines her parents happy together, kissing and dancing high in the heavens, and then her father swinging her mother high in the air. She thinks about her mother—how she was always there for her, being the best mom she could be. "I forgive you mom, and I love you. My father is Jonathan Parker," she utters.

She feels the compassion of the moment and the heat from the love that she knows awaits her, when Jake will hold her in his arms.

But she also knows that Moishe is right; there is still a coldness in her—that ball of fire that brews when her anger strikes a passion inside of her that is beyond her control. She picked up the paper and pencil and then begins to write.

As a child, I used to dream of being someone famous ...
Now I am.

The End

Printed in the United States
By Bookmasters